WOMAN *of* SUNLIGHT

Books by Mary Connealy

From Bethany House Publishers

THE KINCAID BRIDES

Out of Control
In Too Deep
Over the Edge

TROUBLE IN TEXAS

Swept Away
Fired Up
Stuck Together

WILD AT HEART

Tried and True
Now and Forever
Fire and Ice

THE CIMARRON LEGACY

No Way Up
Long Time Gone
Too Far Down

HIGH SIERRA SWEETHEARTS

The Accidental Guardian
The Reluctant Warrior
The Unexpected Champion

BRIDES OF HOPE MOUNTAIN

Aiming for Love
Woman of Sunlight

The Boden Birthright:
A CIMARRON LEGACY Novella

Meeting Her Match:
A MATCH MADE IN TEXAS
Novella

Runaway Bride:
A KINCAID BRIDES
and TROUBLE IN TEXAS Novella
(With This Ring? *Collection*)

The Tangled Ties That Bind:
A KINCAID BRIDES Novella
(Hearts Entwined *Collection*)

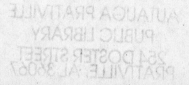

WOMAN *of* SUNLIGHT

MARY CONNEALY

BETHANYHOUSE

a division of Baker Publishing Group
Minneapolis, Minnesota

© 2020 by Mary Connealy

Published by Bethany House Publishers
11400 Hampshire Avenue South
Bloomington, Minnesota 55438
www.bethanyhouse.com

Bethany House Publishers is a division of
Baker Publishing Group, Grand Rapids, Michigan

Printed in the United States of America

Library of Congress Cataloging-in-Publication Data
Names: Connealy, Mary, author.
Title: Woman of sunlight / Mary Connealy.
Description: Minneapolis, Minnesota : Bethany House, a division of Baker
    Publishing Group, [2020] | Series: Brides of Hope Mountain ; 2
Identifiers: LCCN 2019040931 | ISBN 9780764232596 (trade paperback) |
    ISBN 9780764235511 (cloth) | ISBN 9781493421688 (ebook)
Subjects: GSAFD: Christian fiction. | Love stories.
Classification: LCC PS3603.O544 W66 2020 | DDC 813/.6—dc23
LC record available at https://lccn.loc.gov/2019040931

Scripture quotations are from the King James Version of the Bible.

Cover design by Dan Thornberg, Design Source Creative Services

Author is represented by the Natasha Kern Literary Agency.

20 21 22 23 24 25 26   7 6 5 4 3 2 1

Woman of Sunlight
is dedicated to Lauren,
my precious new granddaughter.

1

November 1873
Hope Mountain
Near Bucksnort, Colorado, Near Grizzly Peak, Colorado

Y ou look awful." Mitch Warden poured himself a cup of coffee and studied Ilsa Nordegren's face as she stepped into the kitchen.

Her face was peppered with half-healed blisters left from having chicken pox, but she resisted the urge to slap her hands over her scabby cheeks.

For that matter, she resisted the urge to slap Mitch.

"You're the reason I look so dreadful. You brought this sickness to me." A cranky side of herself that she really hadn't known she had made her shove Mitch back. He didn't even move, but she felt good doing it. "No one ever got sick before you came home."

He'd come down with it first and given it to Ilsa. He'd brought it with him when he came home from back east. He'd found his family's Colorado ranch deserted, but he and his chicken pox had followed his family to the top of Lost Peak—that's the name Ilsa's grandpa had for this place, but the Wardens had always called it Hope Mountain.

She glared at him. "You look awful, too."

He didn't really. He wasn't all the way healed—but he was two weeks ahead of Ilsa. And truth be told, he was a good-looking varmint. Not overly tall, but tall compared to her. Dark blond hair. A nice square chin and brown eyes that made her think of the rich wood of an old oak.

But all that wasn't a good enough reason not to insult him back.

"Mitch, hush." Isabelle Warden, Mitch's mother, who made everyone call her Ma, spoke without turning around, and without stopping her work peeling apples for a pie.

Mitch set his tin coffee cup on the kitchen table and poured a glass of water, then handed it to Ilsa. "Drink this."

He kept pushing water and broth at her even though her fever had gone down over two weeks ago and all her blistered pockmarks had dried up and scabbed over and she was eating plenty of food and had been for days.

But she really did look awful. And Ma had a mirror, something Ilsa had never seen before, so she couldn't lie to herself or smash the mirror, which would be wrong and wouldn't solve the problem anyway.

But she was getting better every day. The red was gone from her face—well, her whole body, but no one saw the rest but her—and her strength had returned.

Still, Mitch treated her like she was in desperate need. The galoot probably felt guilty and well he should.

"You can quit being a doctor now," Ilsa said. "I'm back to being the doctor for everyone here." It was true that Ilsa had more doctoring skills than anyone else. She'd been taught them by her grandpa before he died, and he'd learned the ways of healing from native folks he'd lived with long ago.

Mitch held the water in front of her face. She snatched it away and gulped it down just to make him stop.

She thrust the now-empty cup back into his hands.

Mitch set it aside, picked up his coffee, and took a long sip as he studied her, most likely for signs of thirstiness.

To get his mind off her awful speckled face, she said, "As soon as Jo and Dave get back from town, I'm going to ride with them to visit Ursula. I'm well enough."

Josephine was her older sister, newly married to Mitch's brother, Dave. Ilsa always called her Jo. Ursula was her even-older sister who had turned into some kind of lunatic hermit.

Ilsa and her sisters had lived up here completely alone after their grandparents died, leaving the three girls on their own at a very young age. And they stayed up here because of their grandma and grandpa's terrible warnings to never leave the mountains because there was deadly danger in the lowlands.

Those had been good days.

Then the Wardens had moved in, and soon after, along came their pest of a son Mitch.

Mitch slammed his cup on the table. "You are not up to riding to see your crazy sister any time soon. You're barely up from your sickbed."

"My sister isn't crazy." Honestly, some days Ursula seemed as crazy as a rabid skunk bear, but Ilsa ignored that and glared at Mitch. "You don't get to tell me how I feel or where I can go."

Nobody did. Not once since her grandpa died. Her sisters had let her come and go as she chose, and it suited her.

"Well, somebody's got to tell you when you don't seem to have a lick of sense."

"Mitch," Ma snapped, turning away from her apples, "go out and see if your father and Dave are coming up the trail."

"Ma, you know there are sentries who'll let us know if—"

"Go," Ma snapped, then pointed a very motherly finger toward the door. She'd been throwing Mitch out a lot lately. "And don't come back until you can be polite to Ilsa."

Ilsa was always glad to see him go. And considering Ma's order about being polite, he'd be gone awhile. Maybe forever.

Not that Ilsa really understood what polite was. It must have something to do with him being so cranky.

Mitch picked on her, nagged her, and found every fault in her. The man was just watching her too closely, and she felt much better when he was gone.

Ilsa knew she treated him a lot like he treated her. But he deserved it and she didn't. Anyone could see that.

He snorted like a caged bull, then stormed out, slamming the door.

"Your son seems easily upset," Ilsa said. She'd had no practice understanding what people were thinking. She'd gotten the impression others could look at someone in the face and say, "he's mad . . . he's worried . . . she's sad."

Well, Ilsa knew what a frown was and a smile. But beyond that, she and her sisters had always just said what they thought straight out.

10

She didn't understand gleaning details from watching someone's face.

"He most certainly does." Ma gave her the oddest smile. And why was it odd? Ilsa couldn't say.

Ilsa helped with the apples. Soon she heard hooves galloping away. Mitch had saddled up and was off.

"I have some eggs and bacon keeping warm in the back of the fireplace. Let me get you some breakfast." Ma made food so deliciously. Ilsa paid rapt attention whenever cooking was involved. She was learning more from Ma every day.

As she ate the wonderful food, Ilsa thought of how much she stayed inside these days. It wasn't normal for her. The woods and treetops, the caves and trails, were as much her home as the inside of a cabin, and she missed being outside until it was a kind of hunger. She'd spent far too much time indoors since she'd gotten sick. She wouldn't have minded going along with Mitch, except she'd've had Mitch for company.

Anyway, Jo and Dave and Quill Warden, Dave and Mitch's pa, weren't coming yet. The sentries would've let them know. Ma just wanted peace. Ilsa would have liked to check for herself, though. She was anxious for Dave to get back because he'd taken Jo with him. And Ilsa wanted to see her sister again and go back to their cabin.

This one had too many grouchy men in it. One too many.

The cabin they were in was built near where the forest started on the northeast edge of a huge, grassy meadow. The trail down the mountain opened after a short ride into the forest on the far side. Ilsa expected the ride to take him a long time, especially since his mother throwing him out had so obviously been intended to keep him out.

If she couldn't go see Ursula, she could at least get out of the confines of this cabin. A long, cold walk would suit her right now. With that in mind, and without asking Ma, who could be counted on to always have some rule Ilsa didn't understand, she slipped into her coat, grabbed her bonnet and gloves, and was outside and running before Ma could say anything.

She dashed into her beloved forest. The first tree she found to her liking, she scampered up, light and easy as any woodland creature, then perched on a broad branch to watch the cowhands and cattle and Mitch riding wild across the meadow.

She drew out her knife, one she'd carried since before Grandpa died, and studied it. After years of sharpening with her whetstone, the blade was almost needle thin.

Afraid every day the blade would break, but unwilling to let it grow dull, she sharpened it as Grandpa had taught her, then gently replaced it in the little leather pouch she'd sewn into the pocket of the strange dress Ma Warden had made for her.

Then she tugged on one of the many thick vines she'd braided and hung here and there, and swung from where she sat to the next tree. Branches slapped at her, and the wind blew through her hair. Her heart nearly sang from the pleasure of swinging, moving fast far above where anyone would notice.

She followed Mitch.

She didn't have braided vines everywhere. But when she'd reach a tree that lacked one, it was because she'd come to a clump of trees with branches woven so tightly to each other they were nearly a solid floor far above the ground.

She'd run along up high, then she'd find one of her vines and swing again. She was always joyful when she was swinging.

The treetops were where she went when there was tension at home, as there sometimes was between her tough middle sister, Jo, and her anxious and bossy big sister, Ursula.

Now, having fun for the first time since she'd been sick, she swung through the forest that edged the meadow, almost as fast as Mitch galloped.

The top of the trail, where Jo had gone down—breaking the most forbidden rule her grandparents had ever made—was hidden by a stand of trees that marked the southeast corner of this meadow.

Mitch rode into the woods and vanished from sight for a time. Ilsa swung along until she caught up to him and crouched to watch. She loved to stand back and watch.

Cranky Mitch had slowed his horse to a walk and continued toward the top of the trail. She hoped the long, hard ride had cooled him off.

2

Mitch was turning into a hothead.

And he'd always considered himself a man with cool control. He'd even had the calm reserve to survive two murder attempts. Those were the goads that made him decide to leave the city behind and come home to the Circle Dash Ranch where he'd grown up . . . the place his heart had longed to be for years.

He'd fought in the Civil War, succeeded in the cutthroat business world of New York City, survived attempted murder, and then he'd crossed a continent carrying thousands of dollars in gold and changed his name again and again, leaving no trail—and through it all, he'd stayed calm and cool.

And now he couldn't stop steaming over a woman like a boiling pot with the lid clamped on tight.

She was a little fairy princess. Short and fine boned with a tangle of dark curls and eyes so blue they were like looking in the heart of a flame. And she could vanish in the woods as quick and quiet as any wild creature.

Because that's what she was. Completely untamed.

Ilsa drove him crazy with her peculiar ways, but he couldn't just walk away from all her strange notions because he owed her, since he'd almost killed her.

Apparently, guilt made him hot with anger—which wasn't fair to her or anyone. It surprised him to realize it. On the other hand, he hadn't spent much time feeling guilty while he ran roughshod over business competitors.

How could he have known he was going to get sick? He'd been fine when he got home. He'd stayed fine until he'd been home nearly a week. Then all of a sudden, he'd turned feverish and within a day, he was covered with itchy blisters.

He'd tried to make up for Ilsa catching his chicken pox. He'd crawled out of his sickbed to help care for her. Still weak from his own recent fever, he'd worked day and night to get her through.

And now she wanted to overdo it. . . . He'd done the same thing, but that didn't make it right. Riding for hours through the cold to go see her crazy sister Ursula who'd moved into some odd stone house far from everyone else was a poor excuse for an idea.

Besides, he was a strong man. She was a delicate woman. She needed someone to tell her to stop being a half-wit and just, for heaven's sake, give herself a little more time to heal.

He was getting angry again. But someone needed to forbid it. When no one else seemed willing to talk sense into her, he gladly took the job.

And for his efforts to keep her from relapsing—maybe dying—he'd gotten thrown out of the cabin by his own mother. It was by no means the first time.

Checking the trail was a wasted effort, and there weren't even any windows open on that side of the cabin for Ma to see if he minded her.

But she'd know if he didn't check the trail. Somehow.

Mighty strange being treated like a boy again after ten years on his own. No one in New York City would have dared to order him around, but he'd obeyed that Mother's Finger pointing him out the door.

All he could think was, she was making apple pie for dinner, and if he didn't mind her, she might not give him a piece.

Which was pure mean of her because he hadn't been home that long.

Mitch might've gotten his ruthless streak from his mother.

He reached the head of the trail Pa, Dave, and Josephine had taken down the mountain. They'd left three days ago to go to the land office in Bucksnort to buy the meadows they'd found up here in these peaks.

Land that would sell for pennies an acre because it looked like rugged, mountainous wasteland on the maps in the land office.

Only the Wardens knew about the lush high valleys. Well, Ilsa and her sisters knew, but they'd never bought so much as an acre, and neither had their parents or grandparents.

Dave and Pa would get some, and they'd buy Mitch a big chunk of it, too. Which would only cost him a small portion of the fortune he'd made in New York City.

He reached the trailhead. Looking down, he noticed the tracks Pa and Dave had left. They'd talked long and hard about whether buying this land was worth those tracks. Pa had been shot only weeks ago by men planning to steal his land and cattle. If there were still people looking for Pa, those tracks would give their position away. The tracks would be covered soon enough, as soon as more snow fell, but for right now, they were as good as a map.

He saw something move to his left and turned to study the woods. Nothing. But there was something. His eyes drew upward, and he studied the tree branches.

A sudden move off to his right had him twisting in the saddle, hand on his gun. Alberto, Pa's foreman, stood guard in an overhead spot where he could watch this trail for intruders.

Alberto was waving at Mitch. When he caught Mitch's eye, he pointed downward, and Mitch's first thought was that Pa was coming back. About time.

No one was visible yet, and he looked back at Alberto, who shook his head almost violently and pointed a rifle at the trail at a spot beyond where Mitch could see.

Alberto wouldn't be drawing a bead on Pa. That meant whomever he was watching was an intruder.

Mitch backed away from the trail, watching for the moment the men would be visible. When his horse was back far enough, Mitch dismounted, snagged his rifle out of the saddle, and slapped the critter on the rump to send it running for the corral.

Mitch picked a chest-high boulder to use for cover and rested his rifle on it. Hooves clomped softly on the snow. A saddle creaked. The metal on a bridle jingled. Mitch slipped the leather thong free that hooked through the trigger of his gun, holding it in place. He eased his six-gun out of his holster, then put it back, to test that it was loose. He didn't want it getting hung up if he needed to draw.

He leveled his rifle on the trailhead. The riders rounded into sight. Watchful men. One tall, lean, gray-haired. He wore two guns tied down, and was looking at Alberto with his empty right hand raised while his left guided his horse.

The other saw Mitch's rifle instantly. Mitch saw him speak to his saddle partner. The one watching Mitch was younger and had hair black-as-night. He wore a black, broad-brimmed hat with a white, blue, and red beaded band. He was dressed in buckskin and wore two guns tied-down just like the older man. He kept his hands firmly on the reins, making no move for a weapon.

Everything the men wore was sharp-looking and new, and they carried good guns, the finest money could buy.

Both rode bloodstock quarter horses steady enough to climb the trail. Mitch hadn't even tried to get his own horse up here.

Neither man had the lean, hungry look often seen on men hunting work.

Mitch watched their alert, knowing eyes, and they put him in mind of a man who'd taken a shot at him back in New York City. These men were in Western garb, but they had the same fine guns, the same cold gaze.

It couldn't be about his trouble back in New York. He'd taken great pains to prevent anyone from following him. But Mitch wasn't a man to ignore his instincts and New York came to mind.

Much more likely these men were here hunting Pa, sent by that land-stealing Bludgeon Pike.

Mitch calculated and considered these men from all angles between one breath and the next.

They were most of the way to the top of the trail. A few more of the fine horses' long strides would gain them the boulders strewn up here. Once they reached the boulders, they'd have shelter and be out of Alberto's line of fire. Mitch would have to face the two men alone.

Mitch didn't step out and talk friendly.

"Hold up." Mitch briefly raised his rifle off the boulder. "We don't cotton to strangers. Turn around and ride back down the trail."

"We've come a long spell, mister." The horses kept coming, slow and steady, no sudden moves. "Our horses are tired, and our bellies are empty."

"Your horses look fine, and you're not so thin it'll kill you to miss a meal. Bucksnort is a little Colorado town a few hours to the south." More like a long half of a day's ride. "Plenty of places to eat and rest a horse there."

The horses came on.

"One more step and I fire." Mitch's gut twisted because he was going to have to do it. He saw the ugly intent in these men's eyes. He didn't want to kill a man. And he needed at least one of them alive so he could find out who sent them. But he took their measure and figured them for hunting trouble. They were going to push this into a shooting. That's exactly what they'd come for.

Some unseen signal passed between the men. Mitch realized their steps had taken them not only forward but also to the side of the trail Alberto stood over.

They opened fire, then dove off their horses, on the side away from Mitch. The horses blocked the men, and it sickened Mitch to kill such beautiful horseflesh, and for no purpose because the men were sheltered anyway, so he held off. It gave the intruders time to run up the trail behind the horses. Mitch watched for an open shot.

Alberto fired three times. All that shooting would bring the cowhands running. Alberto disappeared from overhead, likely looking for a better angle.

The horses surged forward, panicked by the gunfire, and the men made it to the boulder closest to Alberto's overlook. The horses thundered into the high meadow.

Mitch fired at a hand holding a rifle leveled from behind the boulder. A man howled. His rifle flew to the side, broken.

The howling man switched to a pistol. Pistols were not as accurate, and he fired with his left hand now, but he was good left-handed, and the bullets would kill you just as dead.

Mitch's blood cooled to sleet. His hands settled on his gun—steady as the stone that sheltered him.

He saw the angle of the guns, heard the direction of the bullets, judged the size and shape of the boulder that sheltered these killers.

He heard every galloping step of the horses, smelled the sharp, bitter brimstone of the gunfire. He felt the wind buffeting him and saw the winter-cured grass dancing in the breeze.

He was aware of everything—every sound, smell, touch, and sight that surrounded him. Each move he made was calculated in fractions of a second, and he made all his decisions, took everything into consideration, without giving any of it conscious thought.

He'd always been like this under pressure, ever since he was a kid hunting dinner with his pa. Thinking, reasoning, the whole world so sharp and clear it nearly hurt his eyes. His mind working as fast as the trigger on his Winchester.

He also knew people were coming. Circle Dash cowhands were racing to back him. Alberto would be back in the fight soon. His ma would come, Ilsa might, too. He couldn't let them get shot, and it wouldn't take long for them to get into rifle range.

The intruders crouched completely behind the boulder with only a gun showing from each: one fired his rifle, one his pistol.

Bullets shredded the air over Mitch's head so it was impossible to do any more than what they were doing— stick out a gun and fire. But he couldn't aim, and he was burning through his lead.

He had to end this, and do it fast, before anyone got hurt. He was crouched below the top of the boulder, but he could see up and realized what it meant that they'd picked a boulder so close to the rock wall behind it. And like a light snapping on, Mitch knew what to do. He aimed for the wall over the men's heads and fired. Bullets whined off the rock, ricocheting in all directions. Dangerous, deadly business, and he hated to think where a wild bullet might fly.

He fired and fired, unloading his rifle on that rock, changing each angle slightly, hoping to salt that thin space between the boulder and the wall with a hornets' nest of stinging lead.

—o◯o—

High above, Ilsa ducked behind a tree trunk as gunfire exploded below her.

She didn't know much about guns, but she knew it was a gunshot that led to the hole in Quill Warden's gut.

Rocks exploded, a rifle shattered and broke. She was smart enough to know she wanted no part of a bullet.

The guns whizzed with even more speed than one of Jo's arrows.

Everything was below her, so she risked a look around and saw from her perch two men shooting at Mitch.

Rage like nothing she'd ever felt before roared to life in her as she watched those men try to hit Mitch as someone—maybe these very men—had hit Quill.

She studied where those men hid, firing over the top of that huge stone, and where she was and the woven-together tree vines hanging between here and there.

And then she spotted something else.

Another howl. Mitch thought it was the same man. Then he could hear two guns again, but it was one man firing with two hands.

Mitch kept up the barrage. Then his rifle clicked on an empty chamber.

He dragged his pistol from his holster and rained death down on the one gunman still shooting. He heard one gun go silent while the second still fired. Mitch wasn't the only one low on bullets. Or if they had them, they might've been in their saddlebags.

The last gun pounded on. Mitch slowed his firing, hoping they'd run out of ammunition before he did.

He had bullets slipped into loops on his gun belt. When the man firing at him fell silent, Mitch paused to reload. When both guns went silent, something swung overhead. He brought his gun around, trying to see an attacking man. Instead, a swift, silent bird swooped so it skimmed behind the boulder where the gunmen crouched. A man cried out, and there was silence.

The bird—no, Ilsa—that was Ilsa swinging down on the gunmen—Ilsa didn't emerge from behind the boulder.

With a bellow of terror, Mitch leapt up and charged toward the rock.

He heard footsteps coming from behind and glanced back to see Jimmy Joe come running.

Parson Fred was fifty feet behind him with his gun drawn. Alberto popped out off to Mitch's right and had a good, clear look at the men behind the boulder.

The look on Alberto's face would have made Mitch laugh if he wasn't mute with fear.

He or Jimmy Joe or Fred would have ended this fight in a few seconds if it hadn't ended already.

He turned and saw Ma charging across the meadow on foot, carrying a rifle.

Then he rounded the rock to see Ilsa scowling at a broken-off knife while she crouched beside the older of the two outlaws. The man was bleeding out like a gutted elk.

"What are you doing?" Mitch wanted to grab her and shake her. But when he took one threatening step forward, her eyes came up to meet his and he stopped.

Something in her eyes . . . if he got close enough, he might hear her growl.

Or no, that wasn't right. An animal didn't feel emotion when it killed, did it? No, she was more of a . . . barbarian. A one-woman Mongol Horde. His very own Hun.

Whatever she was, Ilsa was in the grip of something savage. He hoped she was furious about her broken knife, but he wasn't sure.

Alberto didn't approach her, so he must've seen it, too. She needed time to calm down, and Mitch didn't want to give it to her. He wanted to hug her and check her for wounds . . . though he could see good and well she was fine.

He wanted to blister her hide . . . hard to do with a woman already covered in blisters.

She'd swung in from the treetops. Into a gunfight. She'd brought a knife to a gunfight.

What's more, she'd won.

The silence stretched. The savagery faded from Ilsa's eyes. Just how untamed was she?

Finally, the spell was broken by Alberto. "Never seen 'em before." He came on down the slope, his eyes now on the gunmen.

Mitch closed the distance between himself and those killers. He needed to know who sent them. Both were still alive but bleeding bad.

He hoped they lived to hang.

Reaching the younger man first, Mitch saw a bullet crease on his head—or maybe a cut from a piece of shattered rock. There were other wounds, but none looked deadly. The man was unconscious, but breathing steadily.

Mitch's eyes went to the older man, and he looked into blue eyes opened to slits that burned with volcanic fire.

This was the man who'd kept up the shooting the longest. He didn't move at all, not a twitch of his arms and legs, he didn't even turn his head, only slid his eyes in Ilsa's direction, then Mitch's.

He lay sprawled, bleeding, and, Mitch knew, dying.

Alberto stepped past Ilsa and stripped the blue-eyed man of weapons. Jimmy Joe rushed in to disarm the unconscious gunman.

"These men look like professional killers. Hunt for hideout weapons."

Mitch stepped to the conscious man's side. Ilsa sat near his head across from Mitch. Alberto, with the guns, stepped back behind Ilsa as if he was wary of getting close to her.

The older man had a gunshot high on his chest, another in the middle of his gut. These weren't wounds a man survived.

Mitch dropped to his knees. "Why did you come in here shooting? What were you after?"

The question he really wanted to ask was, Who hired you? But that was because of New York. This man could have come in shooting for his own reasons. This couldn't be about New York.

The man's mouth went tight. Almost like he was defiantly holding back words, planning to take his secrets to the grave.

Impatient, Mitch searched him and pulled money, a lot of it, out of the man's pockets. A small, full pouch. A quick glance told him they were twenty-dollar golden eagles.

Weighing it quickly with one hand, Mitch estimated about five hundred dollars. He'd taken a thousand dollars off two separate hired gunmen in New York. Could it possibly be a coincidental amount of money? Mitch's mind just wouldn't stretch wide enough to allow for that. But how had they found him? He'd been so careful.

"Jimmy Joe, see if the other one has this much money."

"Yep, a bag of gold just like the one you're holding." Jimmy passed it to Mitch. After they talked to the sheriff, Mitch figured to split all of it between the cowhands—men who'd charged toward blazing guns to fight on Mitch's side.

Five hundred dollars in each bag. A thousand dollars must be the going price for murder. Do it on your own, you get the whole price, bring a saddle partner, you split it.

Die or get caught and you got nothing.

Mitch's low, coiled worry twisting like a worm in his belly was growing into a six-foot Rocky Mountain rattler of writhing dread.

These men had to have come for him. He might be wrong, but he had to figure it that way for now. And that meant more men would come.

Mitch had already brought sickness to this valley, now he was bringing death. He dug deeper into the man's pockets and found a notebook full of writing. Thumbing through it quickly, he found two things.

A record of payment of one thousand dollars.

And a name.

That ended every doubt in his mind. Mitch had found enough to believe the attacks in New York were paid for by Pete Howell, his business partner and the man who had taken up with Katrina Lewis, the prim and delicate New York socialite. Katrina, a woman Mitch had thought he could love. Pete, a man he'd thought he could trust.

The two had teamed up and tried to take everything from Mitch, including his life.

There'd been enough evidence to prove Pete's guilt to Mitch's satisfaction, but not enough to prove it to the police. Mitch had hired Pinkerton agents to continue the investigation. And before he left New York, he'd made business arrangements so Howell would lose everything. Spoiled, vain Katrina would find herself stuck with Howell, a man who had no money.

It'd taken Mitch a while to think of her as spoiled and vain. She'd been fragile. A cool, perfectly mannered beauty.

Pete had convinced her to switch her allegiance, her love, to him instead of Mitch.

On the way here, a financial panic had rocked the whole country.

It was ironic that the best thing Mitch could have done, had he known about the coming nationwide sweep of bankruptcies, was to convert everything he had to gold.

Mitch sold high, while things were roaring along. What little Pete had left was swept away as banks failed across the country.

Pete deserved to be in jail. Deserved to hang. He certainly deserved to be financially ruined.

Yet he'd still come up with a shocking amount of money to hire gunmen. And he'd somehow found Mitch.

Ma reached him then. He looked up at Ma, then he glanced at Ilsa. His life from back east was catching up to him—which meant it would catch up to his whole family.

Furious, he turned to see the older man had died without betraying those who hired him.

MARY CONNEALY

It didn't matter, the notebook was enough for Mitch, but would it be enough for the sheriff?

"Bludge Pike's men found the trail your pa left down the mountain." Ma lifted the rifle, aimed away from everyone, and jacked the bullet out so there wasn't a chance of it going off. Ma was careful like that. Looking grim, she added, "Quill was so stubborn. He had to buy this valley. He never should have gone to town."

"Looks like we're going to town again," Mitch said, looking at the dead man and his unconscious partner.

"What?" Then Ma looked at the two men.

Mitch saw her realize the men had to be taken to the law. He didn't correct her assumption about Pike. She might be right.

Ilsa stirred then. The last of that savage look faded from her eyes. In its place emerged the woodland creature who flitted around and drove him crazy.

She often reminded him of a butterfly. Turned out, she was a butterfly with a hideout knife.

"Can I go? I've never seen a town before. Are we going to New York City?" Ilsa gave her broken knife another disgruntled look. It had snapped off down to the handle.

"We're not going to New York City. Why would you think that?"

With a shrug, Ilsa said, "You said you came from there. It's the only city I've ever heard of."

Mitch shook his head violently. "We're going to Buck-snort. And you can't come. Stay here where it's safe."

"Ma?" Ilsa was nothing but a tattletale. Like a pesky sister.

Then he saw those blue eyes flash with life and energy

29

and that strange fairy quality with only a faint remaining trace of barbarian—which he found shockingly appealing—and didn't feel like any kind of brother.

Ma patted Ilsa on the shoulder. "We'll all go."

"Before we leave, can I get another knife?"

"We'll see what we've got on hand. If we need to, we'll buy you one in town."

Ma slid an arm around Ilsa's waist and relieved her of the knife handle, tossing it aside. "Let's go get you a clean dress. I'll see about soaking the blood out of this one."

Ilsa reached back for the knife handle. "My grandpa gave me that knife. It is my most precious possession. Actually, it's almost my only possession."

Maybe it was the knife that had her so upset. His little Hun didn't like being disarmed.

Mitch heard them talk as they walked back toward the house.

"You have two dresses now, so you have two other possessions," Ma said.

"Nothing as useful as my knife."

Ma answered, but Mitch couldn't make out the words. Just as well, he probably didn't want to hear what they were saying anyway. He rubbed his face hard, wishing he could scrub a whole lot of trouble off like dirt.

He did yell after them a short, simple truth. "Neither of you is going!"

They didn't even turn around.

3

The Bible says, women ought not 'usurp authority over the man, but to be in silence.' You're both a couple of sinners before the Lord." At least Mitch got to lead down the snowy, slippery trail.

"Don't you quote the Bible to me, Mitchell Warden." Ma shook her finger at Mitch.

"How can you do that and not fall off?"

Mitch glanced back to see Ilsa staring at Ma's finger while she clung to the saddle horn with both hands.

Ma went on. "That's about a man having authority over his wife, not just any random woman, and certainly not a son over his mother."

Ilsa rode her horse right behind Mitch and ahead of Ma. He looked back constantly, afraid she'd fall off. It was so steep, if she did, she might beat them all down the mountain, rolled into a snowball the size of a house. The woman didn't know a lick about riding. "You shouldn't be here, Ilsa. It's your first time down this mountain, and you're on about the steepest, slickest slope I've ever seen. This trail is just looking for an excuse to kill someone."

Mitch figured it'd probably be him.

"Don't let him upset you, Ma. The Bible story that comes to mind for me is 'The Fox and the Grapes.' He's not getting his way, and he's acting like the world is a cluster of sour grapes."

Mitch twisted in his saddle. "That is not in the Bible."

Ilsa's eyes narrowed. She clung to the saddle horn for dear life, and considering her lack of riding skills and the treacherous path they trod, that wasn't a bad idea.

But she got real brave and let go for one moment to jab a finger right at him. "Heretic."

She practically growled. He was afraid of her when she growled.

Looking on past her to his mother, who came third in this parade of fools, he said, "Ma, you can't let her go on thinking a bunch of fables are in the Bible. Do something." His eyes went farther back, and he saw Alberto trying not to laugh. And laughter wasn't a real normal reaction considering Alberto led two horses, each with a man draped over the saddle.

One dead, one still knocked into a sound sleep.

Ilsa the Wild thinking she owned two Bibles—different books, like the Bible was a two-volume set. The women really had been cut off from the world for too long.

Ma said with patient amusement, "Ilsa, he's right. I know that second book you have is full of wonderful tales, most with strong biblical morals, but there is only one Bible."

Ilsa loved Ma. And Ma loved Ilsa. Ma just might love Ilsa more than she loved Mitch.

That didn't stop Ilsa from turning and pointing at Ma. "'Get thee behind me, Satan.'"

Then she faced forward. "You all need to set aside your confusion, or you'll never get into heaven." Ilsa sounded mournful about that. Which was sweet of her.

"She's trying to save our souls, Mitch. Try to remember that."

Mitch rolled his eyes heavenward. Since he was facing forward, he figured he could make all the faces he wanted. God could see him, but he suspected God was on his side.

The trail was a long one. And Mitch was glad he was riding one of Pa's mountain-bred mustangs. His own horse was an animal as beautiful as the quarter horses their attackers had ridden. He'd told Pa about leaving his horse, and a packhorse, in a hidden corral at Pa's ranch, and Pa said he'd check on them when he went down the mountain.

The bottom of this trail was a good stretch away from their ranch house, and if they skirted around, no one would see them pass by.

Unless they were skirting around.

Shaking off the worry about the tracks, Mitch hoped his horses were still there.

He'd bought them in Denver, and they'd never run wild in the mountains. He wanted to bring the critters to the highlands when he came back, but he wasn't sure they could climb this trail.

The group reached the bottom and found the snow deeper down here than up high. They were leaving new tracks. A trail as clear as a road should anyone ride this way. It snowed heavily a couple of times a week. Mitch hoped it snowed soon to cover their trail.

They took a few minutes to tend Mitch's lonely horses

in the corral set well away from the ranch house. Then, on a whim, he saddled one of his horses to ride it to town. The animal needed the exercise. They might want supplies, too, so he took the second as a packhorse. He led the group on toward Bucksnort.

Ma rode up beside Ilsa, and the trail widened enough they both came up beside him and rode three abreast.

Ma pointed at three sets of hoof tracks leading straight south. "The trail is broken here by Pa, Dave, and Jo." She looked back at Alberto . . . riding alone . . . leading the packhorses.

"And here by those two men. They rode in from the east." Mitch followed his pa's tracks.

"The trail gets narrow ahead so the three of us can't ride abreast," Ma said. "Alberto, I'll drop back and ride beside you then."

Alberto nodded.

He wasn't a big talker, and Ma was. Mitch could tell Alberto wasn't all that eager for her to join him. Or maybe Mitch just assumed.

They rode along in silence awhile. But Mitch felt the weight of that silence, and his thoughts went to the men he'd shot. One of them he'd killed. Or Ilsa had. Or they both had. And Ilsa, what was there to say to her?

The men had come on orders from New York City to kill him.

Somehow his business partner, Pete Howell, had found him. Mitch had gone to great lengths to cover his tracks. But somehow Mitch had left something behind that led these men, hired by Howell, out here to Pa's ranch. Mitch hadn't trusted many people back east, so he'd told no one where he was headed—they shouldn't have even known his real name. What had he left behind?

"Ilsa." Ma's voice reminded him of the weight of the silence. He'd thought it was because of the trouble following him. Trouble he hadn't admitted to yet.

He had a lot of thinking to do.

Then he had to apologize to his family.

Then he had to leave.

If he couldn't get this finished, he might never be able to come back. Trouble would follow him, so he had to lead it away from here.

But Ma wasn't talking to him. She was on his right, and she looked across him to talk to Ilsa on his left. Was she going to bring up Ilsa killing a man? A man who was probably already as good as dead, judging by the bullets in him, but still, Ilsa had done it. Or had she? If she did, she had to be upset.

He hoped she was upset.

She didn't seem all that upset.

"There's no harm in having a beloved book full of wisdom that you cherish. But there is only one Bible."

That's right, in his pondering, Mitch had forgotten about the two Bibles.

Ma went on. "The Bible is the Word of God. It's holy. The book your family has is in many ways filled with wisdom that comes from the Bible. But it isn't correct to call it a second Bible." Ma turned in her saddle to meet Ilsa's bright blue eyes.

"My family and I are Bible-believing people. And it hurts me to be called Satan and hear my son called a heretic. We love God and have made our peace with Him. I don't know if I can convince you that there is only one Bible, but I hope and pray I can convince you to stop calling us unkind names."

Mitch looked right at Ilsa as she listened.

Ma wasn't done. "The Bible tells us to believe in Jesus Christ in order to have eternal life. To believe He died for our sins and to accept His sacrifice as our way to heaven. That's the foundation of all Christian faith. If you think there are two Bibles, and I think there is one Bible, but we both believe in Jesus, then we've done what's needed. I believe that, and you should offer me that same kindness of accepting what I believe."

Mitch whispered to Ma. "Are you sure? There's a verse about not adding a jot or tittle to the Bible."

Ma shrugged. "I'm sure about believing in Jesus. I just hope they're not so mixed up they're worshiping the goose that laid the golden egg."

They both turned to see what Ilsa would say. "I won't call you a heretic or Satan anymore. I'll just pray for you to see the truth."

It kind of made Mitch want to hammer his head against something really hard. His saddle horn was right there handy. "Ilsa, there are not two Bibles. Now, you listen here. There is—"

"Mitch, let's leave it until later. I hope, well, that is . . . there is . . . we should . . . Umm . . . in time we can figure it all out. I hope. Maybe we should have asked Parson Fred if he'd . . . I think if . . ." Ma's voice faded to sort of a weak ending. Then in a more normal voice, she said, "Let's pick up the pace and get to town."

Mitch didn't know what else to do, so he nodded and

kicked his horse into a trot. He saw Ilsa falling off her horse.

"Mitch, I—" She quit talking to squeal.

He reined his horse back so Ilsa caught up to him. She was toppling in his direction, so it was easy to grab her and drag her right onto his lap. He caught her horse's reins.

With another kick, Mitch's horse started galloping.

Ma laughed as she fell in behind him.

Ilsa looked him right in the eye. "Why did the horse start being all bumpy like that? It's not like that now."

"It's called trotting. It's a little faster than walking but not as fast as galloping. Usually a horse trots for a few paces until it breaks into a gallop. There's a trick to hanging on through the trotting. I'll teach you how when we get back to the top of the mountain. For now, just hang on to me and come along for the ride."

And, put like that, some shocking notions flooded into his head. Deeply, profoundly, wildly improper notions.

His arm tightened around her back. He didn't really plan it, but he pulled her close enough that their noses almost touched.

As they moved along, Mitch looked at her speckled face and said, "I'm really sorry I gave you my chicken pox."

His already-tight hold squeezed a bit more. "Really sorry, Ilsa. I had no idea I'd been near anyone who was sick, but then maybe they showed no symptoms. I probably gave it to you before I knew I had it."

"My grandma always made Grandpa stay away when he'd gone to town."

"That's called a quarantine. It's usually only called for

when a disease is identified, not every time someone has been near another person."

"It seems like he was gone more than he was home. And now we find he built a cabin far away from where we lived. I wonder if he came home much at all. I was so young I can't really remember. He was there some. I know that, but I'm not sure how much."

"He stayed away even after your grandma died?"

"He was there more after that. He went down to New York City much less often."

"No, Ilsa, it's—" His voice broke as he choked back a laugh. "No, he didn't go to New York City. You know about that town because that's where I lived, and I've mentioned it, but there are lots of towns down here off the mountaintop. New York City is a many, many days' ride away. Your grandpa wouldn't have gone there. Most likely he went to Bucksnort just like we are."

"And your pa and Jo and Dave went there?"

"Yep."

"And they said they'd be back in three days."

"Yep, and Pa was giving himself lots of time because he's not at full strength. When I was a youngster, we rode in to Bucksnort and back in a single day. Up before dawn, home long after sunset, but we'd make it. We only went a few times a year, and we'd stock up on supplies that lasted for months."

"But, if Grandpa only had a three-day journey, maybe even less, why was he gone most of the time?"

Mitch had heard a few things about Ilsa's grandparents. They told the girls, Ursula, Jo, and Ilsa, he had to stay away after trips to town so he wouldn't bring home a sickness, but in truth, Mitch suspected her grandpa found peace in his remote cabin. Her grandma was probably in no hurry for him to return. But Mitch was afraid saying that would make Ilsa feel bad. Then they'd end up arguing.

Now that he'd seen her in action with that knife, he was less inclined to bicker with her.

"Some of the time he was probably trapping. He was a mountain man, wasn't he? He probably had trap lines run far and wide." And Mitch thought that might be a part of the truth, too.

"After Grandma died, he took on all her worst warnings about staying on the mountain. And he worked hard to teach us how to live without needing supplies from a town. And he read from—" Ilsa glanced at him and arched one accusing brow—"he read from both Bibles every night."

Mitch clamped his mouth shut.

"And we took turns reading, except now it seems none of us knows how to read. Your ma said she'd teach us, and she's already given Jo a few lessons. But I kept falling asleep, so now I'm behind."

He didn't want to say it, but he felt like something needed to be said. "Ilsa, it about scared the life out of me to see you swinging down on that man. You could have been shot."

"No, I was watching. Your guns had both gone silent."

"We were both out of bullets."

Nodding, Ilsa said, "I waited. I saw what a bullet did to your pa."

"If you want to talk about it, I'll listen. You must be upset."

"I was terribly upset. Half-mad over it."

That gave Mitch some comfort. "I don't blame you." He swallowed hard. "It was my gunfire that probably killed him. Not you."

She jerked up so she looked him straight in the eye. "Of course it was you. I barely even touched him. My knife hit the boulder he hid behind and snapped off before I could get into the fight. I was lucky they'd both been stopped."

And thinking of her alone back there with two armed gunmen, her knife broken, almost made Mitch start howling. Fighting down the panic, he thought of her diving in like she'd done. He had to think of something besides the danger she'd put herself in trying to protect him.

"D-do you swing around like that a lot?"

"Oh yes. I've spent years braiding thin branches, sometimes heavy ivy vines, even thin roots work. And I tied them up in trees. Some trees have branches so thick, so woven together, that I can run along on them almost like I'm on the ground. Where there are gaps in the branches, I've got swinging vines. Moving around in the treetops is much faster than being on foot. I prefer it up there."

Mitch wanted to ask her more about planning to attack that man and how it'd made her feel. He wanted to scold her about taking such risks.

For now, though, she seemed content riding along in his arms. And he was mighty content himself. He decided to put off the scolding.

Even annoyed as he was with this saucy, savage fairy princess, he didn't loosen his hold on her. In fact, as they rode along and he felt her solid and alive in his arms, his eyes were drawn to her lips. So close. So perfectly close.

And then they were closer still.

4

"Mitch, what're you doing?"

Ilsa jerked her head away from Mitch, who had suddenly been so close to her. Which had seemed fine until her big sister came riding down the trail.

"We had some trouble, Pa."

Ilsa sat up and looked at Jo, who was a married woman now. And had gone to a town. Not New York City it seemed, but a town nonetheless, and here she was alive and well. Of course, they'd need two weeks to be sure she'd live.

But for now, here Jo was, riding beside her husband, Dave, and her father-in-law, Quill Warden.

"What kind of trouble?" Quill asked. His eyes slid from Mitch to Ma to Alberto and to those horses carrying men draped over the saddle.

Ilsa was struck by how much Mitch looked like his pa. Both of them much shorter than Dave. They were stocky and blond—not yellow haired like Jo or white haired like Ursula, but light. They both had brown eyes and were built sturdy and strong, and had a way about them that spoke of an iron will and bone-deep confidence.

"How was town, Jo?" Jo looked so different from Ilsa. They were both small, but Jo had blond hair, and Ilsa had black. Their eyes were blue, but Ilsa's were a darker, brighter blue.

"Why are you sitting on Mitch's lap?" Jo's gaze slid between Ilsa and Mitch.

"I was riding alone." She jabbed a finger at the horse Mitch had scooped her off of. "But we started—" She turned to Mitch. "What did you call it?"

"Trotting," he said, in a voice so dry she was tempted to give him a drink of water.

Ilsa turned back to Jo. "That's right, trotting, and I was falling off—"

Jo's eyes went wide. "Trotting is hard. And dangerous."

Jo had never ridden before she'd met Dave—well, not since she was a child and then on Grandpa's plodding old horse who'd rather stand than walk. Jo had never gone down the mountain until she'd met Dave. She'd never met anyone other than family before she met Dave.

And then, so fast Ilsa's head could nearly spin, Jo was a married woman, and here she was coming home from town.

Alive.

"Trotting isn't dangerous if you know what you're doing. You just need lessons on how to ride is all." Mitch had pulled his horse to a stop.

"We're not even walking now." Ilsa poked him with the same finger she'd used to point at the horse. "You can put me back on the horse."

Mitch plopped her on her own saddle as if he couldn't wait to be rid of her. All the while talking about the shooting.

When Mitch finally wound down, Quill said, "You're looking better, Ilsa."

Quill studied her face. Ilsa wished these odd dots all over her would go away.

"We're on our way to Bucksnort to tell the sheriff what happened," Mitch continued on. "I'll find out if they're wanted men. We'll bury the one and see what the other knows once he wakes up. Then he'll be locked up for life or hanged."

"We'll ride back with you." Quill reined his horse around with impressive skill. Well, impressive to Ilsa. All she did was hold on and ride. Her horse seemed willing to stay with the herd.

Mitch rode beside Pa. Dave started talking to Ma and fell in beside her. Ilsa tried to keep up, but she was busy looking at Jo, who guided her own horse a bit. . . . Ilsa needed to learn to do that. Jo and Ilsa dropped back so they were behind the Wardens and ahead of Alberto and the unfortunate outlaws.

Ilsa couldn't contain her excited questions. Before Jo could talk, she asked, "How was town?"

"There are so many people." Jo's cheeks flushed with excitement. "Swarms of them."

Dave looked back with the nicest smile for his wife. "Only about one hundred people live in Bucksnort, honey. It's really small as towns go."

"One hundred people?" Ilsa clutched her hand to her throat, afraid it might be swelling shut.

43

Mitch must have heard because he called over his shoulder, "New York City has nearly a million people."

Dave faced forward so fast his hat fell off. "Really?" He caught his hat and returned it to his head.

"How many is a million? It must be even more than one hundred." Ilsa regretted her lack of schooling. "Grandma taught us to count to one hundred, but we never figured to have more than one hundred of anything, so going higher was a waste of time."

Mitch closed his eyes, and his shoulders slumped. She hoped a person couldn't relapse with the chicken pox.

Ma said over her shoulder, "Let's just say that New York is a very, very big city. But the town of Bucksnort is big, too, compared to living alone up on that mountaintop all your lives, so I'm sure it will seem crowded."

Mitch punched himself in the forehead with the side of his fist. His pa dragged him by the shoulder to face forward.

Dave called back to Alberto, "Let me tie those horses on my saddle, and you can head back home. You don't need to take this long ride."

Ilsa saw Alberto shake his head. "There's trouble down here from plenty of directions. Another hand riding along to town isn't a bad idea."

"So, you saw one hundred people?" Ilsa asked Jo. "Did you talk to all of them? Was there any fever in town?"

"I didn't see that many, but we didn't go into all the houses. Some folks must've stayed inside. We went in a general store, and there were cans of food sitting right on the shelf to buy. You didn't have to shoot it or pick it from the garden. It was all done for you. And right alongside the food were pots and pans."

She pointed to the big pack strapped on her horse behind her saddle. "Dave bought me fabric. There are several yards of it, and I will make myself a new dress."

Ilsa frowned. "How do you do that? You've never sewn a dress before."

For years they'd gotten by with clothing left from their Ma and Grandma, then when those wore away, they wore Pa and Grandpa's clothes. Ursula was good with a needle and made them fit. Then that was all gone. Until they'd met Ma Warden, they'd made do by tanning hides and wearing trousers—Grandpa had taught them how to sew leather, but they had no way to get more fabric. Jo had found ways to use old scraps of cloth to sew aspen leaf–sized pieces of cloth onto her clothes. It helped her hide in the woods. She had hunting clothes for every season.

"Dave said Ma would teach me." Jo was wearing a dress right now that Ma had made for her before she was allowed to go to town. Ilsa remembered that Grandma had always worn skirts, but they were completely wrong for riding a horse. And Ma Warden fussed if skirts flew up to uncover an ankle. She fussed about a lot of things. Who had made all these rules?

Yes, Ilsa wore a dress, too. Ma had made them each a dress. Even Ursula. But Ursula had left before her dress was done.

Jo's voice dropped to a whisper. "In town, I asked about the second Bible, and no one had ever heard of it. They had the big black Bible for sale in the general store, but there wasn't a second one." Jo leaned closer. "I think they might be right about there being only one Bible."

Ilsa hated to see her sister fall away from her faith.

But she remembered Ma asking her to stop calling people Satan and such, so with her eyes open and with what she hoped was a bland, nonjudgmental look on her face, she prayed frantically for all their immortal souls.

"Let's pick up the pace." Quill's voice was hard. A man used to taking charge. He didn't just look like Mitch. He acted like him. Of course, Dave and Ma could be fairly bossy, too.

Ilsa didn't mind being ordered around as long as no one gave orders she didn't want to obey.

Her horse stepped out, and Ilsa was jarringly reminded that "pick up the pace" meant trotting. By the time Mitch reached her side, she was hanging off the edge of her horse. He scooped her into his arms, handed the horse's reins to Dave, and rode back up to the front alongside Quill. She noticed Jo stuck to her horse nicely and pondered which parables concerned envy.

The trotting ended, and the horse broke into a much smoother run. Mitch and Quill discussed the details of the morning's attack while they rode. When they got to the part where Ilsa swung in to put a stop to all the shooting, Quill gave her a look so strange, so hard, that she felt like he was boring a hole right into her brain so he could look around in there.

"Ilsa," Mitch said, "we shouldn't be talking about such troubles in front of you."

Ilsa thought of the life she'd always lived. Running wild in the woods. Learning to track animals. She enjoyed finding wild birds' nests tucked into the tall grass. She'd watch the babies hatch and grow. The birds worked so hard to feed them, and the little ones would sprout feathers and finally fly away.

She knew how to be patient and watch without disturbing the critters. She'd pick her moment, slip in close, and watch the little birds chirp and tussle. She loved watching them and was mindful not to upset the animals into moving their babies.

Not all animals were soft and timid, though. And she knew what to do with a predator. If he was minding his own business and Ilsa could back away, she did it every time. But if they threatened her, Ilsa could protect herself. She knew wolverines, badgers, bears, and cougars. She knew rattlers and bull elk and wolves. She knew how to avoid a fight, and if it couldn't be avoided, she knew how to survive.

All of that she knew as easy as she took in each breath. But she knew nothing about people, how people thought, what they felt. She couldn't read expressions. Jo and Ursula, Grandma and Grandpa, too, had been so familiar and so direct that there wasn't much need to guess what they were thinking.

Now she wanted to understand Mitch, and listening to him talk to his pa was a good way to learn. "Don't worry about me."

He grinned. "Not sure I can help it."

"I want to know everything. I want to learn about people, how they act, good or bad. Tell your pa all the details about those men and don't worry that you need to keep it from me."

Mitch still looked at her. A furrow appeared on his forehead, and she realized he was thinking and fretting. She could tell—of course he'd just said he was, so that was a big clue. But she was matching his expression to his words. Maybe soon she'd match expressions to thoughts. Maybe understanding other people wasn't going to be as hard as she feared.

He turned to his pa. "I told you some about the troubles that brought me home." He had a vague tone to his voice, as if he wanted to speak of this to his pa but was guarding his words in front of Ilsa.

"Yep."

Ilsa poked him in the ribs. "You didn't tell me. What troubles?"

Mitch gave her a new look. Not worried, not a frown or a smile. She had no idea what he was thinking. She poked him again and that got a little smile out of him.

"It's not a nice story. I had a business partner, a young man I'd helped get a start."

"A start? Like the stuff we use to bake bread? We call that sourdough and sometimes starter."

Mitch laughed. "No, not like that." He hesitated, then said, "In some ways it's like that, though. Your kind of starter is a yeast that makes the bread dough rise. The start I gave Pete Howell helped him rise in the business world."

"Is he really fat and round and white?"

Shaking his head, Mitch kept talking. "I gave him his first job. He was smart and willing to work hard. There were men who gave me a chance when I was just starting out in business, and I thought I was doing for him what they'd done for me. I spent years working for myself, being ambitious for myself. When I gave Pete his start, I saw it as unselfish, thinking of someone else for the first time in a long time. It felt Christian. I promoted him to manager in one of my steel mills."

"*One* of your steel mills?" Quill sounded stunned.

With a small shrug, Mitch said, "You know I was successful back east."

"I knew you owned a steel mill but '*one* of them'? How many did you own?"

Mitch was slow to answer. "I had—eh—five by the end. And was a silent partner in a few other things."

Quill started coughing. Finally, sounding hoarse, he asked, "What else?"

"I owned one bank outright and shares in more. Uh . . . quite a few more. I owned a row of New York City buildings and had prime real estate in other parts of New York and in several other East Coast cities."

Ilsa wasn't sure what prime real estate meant, but she didn't ask. She wanted him to keep talking. She'd save up questions for later.

"I invested in lots of things. Railroads, textile mills, smelting plants, coal mines, and kerosene refineries. Plenty of other businesses, too. Pete Howell knew enough about that to—well—I guess he wanted it all. When I realized he was behind two murder attempts—"

"Two?" Ilsa hadn't meant to ask, but the word slipped out.

"Yep, the second time I caught the man, and he told me Pete had hired him. I found Pete's name in the pocket of the man we—uh—I killed today." Mitch paused and shifted Ilsa around so he supported her and held the reins in one hand, and had a hand free to rub his face for a bit too long.

She was learning he did that when he was upset, so maybe she was beginning to understand him better.

Ilsa didn't have to get much practice studying people to know killing that man had hurt Mitch. "Thou shalt not kill" echoed in her mind, but she hadn't hesitated to fight when Mitch was in such danger. Neither she nor Mitch had had any choice.

"I'd been wanting to come home for a long while, but it was easy to keep buying and earning. When that second man took his shot and then told me Pete's name, I knew it was time to get out. I sold quietly. There were plenty of dollars chasing after what I had. I had no plans to ever go back, so I converted everything to gold and carried it along with me."

"And these men were sent *here* to kill you?" Quill asked, sounding fierce.

Mitch shrugged one shoulder. "I found Pete Howell's name in the pocket of the dead man. And I found the same amount of money split between the two as what I found on both the men who attacked me back east. One thousand dollars must be the price to hire a killer."

A silence fell as they galloped along, and Ilsa couldn't remember any of the questions that had churned in her. Maybe Mitch had answered them all.

"Thanks for riding back to Bucksnort with us, Pa. It's good to have the company."

Quill nodded. "Going with only Dave and Jo was a little

50

quieter, a little sneakier. We slipped into town and bought the land without raising any notice, or not much. We had to spend the night, had to eat, but I'd hoped to get away and get home before Bludge Pike got word we were around. But now, between your business partner sending trouble your way, and Pike wanting to steal my land, we need to stick together and be ready to back each other. We still can't face down all Pike's men, especially with Wax Mosby among 'em."

"And my trouble from New York is taking us straight to the trouble you have out here."

"We have no choice. I didn't want to leave buying that land until spring. I just felt like it had to be settled."

"I like it being in our hands, too."

Ilsa listened to them talk. They were so similar to each other. Their voices had the same tone, though Mitch talked faster, and she'd heard Dave say that was how they talked in New York City.

"And we have no choice but to take these men in to the sheriff. Trouble is," Quill said, "Pike might be coming."

"But there's no way to avoid the trip, not with one man dead and another needing to be locked up. We need to get there fast, drop these men with the sheriff, and get home." Mitch kicked his horse, and the ride got faster.

Ilsa liked listening to them talk. It was so different from her usual, all-women life. But they fell silent as the horses stretched out their legs.

No talking over the thundering hoofbeats.

Just exactly how big was the world down here? And if they had to ride all day to get to Bucksnort, then where exactly was New York City?

Mitch had said New York City was days and days away. Did that mean four days? Or more? She wished he'd said exactly how far it was. And how ever many one million was, it sure sounded like a lot of people. It should have terrified her. Instead, she was intrigued.

She'd probably never get a chance to see it, but she could certainly wonder.

Ursula sent music up to God, the words to the One Hundredth Psalm. It'd been Grandma's favorite—and Grandma was given to singing just as Ursula was. "The Old One Hundredth," Grandma had called it. Make a joyful noise. But Grandma sang songs she knew. It was Ursula who invented tunes for Bible verses and everyday joys and sorrows.

Some days Ursula could barely bring herself to talk for the weight of all her fears, but she could always sing.

And Grandpa had loved to hear the tunes Ursula dreamed up.

After Grandma died, Grandpa had taught all of them everything he knew. He'd done it with an almost desperate fear, because he knew his life would end before theirs, and they had to be able to survive without going down the mountain.

Jo had been the best at hunting. Ilsa had taken to heart all Grandpa knew of healing and herbs. Ursula ran the house, but that had been Grandma's job—Grandpa couldn't teach her anything there. The thing she'd had that was her connection to Grandpa was singing. It soothed him, gave him pleasure. It made him smile.

She had a broom she'd made of fine twigs tied with vines to a stout stick. She had a roaring fire. She had food because, though Jo was the best hunter, Ursula could bring down a deer well enough and find winter dried berries and dig up Indian potatoes. She'd even found a beehive. Jo had brought flour and other useful things that were harder to come by. Ursula had tried to ignore those things, but in the end, it was too tempting, and she'd made biscuits, baked bread, and even tried a pie.

She swept the floor and brushed the refuse out into the hall beyond her door and down the hall out of her way. Just as she'd swept her whole life away.

From the hall, she looked overhead at the aging timbers that formed part of the roof. She was in a strange old building made of stacked stone blocks. She had no idea who'd built it. Much of it was collapsed, with many small rooms with walls partly caved off with their roof gone. But the back of the building reached into a deep overhang so the roof was solid rock overhead and only the front of this room was a constructed wall.

The fireplace was in that wall, and the room was cozy. Jo and Dave had brought blankets and pans, even a mattress stuffed with prairie grass. They'd brought it all, and then she'd demanded they leave.

And here she was alone and determined to stay alone forever. She sang, "'Make a joyful noise unto the Lord, all ye lands. Serve the Lord with gladness: come into His presence with singing.'"

Yes, finally, at last she was alone and safe, and soon enough she'd get used to it and be happy. The song was helping her find that happiness.

Surely the happiness would come one of these days.

On days that happiness seemed out of reach, she had started throwing an ax at a tree. She was getting fast and accurate with it. And if she could find some relief from her worries by hurling an ax, she'd take it.

5

They reached town after full dark. The sun was long set, and it was late. Ilsa had spent time in her own saddle when they walked and time in Mitch's lap when they trotted or galloped. The smooth glide of galloping probably wouldn't have knocked her off the horse, but getting from the walk to the gallop, by way of trotting, was just too much for her.

Mitch assured her he'd teach her to stay on a horse while it was trotting. Right now, they just didn't have time for a riding lesson.

The unconscious man riding draped over a saddle came around after a time, and Alberto spoke quietly to him, asking questions. The man wouldn't speak a word.

They stopped once in the midafternoon to stretch their legs and slip into the woods for a necessary moment. They saw to it that the newly wakened man had his turn for that and water to drink and as much food as they had. Once he was conscious, they let him sit up with his hands tied to the saddle horn and the reins tied to the horse ahead of him, with two men watching him at all times.

As their horses clopped into town, walking past buildings, Ilsa was stunned by the size of Bucksnort. She nearly hurt her neck looking in all directions, trying to see all the buildings. Lights were on in many of them. Music came out of one that was lit up bright as day, but not singing, which was the only music Ilsa had ever heard, and that mainly from Ursula with the miraculous beauty of her voice. This music was a strange, plinking sound, pretty though, and she desperately wanted to go see what it was.

And there were people everywhere. She counted six.

Men walked along smooth boards that lay on the ground along the fronts of each building. Horses stood, tied to hitching posts. Ilsa saw a dress in a window and a pretty bowl, beside them were jumbles of things she didn't even recognize.

Quill didn't look at any of these wonders. Instead, he led the way to a building that was taller and wider than anything she'd ever imagined. A whole row of big windows on top of another row at ground level.

"We'll sleep here at the hotel tonight," Quill said. "I'll get a room for the women and another for the men. After I register, we'll take these outlaws to see the sheriff."

"My brother lives in Bucksnort, Quill," Alberto said. "I'll bunk at his house."

Quill nodded. "Go tell him you're coming, then catch up to us at the sheriff's office. You and Mitch are witnesses. After you've had your say with the sheriff, stay with your brother. I know his house, so I'll stop for you in the morning."

"Quill," Ma said firmly, "I'm a witness, too. And so is Ilsa. Especially Ilsa."

Quill gave Ma a serious look. "I've heard all about what happened, Izzy, but do we have to include her? The jail is a rough place. I don't like her or any of you women coming in. There may be others locked up. And the sheriff isn't an easy man. If he speaks harshly in front of either of you, I won't put up with it. After I punch him, I may find myself behind bars."

Ma smiled. "We're going. Let Dave and Jo check in while we get on with delivering these men. There are already folks noticing we brought in a man draped over a saddle and another one tied up. We don't want to linger."

Ilsa looked around. Men who'd been walking had stopped and turned to watch them pass. Doors on the building with the music swung open and two more men stepped out. There had been a buzz of voices, now there was silence. The music cut off.

"You're right, Izzy," Quill said. "Dave, handle the hotel. Keep Jo at your side."

Mitch took the reins of the horses Alberto was leading while Alberto rode off to his brother's house. Quill turned from the hotel and rode around the corner of a row of buildings. Ilsa, Ma, and Mitch followed.

He'd gone past several more buildings before he came to one with bars on the windows.

Ilsa had never seen a person besides her grandparents and her sisters until the Wardens moved into her high mountain home. She'd never been to a town. Now here she was, finally down off that mountain, seeing people, and the first place she'd see was the inside of a jail.

It wasn't really how she'd dreamed this trip would be.

Mitch was so glad to see bars on those windows he almost collapsed.

Falling off his horse would've been just plain embarrassing, but the day had almost finished him. It'd started early with a shootout and was now finally, maybe, almost over.

The only thing that distracted him from pure exhaustion was holding Ilsa in his arms. Even now, with her safely on the ground, he could feel the weight of her. He had the fleeting thought that if he could just hold her forever, maybe he could push back the thought of this morning's madness.

Did she have the same thoughts circling because of her attempted attack on those men? If she did, he couldn't tell. She said she was upset about her broken knife. And he hadn't noticed any stab wounds. He had to hope she had nothing weighing on her conscience that she couldn't talk about.

He thought again of her in his arms, that moment when they'd been too close, right before his pa rode up. Pa's arrival had stopped Mitch from doing something really stupid, like kissing her.

Pa put an end to his circling thoughts of Ilsa when he pushed open the jailhouse door and hollered, "Hale, we've brought two men in. One dead. One wounded. We need to turn them over to you."

"What's happened here, Quill?" The sheriff pushed out past Pa. His gaze ran over them all until it reached the dead man and the other prisoner.

"These two men attacked my son." Pa jabbed a finger

at Mitch and the sheriff's eyes swung to him. "Dave and I were headed home when we met them coming in."

Sheriff Hale nodded, taking a few steps closer to get a better look at the outlaws.

"We rode back here with them. These men shot wild when my wife, this young lady, and our cowhands were close at hand with no mind who got hurt. But we believe they were after my son Mitch. It's trouble that's followed him here from New York."

That earned Mitch a sharp look from the sheriff. Mitch quickly explained what had happened, and Ma and Ilsa told their stories.

Mitch and Pa helped untie the prisoner. When they stood him up, his knees buckled, and he sank.

Then the man whipped one leg out to knock the sheriff down and grabbed for his gun. Mitch slammed a fist into the outlaw's face, then stomped hard on his wrist to knock the gun loose.

Pa was there before Mitch could swing another fist. He caught the varmint by the back of his shirt, yanked him to his feet, and marched him fast into the jail. Mitch guided Ilsa and Ma through the door in time to see Pa shove the man into the cell and clang the door shut. The sheriff was there with a key and clicked the lock.

Hale turned to go back out, and Mitch went to see what he was doing.

Alberto came up and talked quietly with the sheriff, telling the same story Mitch had, but from his own angle.

"I'll have a look at this one." The sheriff grabbed a handful of hair and lifted the dead man's head up to study it.

There was a long spell of silence broken by the music

starting up again in the Broad Beam Saloon. Horses' hooves clopped along the dirt streets of Bucksnort, and men went back to talking. A few had come around the corner from the main street to watch the goings-on at the jail, but they stayed back and murmured amongst themselves.

"I'm going to need you all to tell me what happened again and in detail." The sheriff dropped the man's head and turned back for his office. "But before you start, I can tell you the dead man is Blue Winston. I'll be a while digging out his wanted poster, but it's there and there's a reward. He's a known gunman, and his reputation lends weight to your story."

"I'll see to the horses, Quill," Alberto said. "And get your bedrolls delivered to the hotel."

"Thanks."

"Alberto, can you lead this horse over to the under-taker?" The sheriff pointed down the street a stretch where a man dressed in a black suit looked at his watch, then at the man draped over his horse, then back to his watch. "That's him. Tell him to start building a box but not to bury him before I say so."

With a silent nod, Alberto led all the horses away.

They stepped inside, and the sheriff walked up to the cell bars. "And I don't know him on sight, but word is a man named Kansas Cassidy rides with Winston. By de-scription, I'd say this is him. Men known as willing to kill for a price. Both are wanted. You've taken two dangerous hombres off the range, Mitch."

The sheriff turned and reached out a hand.

Mitch shook it.

Ilsa reached her hand out, too. The sheriff looked at it awkwardly, then took hers and gave it a hardy shake.

"Ladies, have a seat."

Ma and Ilsa took two chairs that sat facing the sheriff's desk while Pa and Mitch stood behind them. Pa leaned against the wall, and Mitch thought he looked all in.

Settling into the chair behind his desk, the sheriff said, "There'll be a reward for Cassidy here if this is him. Blue Winston broke jail for another murder charge, and he killed a lawman up near Colorado City when he done it. Word is Cassidy helped with the break. There were witnesses, but no one had ever seen Kansas Cassidy before. If those witnesses can swear this is the man, he'll hang. I've also heard Winston was one of the best trackers in the West."

Then the man reached low and behind him. He took a stack of wanted posters off the floor. Mitch saw two more stacks a foot tall. Looking for the poster of Winston could take a while, and Sheriff Hale knew enough he didn't need to see one, he was probably just curious about the amount of the reward.

"We'd be pleased," Pa said, eyeing the stacks, "if we didn't have to stay in town for a long stretch. We'd like to get home before snow closes the trail."

Mitch noticed Pa didn't explain that they didn't live on the Circle Dash just now. No doubt Sheriff Hale knew where the Circle Dash was, and the word about them buying the high valleys might go unnoticed for a time. Maybe until spring.

"I want you to go over it again." The sheriff's eyes went to Mitch. "And explain why someone would hire your death?"

Mitch told his tale. The murder attempts back east. The note he'd found in Winston's pocket. He produced the note and jabbed a finger at his old partner's name.

"I know Pete Howell. And these two outlaws had, split between them, the amount of money mentioned in the note." Mitch got the pouches of gold coins out and handed them to the sheriff.

The sheriff took them, frowning. "Blood money. It's a foul business."

Mitch turned to look at Ilsa, feeling like a fool for not hiding his tracks better. And now danger was on his back-trail. And his family and pretty little Ilsa Nordegren were right in the line of fire.

"It looks like I brought trouble with me." His gaze shifted to Pa. "I'll leave and hope the trouble follows on after me. I can handle it somewhere else. Or—"

Ma slammed a hand flat on the sheriff's desk.

Ilsa jumped and squeaked, then looked at Ma with wide eyes.

"You're not going anywhere, Mitchell Warden," Ma exclaimed. "If there's trouble coming, we'll face it. Just like we have to face those gunmen of Pike's."

"What's this?" The sheriff stood so suddenly his chair skidded back and slammed into the wall behind his desk.

Pa shook his head. "We haven't even talked about Bludge. One of his gunmen, I think Wax Mosby, got a bullet into me."

The sheriff scowled. "Mosby's been seen in the area, and he's even come to town. But far as I know he's not wanted for anything. He's a hired gun, but he stays to the right side of the law."

The growl from Pa was more bear than man. "The right side of the law? He came to our place to accuse us of being nesters who'd moved in on Pike's land."

Pa's laugh was humorless. "As if I haven't been here for years and with a clear deed to my land. But we were warned, a few days ahead, that they were coming to drive us off. We were outgunned, so instead of standing to fight, I ran like a yellow coward. I didn't want to shoot it out with hired killers without plenty of men to back me. I got most of my cattle and hands to the high country and figured to spend the winter making plans, then come back in the spring and have it out with Bludge. When we moved out, we found good grazing land. We came down to buy it, hoping to slip into town and get back up the mountain with no shots fired. I want to handle this legally instead of with guns. But if I have to fight, I'll fight."

Pa leaned on the desk, hands flat, so his head came close to the sheriff on the far side. "Pike's driven me off my land, and that burns bad, Sheriff. I'm not going to let it stand. Pike's been driving off homesteaders with solid, legal claims."

"Rumors got to town, but no one's come in to accuse Pike of anything. All I've heard is secondhand. And what goes on outside of town isn't my concern. Nesters and ranchers don't pay my salary, and I'm plenty busy keeping the peace here."

With a shake of his head, Pa straightened from the desk. "It ain't right. There ought to be some kind of law out in the country."

"We can report it to the US Marshals' office. They're shorthanded in this area, but they can send someone."

"Fine, we'll see if they can bring an army." With a snort of disgust, Pa said, "When Mosby, or whoever it was, shot me, I couldn't do anything but lay down and heal. Pike has a lot of men. I might've won a fight against 'em, but I didn't want to ask my men to die for my land."

"I know your property rights are legal, Quill, and I'll stand by you when it comes time to push back against Pike, but I can't do that if you're all the way out of town, and I don't even hear about it."

"Pike's calling me a nester. I've been out here since Mitch was a tyke and before Dave was born. Pike's on the prod and getting land no matter who he needs to push out. Well, I'm not a man who gets pushed without fighting back."

"Pike called you a nester? He just came into this country last spring and he drove in with twenty thousand head of cattle. Next time I see him here in town, I'll make sure he knows your claim is clear and legal. If he somehow ends up owning your place, I'll charge him with theft and any other crime I can think of."

"You can threaten all you like, but he knows as well as we do that you're only the lawman in Bucksnort," Ma said. "We're our own law out of town, and we accept that."

The sheriff didn't like that. Mitch could see he wanted to protest someone taking the law into their own hands. But he'd need to follow that up with an offer to help.

"The plain truth is," Mitch said, "this is the closest town to our ranch, but it's a half a day's ride away. I don't blame you, Sheriff, for not covering so much territory. It would be impossible."

The sheriff muttered and adjusted his Stetson. "Me and one deputy just can't do it."

"Bludge is our problem, Sheriff," Pa said. "We won't be judge, jury, and executioner, but we will be the law. Catch him if we can, and stop him hard if we can't. Whatever happens, we'll do it legal.

"Talk to him if you've a mind, just to make sure he knows the Wardens will stand and fight. But Bludge isn't our biggest problem."

Considering Pa's barely healed gunshot wound, Mitch thought he was a real big problem.

"The men we brought in today are." Ma jammed her fists on her hips and glared at Mitch, then she turned to Hale. "Are you done with us, Sheriff?"

Mitch watched Ilsa study every move Ma made. Mitch was a little nervous that the woman was intending to copy Ma's . . . forceful . . . way of behaving.

"For now, but I want to talk to you again before you head home, in case I have more questions. But your answers won't change much about the two men you brought in. With this man being wanted elsewhere, we don't need testimony or a trial. We'll bury the dead and send for someone to transport the living, and that'll be the end of it."

Mitch knew they weren't even close to the end of it. He had to deal with the trouble following him, and to do that, he had to get away from here.

6

I like it down here off the mountain. Where else can we go?" Ilsa tugged on Mitch's arm. The jail had worried her, but it had been so interesting.

Mitch looked at her as they walked along, the men's boots thudding on the sidewalk. Ma and Quill led the way, Ilsa and Mitch followed.

There was music playing again from one building, and it was the only one with its lights still lit, except for one light, burning dim, in the big hotel where Jo and Dave had gone.

"That is a lunatic thing to say to me. I'm heading east. You can't come."

"You're not going anywhere." Ma didn't even look back, she just walked on toward the hotel, going down some steps on the corner of the wooden walk and crossing a wide street lined with hitching posts out front of every building. There were steps in front of the hotel, and she went up them, her feet thundering like an oncoming storm.

"Are you going to New York City?" Ilsa tugged on his sleeve.

"Mitch," Quill said, glancing over his shoulder, "don't go back east. You've got financial tricks you can play from here. Do this through the telegraph or with letters."

Quill opened the door to the hotel and held it wide. Ilsa just walked right in. It seemed real nice of Quill to do that.

"That note taken out of the outlaw's pocket might be enough proof to get the law to act. I might be able to handle this without going all the way to New York. But I need a bigger city. I need access to a lawman with some reach across states. Or . . ." Mitch fell silent, his eyes narrow.

Ilsa watched him, waiting.

"Or what?" Quill asked.

"I talked with a Pinkerton agent before I came west. They did some hunting to find evidence against Howell. I could hire them again."

"A what?" Ilsa asked. She was pleased to hear Ma and Quill ask a similar question.

Mitch shook his head. "It's a company you can hire to investigate things. Like the sheriff, but I'd have to pay them."

"Whoever heard of such a thing?" Ma asked.

"I don't know how far west they are now. They have a good-sized agency in most towns back east, and I know they're in Chicago."

Ilsa watched Mitch closely. His eyes shifted back and forth as he rubbed his chin. Looking closer, she could see whiskers on his chin. He'd had a lot of hair on his face when he'd come home. It wasn't a full, long beard like Grandpa had, but his face had been real furry. Then he'd shaved it smooth until he got sick and quit shaving. No shaving when there are chicken pox blisters all over. Since he'd mended, he'd shaved every day except maybe not today because of the trouble.

Chin hair fascinated Ilsa. There were so many things she didn't know.

Pa clapped Mitch on the back from where he walked behind him. "Can we talk about this more in the morning? It's been a long day, and I'm still not at full strength. I doubt you and Ilsa are either."

Mitch nodded. "I won't go running off without talking to you."

Inside the hotel, they found the night manager sitting, reading one of the Bibles. He looked up. "You must be the Wardens?"

Ilsa didn't correct him.

"We got a late supper on in the dining room, if you're hungry. Your son got three bedrooms. One for him and his wife, and he said the women would share one and the men another. Your things are already up there."

"Excellent." Ma took one of the keys he offered. Pa took the other, and they headed upstairs. Ilsa was bubbling with curiosity and questions, but everyone else seemed to think going to bed was more interesting than a town.

Ilsa admitted she was tired, and she also knew she'd never understand people.

Ma snored.

Ilsa had noticed that before from sharing a house with her, but she'd never shared a room.

Shut in the same room with her, she now found that Ma snored louder than a thunderstorm. And Ilsa saw no hope for sleep.

Ilsa lay on her own bed. Dave and Jo had gotten a room for Ilsa and Ma that had two separate beds in it. The bed sagged in the middle, the blankets were scratchy, and Ilsa could have ignored all that.

But the snoring!

Ilsa was used to sleeping in a cabin in the high mountains with complete silence other than the songs of the night birds and the soothing sounds of a mountain breeze.

Finally, her head almost foggy with exhaustion, afraid she was going to lose control and shake Ma awake, she threw off the woolen blanket and sat up. She moved silently, thinking of the unfairness of that when Ma didn't have to be silent.

She was in bed fully clothed, but for her shoes. She picked them up and slipped out of the room.

And there she stood, looking down a stairway that led to the front door. There were three rooms to her left and three to her right. The one nearest past the room she'd shared with Ma had Jo and Dave in it, to her right was Mitch and Quill. The rest, well, who could say who slept in those rooms? And who could say who was downstairs?

She was afraid to go downstairs, and she couldn't go into one of the rooms. Which left her with no idea what to do.

The snoring seemed to get louder behind her. Finally, almost desperately, she went to the stairs and sat down. To pass the moments, she pulled on her shoes.

Despite the day being overwhelming, or maybe *because* it had been, her thoughts went to Mitch leaving.

He was going to a big city.

And she, who had been born on a mountaintop and never allowed to come down, had seen her world expand beyond belief today. She'd been abandoned by her parents, though they had almost certainly died so they hadn't *meant* to abandon her, and raised by her grandparents, until they died when Ilsa was so young she could barely remember them. And they had said over and over that the lowlands were dangerous. The lowlands were full of crime and disease. They must never go down, never. If you go down, you'll die.

The fear had been as solid as a wall, and they had never gone down. The three of them alone. Ursula, more a mother to Ilsa than anyone else in her world. Jo, the provider, the hunter. Ilsa had been, in many ways, their child, though they were only a little older than her.

She knew the animals and plants of her mountaintop as well as she knew her sisters. She knew which plants could be used for medicine, taught by her grandfather, who'd learned it when he lived with an Indian tribe.

Ilsa had only the vaguest notion of what an Indian tribe was.

The animals, their tracks, their nests, their habits, were as clear to her as the spoken word, and she loved her mountain home and missed it. And feared this wide world. But it fascinated her, too. Just as she'd learned about her wild home, she now wanted to learn the ways of people.

She wanted to understand the expressions on a person's face. She wanted to learn about everyone and everything.

Now Ilsa had done the forbidden. She'd come down off

the mountain. She'd seen this huge city. And Mitch said there were other cities, even larger. There was a wildness in her to see those cities. An almost desperate longing to see more of the world.

She wanted to go. And of course, she never would get to.

A squeak from behind made her jump. It wasn't the door Mitch and Quill were in, it was the next one down. But it was Mitch standing there, fully dressed, looking at her.

Leaping to her feet, desperately happy to see a face she knew, she rushed the few steps to him and asked, "What are you doing in there?"

"Shh-shh." Mitch held up a hand as if to push her back. He didn't touch her, but she quit talking immediately.

"You'll wake up Ma and Pa."

Ilsa felt the painful truth of that. Wasn't she out here in the hall because she didn't want to do that?

"You can't be out here in the hallway." Mitch looked left and right with a line of furrows on his forehead.

"Yes, I can." She spoke the obvious. "Here I stand, in the hallway."

With a tight, hard shake of his head, Mitch said, "I mean it's not . . . um . . . there are rules for the behavior of young ladies. You're breaking one of them."

Ilsa had never had many rules in her life. She remembered how Ma Warden didn't like her ankles showing. Ma said that was a rule. Had her ankles been showing while she sat on the step?

"What rule are you talking about?"

Mitch squinted his eyes at her, and she thought maybe,

in the dim lantern light of the hallway, she saw his cheeks turn a bit pink.

"Th-the rules about . . . about how a young woman should . . . should conduct herself in matters of . . . of propriety." Brash, fast-talking Mitch seemed barely able to get the words out. And, unless he had a fever—and she really hoped he didn't because she'd probably catch it—he seemed to be blushing.

And talking in strange, unfamiliar words.

"What does *propriety* mean?"

Mitch clapped an open hand over his eyes, then dragged the hand down, past his nose, his mouth. "It doesn't surprise me in the least that you don't know."

"That's not really an answer."

"I-I'll explain." Nodding, Mitch seemed to be forcing words from his mouth. "What I mean is, a woman should not be alone. It's not safe. A man could bother you."

"You're bothering me quite a bit right now, so that's the truth. But I see no point in waking up your ma so she can watch you bother me."

Mitch's jaw went tight. Ilsa studied it, wondering what in the world the man was thinking.

"I'd like to bother you, Ilsa."

"That is still not an answer."

"Oh, it's an answer, all right. But you're too innocent to realize it." Mitch paused. Cleared his throat. Cleared it again. "A young woman who is not married, well, the thing is, if someone saw you out here alone, they might— that is, a woman, if a man came upon her alone in the night and then someone else came along and saw the man and woman alone in the night—"

"You mean alone like the two of us are right now?"

Mitch's throat moved as if he were swallowing something that wasn't going down easy.

"Yes, exactly like the two of us are right now. If someone found us alone together in the night, well, people might think we were being . . . doing . . . that is . . ." Mitch fell silent as if he just could not put his worries into words.

Ilsa leaned close and whispered, "I thought you were sleeping in the same room with your pa?"

Mitch shook his head and started talking again, so it was good she changed the subject. "After you and Ma went to bed, I went down and asked if there was another room empty."

He leaned closer and whispered so quietly she was almost reading words shaped silently by his lips. "Pa snores like a cave of grizzly bears."

Ilsa straightened away from Mitch and giggled. She slapped her hand over her mouth, but the laughter was there, just muffled. Mitch's eyes gleamed as if he wanted to laugh himself.

"Ma, too, as I recall," he said.

Ilsa nodded from behind her hand just as the door next to Mitch, opposite the one Quill was in, clicked open.

Grabbing her wrist, Mitch yanked her into the room and shut the door swiftly and silently, and pressed her back to the door.

"What—"

Mitch clapped *his* hand over her mouth this time. Heavy boots walked past Mitch's door. Mitch looked at the floor, his eyes unfocused. Listening to the man walk by.

Ilsa didn't know exactly what Mitch was trying to say

about it not being right for a man and woman to be alone together in the night. But she was very sure if it was wrong to be alone in the hallway, then it was also wrong to be alone in his room.

Time to go back to Ma, snoring or not.

She listened as the man turned and began walking down the stairs. Where was he going at this late hour? Or was it an early hour? Ilsa wasn't sure. She often rose before the sun. Maybe morning was coming, and this endless night would pass.

Mitch slowly lifted his hand from her mouth. His hand closed and opened in a way that drew her eye. He looked at his hand, then those brown eyes shifted to meet hers. His hand quit opening and closing and rested on her upper arm. He rubbed up and down, and Ilsa thought of that moment when she'd been riding with him. A moment when he'd seemed too close, then closer yet.

Now his hand caressed her arm, then the other hand lifted to her other shoulder and slid around to her back.

In the dark of his room, with those footsteps fading, Mitch said quietly, "I lived a life surrounded by people I couldn't trust. I realize now many of them just told me whatever they thought I wanted to hear because I paid their salary. And I'll admit, I did tend to fire people who disagreed with me because, of course, I thought I was always right. For years, I've heard little but 'yes, sir,' 'right away, sir,' 'whatever you think best, sir.'"

"That seems nice." Ilsa rested one hand on his broad chest and patted him because he seemed unhappy with himself. "I wouldn't mind if you'd start saying yes more often."

"Oh, I don't think that'd be wise at all."

"Saying yes to me? I am sure I would like it very much."

"I'd make sure you liked it *very* much."

Ilsa wasn't sure, but the way he said it made her wonder if he was talking about something completely different than she was.

Mystified, she said, "If, instead of scolding all the time, you say yes to me, of course I'd like it."

The room was nearly pitch dark, shrouded in deep shadows, but she had fine vision in the night. Her eyes had adjusted, and she could see him well, and hear the rise and fall of each breath. Smell him. His scent only made her realize how, until just recently, she'd never been near a man. And never close enough to be so surrounded by all these impressions of him.

His hands slid up and down her arms, both of them now.

"All those years, and now I come home to find a woman with wide-eyed innocence, who speaks her mind, even when I don't want to hear it. I find that refreshing, and I am enjoying it."

"I don't remember you enjoying it particularly."

He gave a small, gentle laugh. His hands relaxed, then tightened. "You have to get out of here, Miss Ilsa."

She most certainly did.

"Your hand over my mouth to keep me quiet made me suspect you were trying to let that man go past without him seeing or hearing us."

"Yes, as I was trying to say, it is against accepted rules for a young, unmarried lady to be seen in the night, alone with an unrelated man."

"Is it against these rules for that man to be alone at night?"

"No, the man can be alone, just not women."

"Why on earth is there such an unfair rule?"

Mitch was silent. Ilsa suspected it was because he didn't have an answer any more than she did.

"Well, we're alone, but no one can see us in here. So then is this not against the rules?"

"It is most definitely against the rules." Mitch closed his eyes. His hands opened and closed on her upper arms. "You go back to Ma's room, and you stay in there no matter how loud she snores."

"I was daydreaming about smothering her with a pillow. I thought it best to get out."

A chuckle escaped Mitch's lips, which drew her eyes to them.

"Go on right now, before it's too late." Mitch was still holding her, in fact, if she wasn't mistaken, he might be holding her closer than before.

Although it might have been her moving closer, not him.

"Too late for what?"

Mitch reached around her and grabbed the doorknob. At that moment, footsteps sounded down at the bottom of the steps, the man returning, maybe from the privy?

Mitch's hand froze, his eyes sharpened. As he stood, hand on the doorknob, he surrounded her more than ever. He was closer than ever.

She spoke an obvious truth. "I can't leave now."

"No, you can't." He released the knob, and his arm slid around her waist. "It doesn't matter, it's already too late."

The man was on his way up.

"You said that before. Too late for—"

"Hush." Mitch's lips descended on hers.

Ilsa hadn't expected that.

The man came on. Maybe Mitch just wanted her to be quiet, and his hands were too busy with other things, so he couldn't cover her mouth with one of them.

Then his hands moved to raise her arms up and tug them around his neck. He tilted his head, slid both his arms around her waist, and pulled her close.

And she forgot there was anyone coming. In fact, she forgot there was anyone else in the whole world. All she could think of was the warmth of Mitch's lips, the strength of his arms.

She clung to him like ivy on a mountain oak.

And the door slammed into the back of her head.

7

"Mitch Warden, what is going on here?"

He jumped away from the door, and Ilsa, holding on tight, was dragged along with him.

Plenty was going on here. All wrong. All a huge mistake. He wrestled Ilsa's arms off him, and they stood, still very close, facing Ma.

Good news, she wasn't snoring anymore.

He slung an arm around Ilsa's waist and urged her two long strides forward to get them out of his bedroom. He had a feeling that wasn't going to put Ma's mind at ease much.

How much had she seen? She'd definitely witnessed the wrestling to get them apart. Maybe she could be convinced she'd knocked Ilsa into his arms. Which didn't excuse them being in there to begin with, but maybe she could just keep that to herself.

He opened his mouth to tell a version of the truth that left out the moments before the door assaulted them, but the man who'd just clomped up the stairs must've heard them because he came out of his room. His heavy tread had no doubt stirred Ma awake. At which point she would've noticed she was alone in her room. So she'd come out to hunt down Ilsa, but how did she even know Mitch had rented his own room?

Then Pa's door swung open. "Yep, next door like I said. Oh, you found Ilsa, too. Good."

Not good. Not good at all.

Ma must've enlisted Pa's help in her search for Ilsa, only to find out Mitch was missing. And Pa had known where Mitch had moved to. So, Ma the Bloodhound had probably come to his room to enlist his help in the search.

Well, the search was over.

Pa passed an assessing glare over Mitch and Ilsa, then crossed his arms and frowned as he joined the mess.

The noisy man was on Mitch's right, Pa on his left, and Ma right in front of him. He was surrounded for a fact. Behind him lay only the dream of escape. They'd just follow right after him if he ran back into his room.

Speaking past Mitch, Ilsa, and Ma, the man said, "Hello, Quill. I thought you left town today. You had your son and daughter-in-law with you." The man's eyes slid to Mitch with Ilsa standing right in front of him. "But this ain't them."

"Oh, but you mentioned having another son." The man seemed to be a lunkhead with no notion that this wasn't the time for a friendly visit. "I recall him from when he was a youngster. You must be Mitch."

The man reached out a hand just as a lantern lit up the base of the stairs and a heavy-set woman wearing an apron looked up from below. Next another door opened in the hallway behind the clomping man. There was enough commotion in the hall now to raise the dead, let alone wake the sleeping.

Everyone was fully dressed for the day. What time was it anyway?

They all delayed Mitch having to shake hands with the man who had caused this mess by giving Mitch the notion of dragging Ilsa into his room. Except Mitch had better admit right here and now, this mess was his fault and his alone.

From the newly opened door past the man who was trying to shake Mitch's hand, a couple emerged. The husband was fully dressed right up to his parson's collar and had eyes that, well, they were blazing with a righteous fire that probably goaded many a man to give his soul to the Lord just to get the man to stop staring.

The parson looked at Mitch, Ilsa, the open bedroom door right behind them, then back at Mitch. The parson seemed to come to some conclusion that Mitch feared was way too close to the truth.

The woman at the bottom of the stairs called up with a voice fit to stand in place for the trumpets announcing the return of the Lord in glory, "You folks are all up and going early. Breakfast will be on soon." Her eyes followed the same path the parson's had, and they were wide open and far too eager to take in all the details. Mitch had met her, too, and she struck him as a woman who lived to gossip.

The cook's husband owned the hotel, and between her and her husband, they probably spoke daily to nearly everyone in town. Of course, there were only a hundred people in town. Mitch braced himself for every single one of them to traipse through here before this was over.

The parson was the circuit rider for Bucksnort. Mitch had met him and his family at supper here in the hotel. Mitch now regretted he hadn't stayed and let the sheriff question him for another hour or so.

The parson's two small children came out of the room, too. And then Mitch remembered the man wasn't a circuit rider. Not anymore. Circuit riders didn't bring a wife and children along for preaching. This man was here to stay.

Mitch's folks had introduced Ilsa as Jo's sister, definitely not Mitch's wife. And yet here the two of them stood right outside Mitch's wide-open bedroom door.

The new parson in town made a fine witness to this mess.

Which was when Mitch realized he still had his arm around Ilsa's waist. He let her go—way too late.

From the expression on Ma's face, the cook's face, the parson's face . . . it was way, way, way too late. Have-mercy-too-late.

Mitch realized the clomping man still stood with his hand extended. Mitch wasn't sure if the man was just that patient or if all that was swamping Mitch had happened in a matter of seconds. He shook the man's hand as he felt the force of all the staring eyes press on his spine.

"And this must be your wife, Mitch. Quill, you didn't mention both your boys were married." The man faltered. His brow lowered. "In fact, you mentioned Mitch was from New York City, and he'd just come back from the east, and I'm sure you said alone."

The man said it with the volume of a town crier.

The man gave Ilsa a look of . . . well, Mitch couldn't think of the word exactly, he just looked at her as if he'd

figured everything out. And Ilsa was in Mitch's room for
reasons that were not respectable.

Propriety was sinking its pointy teeth into Mitch's backside.

The expression on the man's face then changed to something Mitch did recognize. The man eased past Ma and
whispered to Mitch, "If you're done with her, send her
to my—"

Mitch's hand lashed out like a rattler and closed over
the man's throat.

The parson's wife jumped and screamed. The children
threw themselves against their mother's legs and cried
in fear.

The clomping man's eyes bulged. Choking, he clawed
at Mitch's strangling grip.

Outraged, Ma shoved past the man and put herself in
front of Ilsa. Mitch should have done that instead of attacking. He let the man go with a low growl.

The parson's wife cleared her throat in a rough, loud
way that could have rivaled Ma's snores, and said, "I'm
sure this young couple is about to make an *announcement*?"

And all Mitch had said to Ilsa about innocence and
propriety and young ladies alone with men in the night
swept over him, and Mitch had no choice. None at all.

Disgusting as the man was, Mitch himself had caused
this.

With a sinking stomach, Mitch forced the words out
with a sincere effort to be calm and accept his fate. "My
fiancée and I shouldn't have been alone in here. I know
it, but I wanted a private place to propose. She said yes."

And hadn't all this started with talk of saying yes? Well, they'd have to live with that yes for the rest of their lives.

"We were just coming to tell you the news, Ma . . . and Pa."

A squeak from the other side of Pa drew Mitch's eyes. "And Dave and Jo."

Behind Dave and Jo, a pair of single ladies looked delightfully scandalized. He'd met them, too. Schoolteachers who shared a room in the hotel as part of their pay.

Prim, middle-aged, fully scandalized maiden ladies.

And the cook said, "I'll make something special for our morning meal to celebrate. After I wake my husband."

She stared a moment longer, clearly torn as to whether she dared leave and possibly miss something else good. Then, as if the news were impossible to keep, she dashed away, maybe to try to get the engagement announcement in this week's paper.

If Bucksnort didn't have a paper, the woman might start one.

They might as well go yell it on the street.

He glanced at Ilsa, who seemed to be confused. She might not know what a fiancée was. But she was sure enough going to find out.

Ma smiled. It was forced, and Mitch knew she was just keeping the lie alive, but she whirled and hugged Ilsa. "How wonderful."

Ilsa, buried against Ma's ample bosom, looked past Ma's shoulder at Mitch and arched a brow. A confused woman who was soon to be a confused wife.

The thought didn't really bring the sickening twist to

Mitch's belly it should have. Maybe because he could still feel her arms twined around his neck.

Mitch heard Jo say something quietly to Dave. Mitch suspected she was asking him what a fiancée was. Then Jo turned with a genuine smile on her face.

Which only proved Jo was as naïve as Ilsa. She squeezed between Ma and Ilsa, which wasn't easy, and hugged her little sister.

The man Mitch had nearly strangled took a few steps back. "My most sincere apologies, Mitch. To you and your whole family. I beg your pardon for what I said." He turned and almost ran into his room. The door shut with a loud click. Mitch heard a key turn in the lock.

The parson came up and gave Mitch a falsely hardy clap on the shoulder. "We'll be ready at the church after breakfast." He turned and hurried his wife and children back into their room.

The pair of women behind Dave and Jo stayed put, whispering to each other, their eyes locked on Mitch and Ilsa, not willing to miss a single detail. Maybe they had an arrangement with the cook.

Mitch reluctantly looked at Pa, expecting anger and disappointment. Instead, Pa looked surprisingly calm. No scolding about Mitch's improper behavior.

Dave was outright grinning as if he enjoyed seeing the parson's mousetrap snap shut on his big brother.

Then he heard Ilsa whispering with Jo, and Ilsa almost shouted, "What?"

With a sigh, Mitch figured that now Ilsa knew what a fiancée was.

She turned to look at him, her face drained of color.

Both hands covering her mouth, just like when she'd been giggling earlier.

Ma wrapped an arm around Ilsa, then shooed Jo ahead of her. With one tight, threatening look back at Mitch, Ma said in a cheerful voice that didn't begin to match her grim expression, "Girls, let's go into my room. We've got a wedding to plan . . . for this morning."

"What?" Ilsa seemed to be unable to add anything to this mess beyond that word. Mitch hoped she was able to come up with a couple more words eventually, like, "I do." He hoped he could come up with them, too.

"Mrs. Warden." One of the maiden ladies cleared her throat, then asked, "Would it be too bold for us to ask if we can attend the nuptials? We do love a wedding ceremony."

Everyone froze. There was an extended silence. Ma rarely let anything get the best of her so this final question must've just been too much.

Pa said, "It's going to be family only, ladies. I'm sure you understand."

Ma fled into her bedroom, herding the girls ahead of her.

Pa grabbed Mitch by the arm and dragged him the few paces to his own room . . . where Mitch should've been staying.

And because right now, a powerful, wealthy industrialist felt like a misbehaving eight-year-old, Mitch let himself be dragged into Pa's room.

Dave came in behind him and closed the door with a tight snap.

8

Mitch's ears were still burning from the scolding Pa had given him. Turned out Pa was just better at faking sincerity than Ma.

And Dave was worse because he took up for Ilsa as his wife's baby sister.

There'd been no question that the wedding would go on, even before they started in on him. But he'd deserved their scorn, so he stood there and took it like a man. A badly behaved man.

And now, here he stood with Ilsa by the arm, waiting for that wonderful moment when everyone settled in, and he got to drag his reluctant bride-to-be up the aisle.

Ma must not've scolded Ilsa as hard as Pa had scolded him, because she wasn't resigned to her fate.

"We are not getting married," Ilsa hissed like a leaky boiler.

Clearly, they were.

Ma and Pa went ahead and sat on the right side of the church. Dave led Jo up to the front and off to the parson's left side. Then Dave put some space between them and stood on the right.

Holding a ring.

This wasn't the first time Ilsa had been wrong, and it wouldn't be the last. "I told you a woman couldn't be alone with a man. Why did you think that was?"

Ilsa turned, blinked. "Because that means you have to get married?"

Through a jaw clenched tight, Mitch said, "Yep."

"But why?"

That sent some very powerful shivers through Mitch's body. She wasn't the smartest little thing he'd ever met. Well, that wasn't fair. She was very bright. What she was, was innocent. She had no idea what was going on, and Mitch knew good and well what had happened. This was his fault. He should have seen her in the hallway and yelled for Ma.

Instead, he was getting married.

Admitting fault didn't stop the wedding.

Now here he stood with a bright, innocent, beautiful young woman on his arm. He honestly wasn't as upset as he probably should have been, considering he was marrying a woman who said she hadn't killed a man yesterday.

And yet, he'd seen her crouched and . . . maybe growling . . . like a predator over her prey.

If a woman could get that upset over a broken knife, she probably got that upset every day.

He hoped he tamed her down mighty soon, but he didn't hold out much hope.

His mind wandered to those moments in his room, and that distracted him from the savage part of the woman he was marrying. Oh, he knew exactly why a man and women-not-his-wife weren't supposed to be alone.

Mitch had to admit that while he was a very cynical man who'd seen most everything, he was as innocent of women as Ilsa was of men. He'd been raised believing in what the Bible taught of such things. And didn't his betraying lady friend, Katrina, just prove how innocent he was?

He'd poured every ounce of his energy into making a fortune and left women alone. Not counting Katrina.

Until last night.

And now tonight they'd be alone again. Restless at the thought, he wondered if they'd go home. He tried to figure out where he'd stay with his wife. He could take her to—

Ma cleared her throat almost as if she could read his mind. Oh, he really hoped that wasn't true.

"I'll tell you later why we shouldn't have been alone," he whispered to Ilsa. Tell her. Show her. He ripped his mind back to the present. "For now, we're getting married."

"I don't want to get married."

Since Mitch was running out of time, and he didn't want a big argument right in front of a man of God, he dug around and tried to find shreds of charm. He'd never bothered much with charm. He was more the go-for-the-throat type. He sure hoped it didn't come to that to get her to say yes.

He found a forlorn part of himself, not that hard to do under the circumstances, and faced her, trying to sound hurt and lonely and wistful and whatever other weakling emotion he could cram into his voice.

"Don't you want to marry me?"

He was a good catch. He knew that. Why didn't she know that?

"No, for heaven's sake. Of course, I don't want to marry you."

She'd be good for him.

Keep him humble.

Keep him from ever marrying someone who liked him. That was just too bad, he'd just have to convince *her* to like him.

Looking at her, trying to plot a strategy for success, he saw that Ma had done something fancy with Ilsa's curly, dark hair. It was pulled up at the sides with little ringlets on her temples, by her ears, and on the nape of her neck. She really was beautiful, and when he'd kissed her and held her last night, they'd fit together so well Mitch was still dazzled.

Ma had fixed Jo's long blond hair in a similar style. Ilsa and Jo were the closest he could imagine to completely untamed human beings, and then throw in their sister, Ursula, the worst—and wildest—of the bunch.

But as he looked at Ilsa now, she appeared completely traditional wearing a dress Ma had made. There'd even been a bath in the early-morning hours. He knew that because he heard Ilsa yelling that she didn't want to sit in a stupid tub of hot water.

Apparently she bathed in the stream and only when the weather permitted.

But Ma had prevailed—they'd probably carve that on her tombstone—and to Mitch's amazement, the bath and Ma's gentle scrubbing had done away with nearly all of

Ilsa's tiny scabs. Now he was marrying a woman who couldn't read, liked to wear trousers, roamed the mountains alone at night, swung from trees like a monkey at the New York City zoo, was far too skilled with a knife, and believed there were two Bibles.

And he'd thought owning and operating factories was complicated.

But thanks to the bath, she was a pretty, sweet-smelling little thing. That struck Mitch as a mighty shallow reason for marrying someone, and yet, right now, he had to admit he was all for it.

The piano at the front of the room tinkled as the parson's wife struck a rolling chord.

"I'm not marrying you." Ilsa said it right out loud. Luckily for Mitch, no one was paying her much mind.

He thought of that man in the hallway. What he'd assumed about Ilsa. Mitch should have punched him. Though what that man had assumed was at the heart of why a young woman needed to always have a chaperone.

Any normal woman would understand this. Which meant he was marrying an abnormal woman, but then he knew that.

"Let's go."

"Good idea. I'm hungry. Let's go home, shoot an elk, and have steak."

Mitch tugged and she came along. But he didn't think she was coming with him to happily marry him. She might just be walking up to where the others were so she could tell them how hungry she was.

How did he explain it? How did he tell Ilsa what that

man had assumed when the woman didn't even know what went on between a man and a woman? How could he explain what it meant when that clomping man asked her to come to his room?

Ilsa didn't know how a courtship usually went on. She didn't even know he was a good catch.

Paid assassins notwithstanding.

"Didn't Ma explain why we have to get married?"

She shrugged, rubbing her right arm against his left, because he held her so close he'd almost taken her into captivity. And when you were marrying a feral woman, maybe that's what marriage amounted to.

"She did."

Mitch drew her to a halt. Turned her to face him. The church wasn't that big, they'd be up front in a few more paces. And as much as Mitch knew they really had no choice in the matter, he wanted her to understand what she was getting into.

"I know this is sudden, Ilsa. But I think you're the most interesting woman I've ever met." And that was absolutely the truth. "I want to marry you and spend the rest of our lives together and make a home." An idea popped into his head. "We'll have babies. Wouldn't you like to have a baby?"

That lifted her chin and put a little sparkle in her eyes. "I would like that."

"Then say you'll marry me. Say you're willing. I'll be a good husband to you, Ilsa. You have my solemn vow."

Their gazes locked. She seemed to be searching for something. Or maybe she just stared while she thought over all he'd said.

It seemed to take forever, but no one up front came and interrupted so maybe it was just the longest moment of Mitch's life.

With a firm jerk of her chin, Ilsa said, "Yes. Yes, Mitch. I'll be a good wife to you, too. Let's get married."

They shared a smile, and Mitch thought his wife-to-be was finally willing, even eager to cooperate because they started forward, and he no longer had to drag her. They got to the front of the church, and the parson began.

"I thought I was going to have to get my shotgun to force this wedding." Pa clapped Mitch on the shoulder as they walked back to the hotel where they'd spent the night. There was a restaurant there, and because this whole mess had started early in the morning, they were in time for a midday meal.

"Pa, I never once protested. I knew what needed doing. I married her with a good attitude and did it fast."

"I was talking about Ilsa."

Laughing, Dave came up on Mitch's other side and slung an arm around Mitch's neck. His little brother was about four inches taller than him. "Thought we'd need to rope and hog-tie her for you to get your brand on her."

His little brother was probably tougher than him, too. He'd also been married longer than him, by about two weeks. Mitch was real tempted to ask Dave what exactly happened on a wedding night. Oh, Mitch knew what happened, he just wasn't sure of how it—well, no matter. He wasn't going to ask advice from Dave so instead he shoved the arm away.

"Where's my wife? Why can't I walk with her instead of you two?"

Pa leaned close and whispered, "I think your ma is having a little talk with her about married life."

Mitch could've asked his pa a question or two. Which was an even more embarrassing idea. "I hope she includes telling Ilsa she needs to stop wearing trousers."

"I don't think that's what it's about, but maybe she'll mention that, too."

Fine, if Ma was telling Ilsa about what went on between a bride and groom on a wedding night, he could just wait and ask Ilsa.

Mitch could see how that might be even more embarrassing than asking Dave or Pa.

For something with the huge potential to be deeply and completely embarrassing, Mitch was sure looking forward to it.

"Now, Mitch," Pa said, "the US Marshal might be the man to see about Pike. The sheriff contacted Rance Cosgrove, and he's headed for Bucksnort. When you talk to him, I want you to ask him how we can get the marshals to enforce the law out in the countryside."

They entered the dining room, talking about law on the frontier, or the lack thereof, while they waited for the women. They had to wait so long that they had a plan all worked out by the time the women finally came in.

Mitch got the distinct impression that Ilsa had understood Ma better this time. Because she looked panic-stricken.

9

"We should head for home." Ilsa followed along by Mitch's side, trailing the rest of the Warden family out of the restaurant and into the entrance to the hotel.

She was married.

The thought was odd. Both upsetting and exciting. It kept her all stirred up, so every time it popped into her head, she veered away from it and forced herself to think of something else. Like going home. She was thinking of going up to see Ursula in that remote stone building.

Maybe she'd stay up there with her.

"Didn't you hear what the sheriff said?" Mitch asked.

Sheriff Hale had stopped by their table as they ate.

"You have to talk to the US Marshal."

"Yes, about the men gunning for me and the men who shot Pa. I'm not going to quit until I put a stop to the trouble."

Mitch caught hold of her hand.

It reminded her a bit of how they'd tied that wounded gunfighter over his saddle. Another person Mitch didn't allow to escape.

If she moved up the mountain to live with Ursula, would her husband have to come?

Mitch and Ursula. What a terrible combination—not unlike lightning and treetops. Ilsa definitely wasn't inviting Mitch.

Considering the grip he had on her, though, he might be planning to invite himself.

"I can't believe Sheriff Hale heard back so fast." Dave shook his head. He held Jo's hand, but it wasn't at all the way Mitch held Ilsa. Dave seemed to believe Jo would stay with him by choice.

Ilsa was a long way from feeling the same.

"It's a modern age," Ma said.

Mitch snorted. "He wired the nearest US Marshals' office late last night. Of course, someone would get back to him right away this morning."

The sheriff had said he'd awakened to a return wire. A marshal was in the area, and he was close enough that he'd ride over and be in Bucksnort before the end of the day. He had questions for Mitch. Ilsa had heard all that and had no idea what it meant. Wire? Marshal?

"I agree some of us should go home, though," Pa said. "With those two gunfighters out of the picture, it'll be a while before there is more danger for you, Mitch. You should be safe until word reaches your old partner that his hired killers failed."

"At which point," Ma said, sounding grim, "he will hire more."

"I hope to settle this before there are any more attacks. For now, I have to stay."

"The rest of us will go on home." Pa looked over his shoulder. "Ilsa included. She shouldn't be here for this."

"My wife stays with me." Mitch's hand tightened, and Ilsa wondered if she'd be bruised tomorrow. If she was, Mitch would be bruised the next day.

"And, Pa, I may have to ride to a bigger city. Maybe the marshal can help me. I'll send a few wires of my own from here. If I don't like the answers I get, I may have to ride to Denver or even Omaha. But I won't do anything that endangers Ilsa. I'll handle all this through hired lawmen. Pinkertons—if Denver has an agency."

"Pinkerton sounds so pretty." Ilsa patted his hand.

Mitch's eyes fell shut as if he were in pain. He opened them and turned to smile kindly at her. She was understanding his expressions a bit more all the time. "You'll like Denver. There are more buildings and people than here. More than twenty-five thousand people."

Ilsa leaned close and whispered, "Is that more than a million?"

Again the closed eyes. Again the pained expression. Now she only had to figure out why he was in pain. She glanced down to make sure she hadn't stepped on his toe.

"I should leave you with Ma, let you get on with some schooling." Then he leaned close and whispered, "But you'll be safe with me. I'm not going near the man who's behind this, and I want you with me."

"Heavy snow's coming, Mitch," Pa said. "The trail up Hope Mountain gets mighty feisty."

Mitch nodded. "We go now, or we go in the spring."

"I want to see a big city." Ilsa looked at Jo and frowned. "But it's so different out here in this crowded world. No trees to climb. No ropes to swing on. People and horses everywhere."

"It really is different," Jo said. "But I think I like it."

"You know what I'd really like to do?" Ilsa turned to Mitch.

"No," he said, "but ask. I'd be glad to do whatever you want. Show you sights you've never seen. Buy you silk dresses and fine stockings."

"I'd like to find out what happened to my parents. It's such a big world, I keep thinking maybe they just got lost. Maybe we could find them and bring them home."

"They've been gone how long?"

Ilsa looked at Jo, who said, "Almost twenty years."

Mitch nodded, then shook his head, then shrugged. He was just moving all over, and Ilsa was as lost as could be.

"They've been gone a long time, Ilsa, pretty good chance no one can find them." Pa clapped Mitch on the back. "Let's go pack so the rest of us can head home."

"I'd like to fill a packhorse with some extra supplies," Ma said. "Fabric for more dresses for my daughters. I finally have daughters."

She rubbed her hands together and giggled in a very un-Ma-like way. "Jo, come with me to the general store."

"The sheriff said we can have the horses of the men we brought in and the money they had on them," Pa added.

"I think we should split that money between our men," Mitch said. "They were put in danger because of my problems, and they came running to help."

Dave nodded.

"We'll do that, then," Pa agreed. "And we can use their horses as pack animals, so get any supplies you need."

"I'll go get them from the livery and tie them to a hitching post out front of the general store." Dave headed out of the hotel.

Ma towed Jo out. Dave turned left, Ma and Jo went right. Ilsa sort of wanted to go with Ma and Jo, but Mitch showed no sign of letting her escape.

"I think I'll stay in town," Alberto said.

Everyone stopped talking and turned to him. Ilsa wasn't sure why.

"It's not just paid killers after you, Mitch," Alberto said. "Someone needs to help keep a lookout for Bludge and his men. I'll recognize Pike, and I've seen some of the hired guns he sent to the Circle Dash."

"I appreciate it." Mitch turned to his pa. "Ilsa and I will either be home straightaway with Alberto, or we won't be home until spring."

Ilsa wasn't following this conversation well at all. "Spring?"

"I'll explain later." He turned to the steps to their rooms. "For now, let's go move your things into my room."

She didn't really mind him being in charge. She had no idea where to go or what to do. While they were in the big city of Bucksnort, she'd let Mitch pick what to do next. She just hoped he didn't snore. She'd have to leave the room, and she might end up married to someone else tomorrow.

Mitch waved his family off.

"Why did you want my things in your room?"

His wife was so sweet and innocent it was giving Mitch a headache.

"You remember that Jo and Dave shared a room last night? That's what married couples do. My ma and pa would've shared a room except you needed someone, a woman, to stay with you."

For all the good it did.

"So tonight, we share a room." He grabbed her hand and almost ran back down the stairs, hoping to head off more questions.

He talked fast. "We'll go see if the marshal is here, and if the sheriff has found the wanted posters. There might be a reward. We might get some money."

Ilsa tagged along willingly, not that he gave her much choice. She started talking, and Mitch braced himself for more questions about the sleeping arrangements.

"I've heard you talk about money before. And there is talk of buying and selling in the Bible, of course. Like when Jesus drove the money changers out of the temple, for example. Or when it says, 'Money is the root of all evil.'"

"That's the *love* of money," Mitch said, thinking of his satchels full of gold hidden in a cave at the base of the mountain. He liked money well enough, but love, nope. Most certainly not.

"There's a story with a wicked servant who buried money in a field."

Which was nothing like hiding it in a cave, so Mitch didn't defend himself.

"He was cast into outer darkness where there will be weeping and gnashing of teeth."

Mitch was gnashing his teeth right now. And then he perked up as he realized how different it was to have a woman who had no interest in his money. No interest in him either, but that hadn't stopped the wedding, now, had it?

He stopped just as he reached the steps down off the boardwalk. He looked around. The entrance to the hotel was empty in the midafternoon. The streets were empty. He slid his arms around Ilsa's slender waist and kissed her.

She was a confused little thing, and it wasn't going to get better for a while. But considering he'd had a woman after his money back east—and she hadn't been the first, just the sneakiest and most cold-blooded—he found Ilsa's complete lack of interest in his money a near miracle.

He heard someone coughing behind him and broke off the kiss to see a man standing behind the front desk where people signed in and paid for their rooms. With money.

Mitch hadn't heard him come in.

A glance at Ilsa's swollen lips and messy hair made Mitch wonder how long he'd been kissing her. He gently but firmly tugged her arms away from his neck. She had a dazed look in her eyes, and she glanced at his lips. It gave him a fierce feeling of pleasure, because she'd been as caught up in the moment as he was.

"Let's go see the marshal." He had things to do before his wedding night, and none of them one bit romantic. Ilsa had no more notion of romance than a fence post. He hoped she never got over that, because Mitch knew most women liked romance. He'd given Katrina roses and jewelry. He'd taken her to the theater and on carriage rides through Central Park. All that had taken a heap of time better spent working.

His eyes slid up and down Bucksnort's businesses. No flower shop or jewelry store. Ma had found a ring at the general store early this morning and bought Ilsa a new knife, so Mitch couldn't even do that.

If Ilsa never learned one speck about romance, it'd be fine with him.

"Two gunmen came to the Warden cabin." Wax Mosby stood before Bludgeon Pike, reporting what he'd seen. Wax hadn't liked the looks of those men and slipped away. He wasn't about to start a fight with two tough-looking strangers, especially when there was a chance Pike had hired them.

Anyway, Wax wasn't a man who started shooting without knowing what was what. He'd ridden to Pike's ranch to make sure the men weren't hired by his boss.

Then Bludge had kept him waiting. The boss liked to make his men wait. It must suit him to wield that kind of power.

Wax had used the time to sharpen his knives and clean his guns.

Now he stood in Pike's office, facing his boss. Wax's hands weren't close to his guns, but he saw Bludge glance at the two tied-down, fully loaded firearms.

"Did you talk to them?" Bludge's blue eyes were colder than the howling winter weather outside.

Wax's eyes narrowed. "No. The way they rode in told me they had no good intentions. I didn't like the looks of them, and I trust my gut."

"Strangers, then?" Bludge slid back a little in his huge leather chair, parked behind his big oak desk. He was a short man, thin, without the look about him of a man with hard muscles honed by riding long hours in harsh weather, wrestling longhorns and dodging hooves.

The only thing that made Pike a rancher was enough money to hire all his work done.

"You didn't hire more men and send them over?"

"Nope. I have enough to handle the Wardens."

Handling the Wardens was going to be more work than the boss thought. Wax said, "Wasn't gonna start any shooting trouble with men that might be working for you."

"What'd they look like? Maybe they're still around."

"They were men who rode easy in the saddle, like they've done it all their lives. They rode bloodstock thoroughbreds and wore fine clothes without a sign of wear. They had expensive guns worn tied down, and I was close enough to see cold, sharp eyes. Confident, lethal eyes." Wax might be describing himself.

"I want you back there." Bludge didn't slap those words out like an order. Instead, he sounded like he was thinking, saying out loud what he wanted but considering whether it was wise to send Wax.

Wax was wondering if it was wise himself.

"I can send more men over with you," Bludge offered. "That cabin's big enough. Then you won't find yourself facing them alone."

Wax didn't like facing two gunmen when he didn't know what they wanted.

They looked like the type to shoot first and ask questions later.

Wax asked his questions first.

"I can handle any trouble they bring, boss. I just didn't

103

want to get into a turkey shoot with men you've hired to help out."

"I've got no idea what they're looking for, but they aren't mine. Since there's a pair, you might need to lie in wait, pick them off from cover. You'll get no complaint from me if you have to gun them down."

Wax didn't dry-gulch people. It struck a chill right through Wax's cold heart to think what Bludge was really after. He wanted death, but he was too yellow to do it himself. Too weak, too much of a coward.

"I was gone last payday, so I'd like my time. Then I'll ride on back. I'll keep an eye open for those two."

Bludge handed over fighting wages. Better than a regular cowboy earned. As Wax walked out, he wondered if those men would still be there. Wax had expected them to find his tracks and come after him. They hadn't. He knew, careful as he was, that good trackers could follow his trail.

Where were they? Who were they? What did they want? Would he run into them again?

He rode away from Bludge's ranch with plenty on his mind.

10

Ilsa sat quietly through the inquisition conducted by Marshal Rance Cosgrove. A short, stocky man who looked like he was made of pure gristle and grit. He had overlong dark hair, sharp black eyes, and a coating of dust from long days on the trail.

Mitch wished he could have sent her away, but he and Alberto both needed to be there as witnesses. For a fact, Ilsa needed to be there, too.

There weren't all that many questions about the actual attack. Mostly the marshal asked about there being a price on Mitch's head. But the marshal had a hard way about him, and he'd asked his questions over and over with a goading scowl.

He wanted just enough from Ilsa and Alberto that it was a good thing they hadn't gone home with Pa. Mitch didn't even try to get the man's help with pressing charges against his former partner back in New York. But he did talk about Pa's trouble with Pike.

The marshal seemed to have no interest in the law back

east, but he listened closely to the tale of trouble at the Circle Dash.

"We're spread mighty thin out here, Mitch," the marshal said.

"I know it. Pa's gone to ground for now, but there'll be trouble come spring. He won't let Pike's attack stand. It goes against the grain to ask our cowpokes to wade into a gunfight that is none of their doing, but they're tough and loyal, and they'll stand if there's a fight. If we could gather a posse led by a US Marshal, we might end this without a shot fired."

"I'll work on it, see if I can gather a crew by spring. There is law out here, Mitch. Enforcing it is the trick."

When Cosgrove finally finished with his questions, Mitch sent his wires.

Then he spent time figuring out how to get from Bucksnort to Denver and couldn't see any way to do it but on horseback, just exactly the way he'd come out.

It crossed his mind that he probably should build tracks himself to get a train in here. He knew a few men that'd gone broke doing that, but he understood the impulse.

Standing outside the telegraph office, he watched his wife wander over to a tree that stood right behind the building. Then he watched her climb it.

Ma had Ilsa in a tidy black riding skirt with a white shirtwaist. And she had on a wool coat, gloves, and a bonnet. She'd cast all of those outer garments on the ground at the base of the tree and just plain dashed up into the branches.

Mitch hoped his little treetop-dwelling wife didn't sprout wings and fly off.

As for getting to the train, it looked like he'd be carrying her on his lap on horseback again. Only this time she was his wife, and it was going to be completely different.

It'd be a nuisance, and hard on his horse. But he was looking forward to it.

Standing outside the telegraph office and looking up in the tree while he waited for a response to his wires, he wondered if she didn't come down, would he have to climb up there and get her? He was a little embarrassed to tell anyone his wife was the next thing to a woman-sized red-tailed hawk.

Alberto came up beside him, watching the tree, too, and frowning like he understood Mitch's dilemma. "Gotta tell you what I heard from Miguel, my brother."

Mitch caught Alberto's tone and tore his eyes away from his high-climbing wife. "What?"

"I told him Bludge Pike had caused your family plenty of trouble, told him about the attack on your ranch and your pa being shot. Miguel hadn't heard about what happened at the Circle Dash, but he knew Bludge had been driving people off homesteads all last summer."

Mitch frowned. "I haven't given Pike much thought beyond standing with Pa."

"You haven't given much thought to the man who shot your pa?"

"I didn't mean it that way." Mitch held up his hands as if he were surrendering. "I'll fight the men who shot Pa with everything I've got. But I've made it worse. These killers are trouble I brought out here. Trouble I tried hard to solve when I was back east, then trouble I worked hard not to draw to my family. I've been wrangling around in my head to put an end to that mess. What did you hear?"

"Bludge just came into this country last spring. The sheriff knew that. He drove in twenty thousand head of cattle without owning an acre of land. He knew this land was good grazing, there weren't many settlers here, and he considered it open range, his for the taking. He came along a southern path, so he beat most of the folks who came to homestead in the spring. Bought up big swaths of land, but by no means every acre, then he acted like he was an established rancher and the homesteaders were poaching on his land—even if they weren't."

"So he'd scare the homesteaders into moving on. And, as long as he kept his trouble out of town, no one bothered him." Mitch thought of the sheriff never leaving town. Hale wouldn't bother Pike even if a homesteader did complain.

Alberto nodded. "There were rumors of killings, but if they happened, no witnesses came to town. He rode roughshod with little resistance until he took on the Circle Dash."

"It worked there, too. Pa ran for Hope Mountain."

"But only a fool thinks your pa is gone for good. But by all accounts, Bludgeon Pike is a fool. Once your pa regroups, makes a plan, and comes down off that mountain, Bludge will have to back off, and the word is, he's a yellowbelly."

"So once Pike starts backing, he'll just keep on." Mitch wondered if it'd be that easy. Wax Mosby came to mind. Pa would have his hands full. "No matter what we do chasing down whoever hired those men to kill me, I give you my word, Alberto, I'll be back here by spring to fight alongside all of you."

Then a thought struck Mitch. "I wonder where Pike came from? He had to have money, or he couldn't have bought all those cows and all that land."

"Nothing I've told you so far is what interested me. You already knew most of it."

That perked Mitch's ears right up. "What did interest you?"

"Miguel said Pike's real name is Morris Canton. Some letter came addressed to him by that name, and one of Pike's men picked it up for him. Seems he must've been told to watch for mail under that name."

Morris Canton? The name went through Mitch like an electrical jolt. He knew that name. "Have you seen Pike?"

"Yep."

"Small man, skinny, blue eyes beady as a rat, doesn't have anything about him that speaks of being a rancher?"

"That's an almighty good description of him, Mitch. Word is he didn't even help with the cattle drive. He hired drovers, then rode a buggy out here, trailing along behind the herd by a few miles so he wouldn't get dusty."

"I know who Morris Canton is. I even know why he's here. He was selling his real estate back east about the same time I was. But he got out because there were charges coming—fraud, extortion."

"Not sure what crimes those are."

Nodding, Mitch said, "Out here there may be shooting trouble. Guns and fists. But mostly men come straight at you with their grievances. Back east, Canton was known to have a gang of men who'd threaten small businesses, 'give us a hundred dollars a month or you'll be sorry.' That's extortion. He had a few policemen on his payroll, and plenty of people were scared into paying, especially after a few businesses burned down and a couple of people were killed. He'd been at it a long time and had made himself a very rich man, but his luck was running out."

His luck started running out when he'd tried his extortion on a business run by the wife of one of Mitch's employees, a shop steward in one of his mills. The man had come to Mitch, who knew just how to put a stop to it. "An empire he'd built on dirty money was crumbling. He sold out fast and, with plenty of cash in hand, took his crimes out west."

Slapping Alberto on the shoulder, he said, "Thanks. I might know a few ways to cause Pike more trouble than he wants to handle."

With a quick jerk of his head, Alberto turned back to the tree. "You've got yourself a fine little wife there, Mitch. Don't mess up what's so fine about her."

With that cryptic warning, Alberto turned to his horse, mounted up, and rode away.

Mitch had to admit he'd been standing here thinking of how he could fix Ilsa. Maybe that wasn't the way he should go on.

But he had to teach her a few things.

How to hang on while the horse trotted.

How to read.

How many Bibles there were.

He wasn't even sure he could lure her back to the ground.

For now, he just left her to her climbing. He didn't want to wander away from the telegraph office anyway. And tomorrow, if necessary, they'd have to ride east for the nearest train station.

Smiling, he imagined how she'd act the first time she saw a train.

He found a strange longing to show Ilsa a lot of things. Fine restaurants and theaters. Tall buildings and trolley cars. Stockyards full of cattle and stores full of beautiful furniture, clothing, and dishes. He wanted to dress her in a lavish gown, take her to a ballroom and dance with her in his arms. He wanted to watch her eyes while he showed her the world.

He hoped Alberto wouldn't count that as fixing her.

Not wanting to upset his parents, Mitch hadn't told them he was almost sure he'd need to go as far as Chicago, where he knew he'd find a Pinkerton agency. The farther east he went, the more his family would worry. But Mitch had worked with the Pinkertons before he'd headed west. They were his best chance of building a case against Howell.

How was Pete paying for his killers? Mitch had pulled all the right strings to leave his old partner bankrupt. Yet somehow, he'd come up with a thousand dollars three times now—of course, the first two back in New York had been before Mitch had cut off his funds. Maybe he'd tucked money away, but there'd be no more coming in, so Howell would've been wise to save his gold.

Yep, most likely they were going all the way to Chicago. And it was brand-new, all rebuilt after the Great Fire two years ago. The city was racing to re-create itself in brick and stone.

The Grand Pacific Hotel was soon to reopen when Mitch had been there. And other businesses, bigger and better than ever, were emerging from the ashes. Mitch had invested in some of the new construction for a time, before he'd sold out. Of course, that was before the Panic. That would've set things back. Even so, Chicago was now home to a quarter of a million people.

Wait'll Ilsa saw that. Maybe she'd learn how money worked before they were done.

11

Ilsa had been alone with Mitch before. Just last night. And now here she was again. Hadn't she learned anything?

"We're going to have to ride east tomorrow." Mitch closed the door behind them with a thud that struck Ilsa as dangerous somehow.

Then he began taking off his long leather duster.

Ominous.

She was letting him make all the decisions and leading her everywhere they went. And she'd been going along because she had no idea what else to do. And of course she liked him. She liked him very much when he wasn't making her furious. And she'd greatly enjoyed kissing him.

That's how they'd ended up married—or at least that seemed to be how.

But right now, with uneasy feelings churning inside her, she thought of one of her Bible verses and decided it was time to have another heart-to-heart talk with him about his confused faith.

"You know, this brings to mind one of my favorite Bible stories."

"What story is that? Am I still the prodigal son?" Mitch hung his duster on a hook on the wall and started unbuttoning her coat.

That seemed overly helpful of him—she was perfectly capable of unbuttoning her own coat.

"No, it's the story of 'The Fox and the Scorpion.'"

Mitch's hands froze. He let go of her coat as the last button opened and he stepped back a few inches. She was able to breathe again as she shrugged her own coat off and hung it up beside his. Her bonnet went next, and she tucked her gloves into the coat pocket.

She noticed Mitch scrubbing his face with one hand almost like he thought there was soap and water involved.

"Uh, Ma talked to you about your book of fables and how much they are *like* a Bible story, but they are, um—" he cleared his throat—"not."

Ilsa remembered Jo had said she was beginning to believe there weren't two Bibles. Already her sister was falling away from her faith. Frowning at her heretic husband, she wondered how she could save him.

She waded in. "That story is about expecting someone to be exactly who they are. It is a companion to Jesus' words, 'Love your enemies and bless them that curse you.' Jesus says we're to love our enemies, but the story explains we should also know our enemies and not expect them to be something they're not. You can see how the stories, well, how they, how they . . . uh, they seem to be—well, now that I think of it—they seem to be the exact opposite of each other. How strange."

Mitch scrubbed his face again. She should get him a wet cloth and a towel.

He sounded a little forlorn when he said, "I have something else I want to talk about now, not a story about a fox and a scorpion."

"I have something, too." His helpful hands reached for the buttons on the front of her dress, and she knocked them away.

Mitch snatched his hands back like she'd drawn a gun instead of giving him the mildest of slaps.

She smiled. "I'd better have my say first."

"What did you want to talk about?"

"I understood enough of what Ma said about a wedding night, and I know enough of the, well, the world of . . . of animals and such, to know we aren't going to . . . to . . ." She swallowed hard, then cleared her throat. Surprising how hard it was to say what should be obvious to him already . . . and yet she suspected it was not.

Squaring her shoulders, lifting her chin, determined to be clear and honest, she said, "We aren't going to . . . behave . . . as a married couple until we've spent more time together. The way we ended up married isn't at all the normal sort of way. I have no interest in you being . . . um." She shrugged. "Being overly . . . familiar on so slight an acquaintance. We will spend the next little while becoming other than near strangers, Mitch. And only then will we carry on as married folks."

His gaze held hers, then something shone in his eyes that seemed . . . agreeable.

"You're right, Ilsa. Of course we shouldn't rush into . . . married things. You're a wise woman for such a sheltered little thing." He rested one hand on her cheek and the other at the nape of her neck and kissed her.

She wrapped her arms around his neck and kissed him back with great enthusiasm.

"Let's get ready for bed now, shall we?"

"Sharing a room with your ma, I slept in this dress for reasons of speed and privacy. I'll do the same tonight. I'm ready for bed right now, except for removing my boots."

"I'd as soon wear my nightshirt." He started unbuttoning.

Ilsa whirled away to look at the door. "This is so confusing for it to be all right for me to be in here tonight with you and your . . . your nightshirt . . . when last night it was wrong. Yes, the parson blessed our marriage. But that doesn't change the fact that things have taken a bewildering turn. It's much more shocking than the time I came upon a bull elk in the woods and it charged and rammed me into a stream, and I almost went over a waterfall."

Mitch made some sound she couldn't understand, and she wanted to look at him to see if he was scrubbing his face without water again. That sound seemed to go with the scrubbing.

But she didn't dare look at him until he was done changing.

"All right. I'm done. I'm ready for bed. You can turn around."

She did, but she turned to the side, away from him, sidled around him without looking at him, climbed into the bed, and pulled the covers up to her chin. Only then did she look at him. He was standing there in a nightgown.

Except it was short. Far too short. She could see his knees, and they were as bare as a baby's backside.

"Where are you going to sleep?" she asked.

Mitch started walking straight for the bed, and her.

Mitch woke up with a woman in his arms.

It was a wonderful moment.

He lay holding Ilsa in the first light of dawn and knew he was in big trouble. She'd been hesitant about married things passing between them, and he knew she was right to insist they wait until they were more comfortable with each other. They'd fallen asleep back-to-back, as far from each other as the bed would allow—which wasn't far. But they had both rolled over in the night, and here he was, waking up with her in his arms.

It was like water pouring over the dry desert of his heart.

He pulled her closer. He hadn't been that upset about getting married because he'd figured it was the next step in his life after he got home and got to know his family again. Ilsa was pretty and sweet and right here to hand. And he liked kissing her. Why not marry her?

But he hadn't counted on caring this much.

Her warm breath tickled his chest as she lay with her head on his shoulder, and it was the best thing he could imagine. Well, second best.

A beautiful woman, held in his arms. Sleeping in his bed. He could imagine one thing more wonderful. But drat it, she was right that they didn't know each other well enough for any carrying-on.

Mitch had spent a long time being tough. Being independent. Keeping his emotions firmly in check.

Right now, he was all churned up inside. Enjoying having Ilsa as his bride. Wanting to protect her. Wanting to be worthy of her. Wanting to teach her not to be quite so strange . . . all without fixing her, of course.

And wanting their own cabin and wanting to add rooms on for a growing family.

It overwhelmed him and scared him to death because if he couldn't keep icy control over himself, he had no idea how to act.

And how he felt about Ilsa was beyond his control.

She stirred.

Maybe because he was holding her too tight. He sure had no plans to crush the little woman—but that was a good example of him not controlling himself.

He looked down and saw blue eyes shining through her wild, dark curls. Brushing one hand through her hair, he combed it back off her forehead, loving its silky length.

"My wife is awake." He couldn't stop the smile. Didn't even consider trying.

She didn't smile back. Instead, drawing one trembling hand to her face, she kissed the tip of her index finger, then touched his lips. There was nothing light about it. Nothing even happy. Her expression was too deep, too serious, too intense.

Ilsa managed to say, "We have trouble ahead of us, but we will face that trouble, then come back to our mountaintop home and begin a life together."

"I want that, Ilsa. I want to have a home with you and fill that home with children."

She hugged him tight.

"I'm not planning on heading for danger. I will handle this through hired investigators, as I tried to do before I came home." Which hadn't worked. But he had that note from the hired killers. Maybe that would make all the difference. "But we have to travel east some to handle this, and while we're traveling, I'll show you a bit of the world."

"I'd like that." She eased away from him, just a shift of her body that said she was ready to get up and get on with solving Mitch's problems.

Mitch tightened his arm and forestalled her escape. He distracted her with a kiss.

She kissed him back with genuine warmth and generous enthusiasm.

"With no schedule to keep, we can leave a bit later in the morning and no harm will be done."

"Good." Ilsa smiled.

Mitch's heart leapt.

Then Ilsa tossed back the covers and hopped out of bed. "Plenty of time for breakfast."

Mitch scrambled to keep up with her.

12

Bludge sent Wax back to the Circle Dash.

Stupid name for a ranch. Like they were running in circles really fast. A dog chasing its tail. Stupid.

Bludge told him to go in quietly and make sure those men weren't anywhere around.

Wax did as he was told. Almost. He was going where he was told to go, he just didn't ride directly there.

He went by way of Bucksnort.

Bludge called the Wardens squatters, called their large, well-built home a nester's cabin. Wax wanted to look at the deeds and ask a few questions.

He figured Bludge for a liar, but he'd check just to be sure before he said something that could get him shot.

Might as well know what he was fighting about.

Wax had no doubt he'd find out the Wardens had a free and clear title to that land—and had for a long time.

Wax now knew Bludge had owned his own ranch for less than a year.

His boss was a lying thief, and he'd hired Wax to do his dirty work for him, which made Wax a lying thief, and it didn't suit him to be such.

Riding up the main street in Bucksnort, Wax figured the Wardens wouldn't come back until spring, wherever they'd gone.

But in spring they would come.

That'd give Wax a comfortable cabin for the winter. And almost no chores because the Wardens had taken off with their livestock.

The Wardens would hole up over the winter, make some plans, maybe talk to some lawmen, hire all the help they needed, then come storming in next spring to reclaim the property.

Wax wasn't going to be in that fight. Instead, he'd pick up his winter pay, months of it, and ride west for California.

He'd shave his beard and moustache, which he hated doing. He loved to keep them waxed. Loved it so much it'd earned him his name. His beard was light colored like his hair but darkened by the wax and worn in a point. His moustache was also carefully waxed so it curled out on each side.

He loved that beard and moustache, but he'd give it up and change his name and live a life farther west, where no one knew him as a hired gun.

And then he saw him.

Wax swung off his horse and led the animal sideways toward a hitching post, all while watching the man.

The man with a pretty black-haired woman on his arm.

Only weeks ago, Wax had seen this man perched high on a cliff above the Warden property. He'd been overhead like an angel. A guardian angel who watched over the Warden place.

An avenging angel.

Wax had been walking into the house, behind two of Bludge's hired thugs, and because Wax was a watchful man, he'd looked around, into the woods, low and high. And he'd seen this man looking down at him. Just sitting there, looking, from a place no man should be. It'd sent a chill through Wax that woke up again right now.

Wax hadn't said anything to his saddle partners. He hadn't gone climbing up there to find out who the man was. He hadn't drawn his gun and started shooting.

Why? Why had he just pointed at the man, letting the man know Wax saw him, then gone inside? Because Wax had the uncomfortable notion that the man up there wasn't human, he was an angel sent from God to watch over Wax and judge him. You didn't start shooting at avenging angels.

And now to see him again. It twisted something in Wax's gut. A superstitious impulse he wasn't proud of. But why had he been up there, looking down, watching the abandoned Warden place? Pushing aside the sense of the man being other than human, Wax had to ask himself if the man was connected to the strangers Wax had seen at the Wardens'. Those men had made Wax run—but not before he'd taken a long look. Wax didn't think this man was either of them.

Maybe he was one of the Warden hands sent to stand sentry over the place and report back. If so, the Wardens might know Wax had been there with only two men. They might know he'd later been there alone. They might be planning an attack right now.

Wax had seen this man, and the man had seen Wax. But they'd been a long way apart.

Wax had eyes like a golden eagle with a high-priced telescope. But how sharp were this man's eyes? Would he recognize Wax? Would he demand to know what Wax had been doing at the Warden house?

Maybe it was time to get that shave right now just to change his appearance. But if everyone knew what he looked like barefaced, that did some damage to his plans to change his looks when he took off in the spring.

The West wasn't that full of people, and memories were long. Stories told and retold around a campfire could spread far and wide. Wax was a known man, especially distinguished by his heavily waxed beard and moustache.

The man went toward the sheriff's office, which was off the main street. Whoever that was, and the woman with him, they vanished from sight.

They'd come out of the hotel. Wax studied the situation and knew the best places in town for gossip were saloons and barber shops.

It was early in the day, so the saloon wouldn't have many people in it, if any.

He touched the stiffened hairs, drawn to a waxy point on his chin. Maybe for a few days he could give up the wax, maybe get his moustache trimmed, the wax washed out, and a haircut. That would change his appearance enough to not draw that man's attention.

Wax would do some listening, some watching, some waiting.

Then his eyes went to the end of the street. A box built by an undertaker stood up, lid off, with a man inside.

Just as Wax had known that man from the mountainside, he knew the dead man. One of those sharp-eyed men who'd come to the Warden place and made Wax run.

One of them dead. And the avenging angel heading for the sheriff.

Wax wondered what it all meant, and he intended to find out. He hoped the barber was in a talkative mood.

Ursula heard hoofbeats, and her song died a quick death, replaced with true joy.

What flooded through her was surprising. Hooves were a stark reminder that she had no right to joy. Searching for joy in her favorite Bible verses set to music . . . and not finding it . . . was her due because she was a betrayer who'd turned her back on her sister Ilsa when she was sick and maybe dying.

She rushed to the heavy elk hide that hung over the doorway, then skidded to a stop, breathing nearly in gasps. She forced herself to calm down and arrange her expression so she didn't look desperate to see someone.

She'd chosen the life of a hermit, but only right this moment had she discovered that she didn't like being alone all the time. In fact, she hated it.

She missed her sisters. But she was so scared. So ashamed.

To go to her sisters, she had to break all of Grandma's rules. Besides, they hated her now, and why wouldn't they? She'd abandoned them.

The hooves came on. The desire to hide fought within her with the desire to run out and see someone, anyone. Finally, when it wouldn't look like she was happy for company, she shoved aside the elk hide and rushed through the broken-down rooms with long-collapsed ceilings of the strange stone building. She reached the farthest forward room and the exit to the place just as Jo appeared through a line of trees that encircled the valley.

Jo, her sister. Ursula knew Ilsa had survived her sickness. Jo had been up to visit several times, and she'd told Ursula she was going down the mountain, going to a town.

That's when she realized she heard a second set of hooves. She caught her breath, hoping Ilsa had come.

Dave emerged from the forest.

Dave, who had brought his cattle up here and a bunch of hired men. Then his parents had come, his father with a bullet in him.

Then his brother had come and brought sickness to Ilsa . . . and Ursula had run away. She'd betrayed her ailing sister to save herself.

She deserved to be alone for the rest of her life.

And then Dave had married Jo. Which meant he'd never go away. Jo was lost to Ursula forever.

Jo slowed the galloping horse. Ursula admired how Jo rode after only weeks of practice. And Dave was even better. Jo was learning so much from the Wardens. She'd always been curious. Ursula should have known she'd never be able to keep Jo home and safe.

Now here she came, with a big smile and a husband riding behind. Dave pulled his horse to a stop and just sat there, well back. Ursula had trained him not to expect a warm welcome.

Something else that shamed her.

Jo swung down, led her horse forward, and tied it to the

hitching post Dave had built. Jo wore a dress with her hair twisted neatly in a bun that showed below a tidy bonnet.

Where had her little sister gone?

There was something in Jo's eyes Ursula couldn't quite understand. Excitement. Ursula's heart sped up as she tried to imagine what Jo was excited about.

She braced herself as Jo strode forward and flung her arms around Ursula. What diseases might Jo be bringing with her?

But it was so good to see her little sister. She'd held back when Jo had come over before. Kept out of reach. Refused to talk any more than absolutely necessary. But today her loneliness overcame her fear . . . and her shame.

With a breath so deep it hurt, Ursula flung her arms around Jo and hugged back with all her strength.

"How can you ever for-forgive me . . ." Ursula's voice broke, and she had to steady herself to go on. ". . . for abandoning y-you when Ilsa was so sick?"

The last word came on a sob.

Jo held on tight as Ursula cried. Those arms around her! They'd never been a hugging family, not even back when Grandma and Grandpa had been alive. Ma had hugged a lot, before she'd ridden down that trail and been swallowed up.

But not Grandma and Grandpa, and trained by them, the girls had never done any hugging.

It was wonderful. It was water pouring down over the desert. It was sun coming out at the end of a long winter. Ursula felt each of Jo's hugs all the way to her soul as if she'd been hungry for a hug all her life and now she was presented with a feast.

"Ilsa got married."

Ursula staggered back and almost went all the way into the stone house, which wasn't that far behind her. "T-to who?"

"Dave's brother, Mitch."

Ursula couldn't stop from ramming ten fingers into her hair in shock. The very idea. "They never did a thing but fight."

Jo looked back to her husband, who had edged closer, but one step at a time, as if Ursula was a timid forest creature, and he wanted to approach her but was afraid she'd run.

Which she had done many times.

"Why *did* they get married, Dave? Ursula's right, they fought all the time."

Dave shrugged. "I think when they met, they felt something for each other right away, an attraction to each other. But it was too soon. They took that strong reaction for . . . for . . ." Dave shrugged again. "Well, they just . . . bothered each other. It finally shook itself out when he kissed her, and he knew that 'bothered' feeling was that he cared about her too much, too fast. Once he admitted it, he proposed marriage."

Jo turned to Ursula. "Once he admitted it and kissed her and got caught kissing her at a time and place they should not have been, alone at night. And there was a fuss that attracted a crowd and before you know it, they're standing in front of an altar."

With a gasp, Ursula asked, "You stood by while she was forced to marry a man she doesn't even like?"

Jo looked back at Dave again.

128

Dave said weakly, "Considering them sneaking off to his room, alone, in the night, and being caught in a pretty . . . ahem . . . well, being caught kissing . . . I'd say they like each other pretty well."

"Ilsa didn't seem unhappy about it. Well, right at first maybe, but she settled down. And Mitch had to talk to the sheriff." Jo quit talking abruptly.

"About kissing Ilsa?" Ursula's hand whipped out and grabbed Jo's wrist.

Dave came up to Jo's side. "No, not about Ilsa."

Ursula didn't like him being this close, but she was too busy worrying about her baby sister.

"You know there was shooting trouble. You saw Pa. Well, there was a bit more trouble, and we had to settle a few things. So, Mitch and Ilsa came to town and ended up married, and, well, the trouble isn't quite solved yet so they stayed down the mountain. Considering the snow that was falling on our heads as we climbed the trail, I doubt Mitch and Ilsa will get back up here until spring."

Ursula looked from one to the other of them. There was something they weren't saying, but she had no idea what, and with a sick twist in her belly, she decided she didn't want to know. Most everything she heard from the Wardens was bad news.

"Ilsa is married to your brother." Ursula heard the flat tone of voice. Grim acceptance. "All the details matter nothing."

Jo rested a hand on her shoulder, and Ursula could barely feel the touch. She was numb right to her soul.

"We're both married, Ursula. And it's a wonderful thing to be married." Jo glanced sideways at Dave, and they shared a smile that Ursula didn't understand. It tugged on something deep within the lonely center of her heart.

"You have to dig deep, find your courage, and come away from this cabin. You can't stay up here alone for the rest of your life. You know Ilsa got sick, but she survived that sickness. Terrible things happened to Grandma long before we were born. She couldn't stand to risk them happening again. To protect herself and those she loved— us—she refused to go down the mountain. But, Ursula, someone can fall into a stream and drown. They can come unexpectedly upon a bear. A branch can break over your head and kill you. Lightning can strike."

"None of that happened to any of us."

Jo's hand tightened until Ursula had to come out of her numb grief. She had to come out of it to jerk her arm away from the bruising grip.

Their eyes met. Sisters. Right now and for the whole winter if Ursula didn't go along with Jo, there was nothing else but being alone. The choice was wrenching. The risk of defying Grandma's rules. The loneliness of turning her back on her sisters.

It almost ripped Ursula in half.

"I'm not going to abandon you, Ursula." Jo sounded different. Stronger. More alive.

"I've betrayed you and Ilsa. I'm not fit to be with people." Ursula hated the way she sounded. Pathetic and needy and almost like she was begging Jo for something Ursula didn't even want.

"If you choose to stay up here, then so be it. But I will be here as often as I can. And a few of Dave's cowhands are living in the smaller cabin in that first high valley we found. They're using it as a . . . as a . . ." She looked at Dave. "What did you call it? A lion something? A lion . . . uh . . . shack? Named because it's up here near mountain lions?"

A smile spread across Dave's face. "Line shack."

The affection between the two of them was so enticing to Ursula, and frightening, and wrong, and right.

"We brought you some supplies." Dave changed the subject. "I'm going to chop wood while you and Jo have a nice visit. Then I'm going to build a door onto your room."

Dave got very busy unloading his horse. Jo shooed Ursula back inside, and they headed for the inner room that still had a roof.

13

Mitch had ahold of Ilsa permanently, it seemed.

She'd been dragged here and there all morning, and now they'd packed up everything in their hotel room—which wasn't much—and he dragged her toward the big building where the horses were staying.

And it wasn't exactly being dragged since she just went right along, it's not like she was fighting him.

If they were back on her mountaintop, she wouldn't cooperate because up there she knew more about where to go and what to do than anyone.

Down here, it was better just to tag along after him.

Mitch worked so fast stowing packs on a horse that Ilsa didn't even try to help. Instead, she went and petted the mare she had been told she'd ride.

A pretty thing. A dirty white color Mitch had called dun. Done with what, she had wondered. Its mane, tail, and feet were dark brown. And, as she petted and talked to it, she found an understanding with the critter. She explained her struggle with trotting and believed the horse heard her.

They were in communion. She was sure of it.

Mitch boosted her up on the horse, then swung up on his. He did it all without a word and led the way out of town in the direction they'd come from Ilsa's mountain-top home.

"We're going home?"

"Yes, we are. Back to the Circle Dash." Mitch spoke quite loudly, considering Ilsa was only a couple of feet away from him.

Almost like he was talking to the whole town.

Wax settled into the saloon with a glass of whiskey he didn't intend to drink.

A man who made his living by having steady hands, clear eyes, and sharp wits had no business taking so much as a sip of whiskey.

The saloon had a good-sized window by the front door. Wax set himself up against the wall and just far enough back from the window that he could watch the street from the sheriff's office to the hotel, and watch the rest of the men in the saloon.

It was afternoon, and there were only layabouts in here, but those were the kind of men Wax always kept an eye on. Well, really, he kept an eye on everyone.

The avenging angel rode right into his line of sight. Wax riveted his gaze but tried real hard not to act like he was watching.

No sense telling the whole town he was interested in this stranger.

The barber had talked endlessly about nothing important, but Wax had managed a few questions. The barber had no idea who the stranger was, though he did have a few things to say about the body that'd been brought in, and more to say about the Wardens—folks he considered friends. As for their trip in just now, they'd been seen going to the land office, then they rode out, only to come right back into town again with that stranger and two men draped over their saddles. One dead, one in jail.

Two men over a saddle? Was it possible they were the two sharp-eyed men he'd seen at the Wardens' place? The man Wax had seen in the coffin was definitely one. Not that many strangers passing through when winter was closing in.

One man dead, one in jail. Both wanted outlaws, the barber said. A US Marshal had already taken the live one away, and the other would be planted in Boot Hill. It chafed that Wax couldn't lay eyes on the other so he'd know if it was the other man he saw—but it stood to reason.

Land office? Wax was interested in that, but he didn't say so. Was Bludge right? Had the Wardens maybe settled into an abandoned place that they were now trying to buy? That would give the ranch the look of being long inhabited . . . just not by the Wardens.

Bludge had told Wax he hadn't hired the strangers, and unless he'd hired those men to come gunning for Wax, Bludge had no good reason to lie. Since they were either dead or gone, it was nothing to worry about. Unless more were coming.

Lots of mysteries here.

He wanted to learn more, so after having the barber

wash the wax out of his beard and moustache and give his hair a good trim, he'd come straight to the saloon. He often picked up information at saloons, but today the layabouts were mostly snoozing in their whiskey, and the bartender gave him a wide berth. Wax knew his eyes had gotten cold, his expression grim.

More and more his reputation kept folks back, and if the reputation wasn't enough, whatever they saw in his face was.

The avenging angel rode past the window slowly, heading north out of town. And he rode beside one of the prettiest women Wax had ever seen. She had a riot of dark curls peeking out from under a fur-trimmed bonnet and wore a wool coat that looked soft and warm enough for even a winter morning on the mountaintop . . . if that's where they were headed. Her coat and bonnet looked new. Not the threadbare clothes of most homesteaders.

Who was she? Where had she come from?

It chafed at Wax that he didn't know either one of them. He'd been in the area since last spring, and he was a man who studied faces and remembered them.

Through the window he heard the avenging angel say they were heading toward the Circle Dash. Wax wondered if he was going to live there, because that was where Wax wanted to spend the winter.

If this was one of the Warden cowhands, Wax had never seen him before. Had the Wardens hired a gunfighter to fight Bludge?

Wax watched the blue-eyed, black-haired woman turn to the man and smile at him. It jarred something in Wax's gut and got him to wondering if he'd ever settle down. If his plan to get out of the gun-for-hire business worked, he'd make a better bet for a husband.

The pair rode out of sight. With a careful, sly glance, Wax saw the bartender had gone into the back room, while the layabouts continued to snore or sip.

Wax lifted his whiskey and with a quick, quiet toss, emptied the little glass under the table. In this filthy place with the scarred-up floors and poor lighting, no one would notice a small wet patch.

He set the whiskey glass on the table with a quiet click, stood, and was out the door before anyone noticed. Not that it mattered. A man could have a drink then leave a saloon if he wanted. He headed for the land office with more questions than just about what the Wardens had bought. He wanted to see what claim Bludge really had on the land he'd been taking over.

There was no rush getting out of town because he knew exactly where that man and his pretty companion were headed.

Ilsa was excited to see Jo again, but there was a twist of disappointment. She liked it out here, and she'd hoped to see a bit more before she returned to her mountaintop. But, even without Mitch hanging on to her hand, she was the same as dragged back toward home.

Their horses walked along awhile—hers content to move along with Mitch's. She didn't know how to steer it, and if she did, she wouldn't want to just head off on her own. So it looked like she was going home.

Then, on a rocky stretch blown clean of snow, Mitch

veered off the trail. Ilsa didn't remember this side trail from the ride in, but she wasn't sure exactly how to get home, so she offered no opinion.

Mitch turned to her. "We're not going home."

"You've changed your mind, then?"

He smiled. "You're really sweet, you know?"

She thought of that outlaw she'd attacked and felt her brow furrow. In the instant she had before she went after the vicious criminal, she'd known his bullet wounds were fatal so she didn't consider trying to kill him, just to stop him from shooting anymore in the time he had until he died.

She'd slammed the hilt of her knife into his gun hand, and he'd dropped the weapon. And then she'd seen that her knife was broken. She'd ruined her precious knife that Grandpa had given to her, and for what? A moment later, he'd stopped moving completely, just collapsed backward and lay with only his eyes moving. She hadn't caused that by slamming her knife hilt into his hand. So she saw no reason to be overly upset about it. But it still didn't seem very sweet of her.

Her knife, though. That was a terrible loss.

To keep from thinking about losing one of the few things she had from her grandparents, she kept her eyes on the trail and realized they were on a nearly invisible game trail in a heavy woods. Once again he was leading, but now he led her along a trail she could see and understand.

Ilsa ducked under low-hanging branches, and her horse picked its way across uneven footing. The trail finally widened.

"I said that so loud in Bucksnort in case anyone comes

in asking questions about us. I want anyone who over-heard me to think we were going home. The truth is, we're going to Denver." Mitch added, "We're going to speed up. Do you want to ride double with me, or can I reach over and hang on to you through the trot?"

"Neither is necessary. Done and I understand each other."

"Done?"

"You said her name was Done. And I've told her about trotting and how hard it is for me. We'll be fine. Let's go."

Mitch's brows arched enough it lifted his hat. Then, keeping an eye on her, he nudged his brown stallion into a trot.

Ilsa whispered to her horse. The mare went from walk-ing to galloping in one leap. Ilsa held on tight and passed Mitch a few paces down the trail. She was sure he ex-pected to grab her and keep her from falling off.

He was the sweet one.

Instead, though his expression was startled, he kicked his horse and picked up his pace to match Done. Side by side they raced along.

Wax slipped up on the Circle Dash, alert, ready for the avenging angel to come sweeping down on him and send him on to glory.

If that's where Wax Mosby was headed after this life.

He doubted avenging angels swept down on the heaven bound.

He came to a spot overlooking the Circle Dash yard. Quiet. An abandoned air about it. Snow had fallen since Wax had left to question Pike, and there wasn't a fresh track anywhere. He'd even lost the tracks of the man and woman who'd announced they were heading out here.

Wax had lived a long time by not trusting anyone. So when someone appeared to have lied, it came as no surprise, but he had to ask himself why. Did the man know Wax was in town?

Had that message been for him? Wax pondered his many questions as he studied the ranch and the mountain that rose up behind it. The man didn't lurk on a ledge halfway up. Wax had a notion to climb up there and see where that man had been going.

The wind kicked up, and snow came in a way that told Wax it was going to be heavy. Not a day for mountain climbing.

He'd held back long enough.

There was no one here.

He rode in and settled his horse for the night, then went in to think and watch and wait and wonder.

Ursula saw the heavily laden clouds. She could feel the snow in them. This night would close the trail Jo and Dave rode in on.

She'd be locked away.

Ursula looked out over the valley from the collapsed front of her stone building. The room she stayed in was standing strong. It was warm from the fireplace and had a solid door, thanks to Dave. But out here, the building was falling in. She had land blown clear near her, but across the valley, the snow was deeper than her head. And the trail out of here was drifted shut and packed high with snow. She backed away from the dismal sight of the trail where Jo and Dave had come several times. Nearly impassable already.

They'd all known it was coming, and Jo had begged Ursula to come back with them, even promised she could live alone in the Nordegren family home they'd all grown up in. Jo and Dave would move in with his parents.

She'd said no.

She returned to her lonely room, and a song came to her lips. As she always did, she expressed what she felt with a song.

It rang with the sadness that was her only companion.

"'My God, my God, why hast thou forsaken me?'"

Those words were in the Psalms, but they echoed Jesus' words as He was dying on the cross. They now came from deep within Ursula into a sad song.

"'Why art thou so far from helping me?'"

Even as she sang, Ursula knew her loneliness, her feeling of being forsaken by God, was of her own making. God was right here, waiting for her to reach out.

Her heart hurt until it felt as if it were being torn from her chest.

Other laments, other heartbroken words, came to her and took shape as songs.

But there was joy there, too. Ursula knew she could have that joy. And she could have her family back . . . though not until spring. The trails were too narrow, too high. They would all be fully closed off now until the sun melted the snow away in the spring.

She could grab that joy for herself, though, right where she was.

The Old One Hundredth.

> Make a joyful noise unto the Lord, all ye lands.
> Serve the Lord with gladness: come before his
>   presence with singing.
> Know ye that the Lord he is God: it is he that
>   hath made us, and not we ourselves; we are his
>   people, and the sheep of his pasture.
> Enter into his gates with thanksgiving, and into his
>   courts with praise: be thankful unto him, and
>   bless his name.

Ursula loved it dearly and had sung it with Grandma many times and found such sweet, uplifting hope in those words.

Now, when she thought of beautiful verses, the encouraging, uplifting words in the Bible, all she could do was hate herself. She'd cut herself off from her family. She'd turned coward and run away, leaving her little sister to live or die without any help from Ursula.

Almost worse, Ilsa hadn't needed Ursula's help. She had plenty of it. Ursula's cowardice had only hurt herself. Left her stranded up here. Her fears a more impassable wall than the snow-packed mountain pass.

"'How long wilt thou forget me, O Lord? Forever? How long wilt thou hide thy face from me?'"

Ursula knew the answers to those questions asked in that old, grievous psalm.

God had not hidden His face from Ursula. It was she, in her deep shame, deep guilt, deep fear, who had turned away from God. And what's more, she knew God would forgive her for all of it. All she had to do was reach out.

And maybe that meant she wasn't worried about God forgiving her. She was just too ashamed to forgive herself.

The stone walls of the ancient building echoed with her loneliness, her feelings of worthlessness, her song.

How could she ask God to forgive her until she was brave enough to face her baby sister and ask for forgiveness? Brave enough to go down and join the people who had moved onto her mountain?

She needed courage before she could ask for forgiveness, and she had none.

14

W hat happened here?" Mitch pulled his horse to a halt on a climbing, twisting trail that curved around a mountainside. They needed to pass over this treacherous stretch, then they'd be on a downhill ride. Hours and hours more of it, but the water tank, the spot where Mitch had left the train on his way here from the east, would be at the end of that trail.

The trail was gone.

"There was a landslide," Ilsa said calmly as she rode up beside him. "There's no way to go forward."

Mitch tore his eyes away from the trail. He knew this land like he knew his own face, and what he knew was, this was the only way to the train tracks.

"We have to backtrack. Find another way forward."

Nodding silently, Ilsa finally said, "I saw a trail that headed into a stretch of forest back a ways. It looked larger than a game trail, and it was heading generally west. Let's go try that one."

"Up the mountain or down? The snow's getting heavy,

and it's going to be a long cold ride. We might want to head to lower ground."

Ilsa reined her horse around on the narrow trail. Now Mitch was behind her. He marveled at how well Ilsa and her horse were working together.

And as he followed her, he considered that he had, despite her innocence, a very tough woman for a wife. She might not know the outside world, but she knew trails, she knew living in a harsh land. She knew survival.

He decided maybe until they'd found their way through this rough stretch, he'd let her be in charge.

His innocent wife, the newcomer to horseback riding, with no notion of the way to go, was tougher than he was. And he knew himself to be very tough.

Mitch either had to stop and sleep, or lash his wrists to the saddle. He was exhausted. They'd ridden hard through the night and all the following day, without Ilsa needing to be carried at all—more's the pity.

"Ilsa, I have to stop. We'll have to sleep on the trail."

"You said we'd get to a train. I really want to see a train, whatever that is."

Mitch didn't even try to explain again. He was struggling to speak in complete sentences. "I hoped, if things went well, we'd make it. I slept out on the trail when I came west. But I didn't want that for you."

Which reminded him again how tough she was. "But that landslide sent us a long way north. You got us through, and now we're headed west again, so we have to cut across the train tracks at some point. But I don't know where we'll find a place the train will stop. We might have to ride all the way to Denver. We might as well admit we can't make it tonight and pull up and sleep." He forced his eyes open and wasn't sure how long he'd been riding with them closed.

Ilsa looked at him. The moonlight was bright enough he could see her arched brow and scowling expression.

She was so cute. Then she just kept going. They were galloping along on a trail that'd gotten wide and showed signs of wagon traffic. This trail had to lead somewhere. They'd ridden away from most of the foothills of the mountains, so the path wasn't treacherous.

"Can we just try to ride a little longer?"

Mitch's eyes fell shut. That felt so good he had to think long and hard before he opened them. The horses were in good shape. They'd alternated walking and galloping. They'd even gotten off and led them for a while and stopped for water and to let them graze.

It was all time Mitch now wished he had back, but they'd had no choice if the poor horses were to keep going.

"Talk to me, Ilsa. Tell me a story about your life. I need noise to keep me awake."

There was a stretch of silence. Mitch's eyes fell shut.

"My parents died before I was old enough to remember them."

That jerked him awake.

"Grandma died when I was three."

"That's a lot of loss for a child."

Ilsa was silent again. "I have only the faintest memories of Grandma. A few flashes are true memories, but most of what seem like memories are probably just stories I've been told by Ursula and Jo."

"It was always, or nearly always, you and your sisters and your grandpa?"

"More often it was just the three of us. Grandpa was gone a lot, even after Grandma died. At the end he settled down more. He complained of aching joints, called it room-a-tiz."

"Rheumatism," Mitch said. "It's a condition that makes your joints ache something fierce. Lots of older folks end up with it."

"That sounds right, then, because he talked of his knees and stayed in the cabin more all the time. He had all these medicines he took to treat himself. He taught me what they all were. Even before he started ailing, he took me with him to hunt plants and roots that he ground up and used in medicine. He said I had a gift. A God-given gift for healing. He called me his little medicine w-woman." Ilsa's voice broke.

Resting two gloved fingers on her lips, she waited a bit, then uncovered her mouth and said, "I'm surprised the memory is so painful. He's been gone for so l-long." Silent again except for the pounding of hooves.

Mitch saw her swallow convulsively and wondered if she'd go on, or if he should change the subject. He wasn't overly fond of a woman's tears. Ma never cried. Well, she'd cried when he'd come home. But mostly she never cried. And Katrina, the woman he'd been seeing back east, who'd also been seeing his partner behind Mitch's back, had been overly prone to tears.

He had compared the two women and much preferred his mother. With Katrina, he'd found himself scrambling to do anything to keep her happy, so she'd be that perfect,

148

cool lady. Wanting to protect her from whatever upset her. He'd told himself that was love. Now he could see it was just confusion and panic on his part. Somehow, Katrina had made him feel like everything that bothered her was his fault. He was always trying not to be a ham-handed brute, and his protectiveness toward her was all twisted up with her stunning beauty.

Were all men as stupid about women?

Here he was married to a rather savage kind of woman. He hoped they got on well, but there was no great supply of blazing intelligence involved in how he'd ended up leg shackled to her.

Clearing her throat, Ilsa went on, "It was the bond between Grandpa and me. The thing that made me feel special. Jo was his little huntress. I was his little medicine woman."

"What was Ursula?"

Galloping along, she gave him a surprised glance and didn't even begin to lose control of her mare or fall off.

"I don't know. Ursula was . . . she was . . . well, everything that Grandma had done was now Ursula's job, and that didn't involve Grandpa overly. He liked when she sang, but I was told that Grandma loved to sing, so that wasn't anything Grandpa taught Ursula. Jo and I helped around the cabin, but Ursula was in charge. She's about seven years older than I am. That doesn't sound like much, but she . . ." Ilsa shrugged. "She mothered me. She mothered Jo, too, a bit, though Jo was more an equal with her."

"That's a really young mother." Mitch heard the love in Ilsa's voice as she spoke of her sisters. And here he was likely taking her half a continent away from them.

"Grandpa never called her his little baker, his little seamstress, or his little gardener. But she did all of that and more. She milked the cows and fed the chickens, gathered the eggs. Cared for all of us. Jo and I mostly left everything to her while we ran off into the woods. I'm more at home there than inside."

"That's a heavy weight for Ursula." Mitch thought of Ilsa's hermit of a big sister.

"I hadn't thought of it before, but—" In the full moonlight, Ilsa gave him a look full of wide-eyed sorrow. "She didn't come when I was so sick. She chose her fear over me."

"Maybe the weight was too much," Mitch said quietly. The talking had helped because he was fully alert again, but he regretted bringing up such sad things. "She knew you had a lot of care. She maybe chose to be alone out of fear, but she stayed with you until help came, then she ran to that isolated house. What a terrible, lonely life for her."

"I need to go see her. Make sure she knows I'm well, we're all well."

"Jo and Dave were going to take her supplies and tell her we got married."

"Can we ask her to come and stay with us?" Ilsa turned and blinked at Mitch. "Wherever we end up living?"

"We'll do that when we get back." He'd said it before, so he didn't repeat that they'd be gone until spring. That was a long time alone for Ursula. Then Mitch remembered how he'd climbed that mountainside to get into the valley. Maybe they *could* get back in.

The notion and Ilsa's story pulled him out of his drowsiness. He picked up the pace as they rode along.

The moon rose high in the sky for a long stretch until the silence once more eased into exhaustion. He fought to keep his eyelids from falling shut. "We've got to stop at the top of this rise, Ilsa, and start looking for some kind of shelter."

They rode up a long, sloping hill, and at the crest he looked down at lights. It wasn't the water tank where he'd gotten off the train on his way home. The landslide had sent them enough off course that they were riding up to a town. In the moonlight, he saw train tracks.

"We made it." His hushed voice carried on the night air.

"Another big town."

It was as small as Bucksnort. He needed to be more alert than he was tonight to explain to her they were heading for Chicago, and they'd be sleeping on the tenth floor of a hotel. He could maybe do some talking once they were on the train.

"We'll catch the first train that comes through." He wished he had the private sleeper car he'd sold. Comfortable way to travel. The weight of the gold he carried in a pouch tied inside the waist of his jeans reminded him there might be a way to make the trip better if he took a little time looking around in the first good-sized city they came to, which would be Denver, unless he'd gotten severely lost.

"We'll catch it?" Ilsa asked. "Like with a rope, the way you caught the horses out of the corral?"

The iron horse. Mitch smiled but only said, "It rolls along on those tracks, those iron rails." He pointed, but he wasn't sure he made much sense. "It'll stop. We won't have to throw a lasso over it."

"Then ride on it?"

He had to admit it wouldn't take much to impress Ilsa. That was a nice quality in a wife.

"Yes, we'll ride on it to wherever we need to go to put an end to my troubles."

He wondered if a train existed that could take him there.

When they finally got to a boardinghouse, Mitch fell asleep next to his brand-new wife so quickly, so suddenly, that he had no memory of closing his eyes.

And he was awakened in the first light of dawn by the blast of a train whistle.

"It's here." He yanked Ilsa up, but she was jumping half-way to the ceiling with a wild look of fear and something else. That feral look that made him worry she was going to pull her knife. But there was no time, and she started getting her boots on before he had to decide if she was going to attack.

He'd disarm her later.

"That loud noise was made by the train. The man who will be boarding our horses told us it might be in this morning. We've got to get out there before it leaves. It might not be back again for a week."

They hadn't unpacked much, so they had everything stowed in a few seconds. They were breathing hard when they ran up to the station. The train was just pulling in; it'd begun whistling a fair distance out.

Ilsa had heard the noise but didn't see the train until they were up the steps to the station.

She shrieked at the huffing and puffing monster slowing down as it reached town. She whirled and dove for the edge of the platform.

He stepped in her way, and she smashed into him. With no time to spare and their meager possessions in hand, he carried Ilsa along to buy a ticket.

Then Mitch hustled her toward the train. He tossed the satchels, bedrolls, and his wife on board, then dragged Ilsa into a seat. He dropped their baggage on the seat facing them.

"Ilsa." The whistle blasted again. Ilsa dove over him. He snagged her and pinned her down until the blast ended.

The train car wasn't overly full, thank heavens. No one seemed inconvenienced by the wrestling match he was having with his wife.

He smiled at about five curious passengers. "She's never been on a train before."

The one woman on board, a gray-haired matron next to a gray-haired man who was most likely her husband, asked, "Should you be sitting on her head like that?"

Ilsa started growling, and he looked down at her savage eyes. He really hoped she didn't pull her knife.

15

Finally, Ilsa stopped struggling. He looked down at her, worried. He didn't want to crush her, after all.

"I'm sorry we didn't have more time to talk about the train."

She blinked those blue eyes at him, and he thought he saw his wife again, not the barbarian she could become. He oughta let her up, but she could be playing possum.

"The wagons in Bucksnort, you saw them, didn't you?" He waited.

She nodded. Not that easy when she was squashed into the thin cushions of the bench seat under his backside.

"They're just really small versions of this."

She arched an extremely doubtful brow.

"I mean they have wheels and carry loads. Much, much smaller than this, but both trains and wagons are ways to ride around. In fact, the train is sometimes called an iron horse."

She growled again. He was trying to explain, but he was clearly not up to the task.

"This is a huge . . . wagon . . . with a roof." He lifted his hand and ran a level palm back and forth a few inches over his head. As if she didn't know the word *roof*. "And an engine."

Engine did nothing for her, and no hand signals came to mind. He was wasting his breath.

He stood and extended his hand. She took it and sat up but made no escape attempt. Neither did she adjust her badly disarrayed bonnet, tame her hair, or straighten the dress that came over one knee and halfway up the other.

He moved slightly to block the other passengers' view of her—because they were watching, and why not? This was easily the most interesting thing going on in the train car. "It's loud and huge, but it's really fast and safe." Usually. He decided now wasn't the time for honesty about train wrecks.

"We can cover hundreds . . ." Numbers again. "I mean, we can cover many, many miles . . ." She couldn't possibly know what a mile was. "I mean we can cover a long distance riding a train much faster than we can on horseback, and the horses can rest up in that stable while we head for . . ." Denver? Omaha? Chicago? ". . . when we get to, uh, where we're going."

Maybe resting the horses would appeal to her. She seemed to like the dun mare he'd gotten her.

The train began climbing, and the engine chugged louder. Ilsa's eyes went wide.

Mitch, who'd been standing to block her from escaping her little stretch of bench, sat down beside her and took her hand.

"I'm sorry." He squeezed her hand gently. "I really am. That was a poor way to treat you. I should have let you see the train and get used to it." Back east, they schooled horses by locking them up near a train yard. Mitch had to admit it'd never occurred to him to treat his wife like a fractious horse, but maybe he should start.

"Then we could have just waited to travel on it when you understood what a train was and were in agreement that we should take it. We could have even ridden the horses to Denver. That's where this train is headed."

"Is Denver as large as Bucksnort?"

"Um . . ." Mitch tried to think of how to explain it. "Um . . . comparing Denver to Bucksnort is like comparing a train to a wagon."

"Denver is much smaller, then?"

"No, Denver is the train. Bucksnort is the wagon." Mitch was tempted to just whack his head on something hard. "Forget I mentioned trains and wagons. Denver is bigger than Bucksnort."

Ilsa seemed to be settling down. A mite. Making no sudden moves, he reached his free hand to smooth her skirts down over her ankles. She hadn't seemed to notice her exposed knee. Then he straightened her bonnet and tucked in her hair.

Smiling, he said, "It takes some getting used to. You know I'd never lived away from the ranch when I headed east. I had to learn all about trains and big cities and . . . well, war, for heaven's sake. Now, that's loud. I did it, learned about it, got used to it, and so can you."

"Do you think so?"

"Just stay right by me, and we'll get through this and get back to your sisters." He didn't speculate on how long it might take.

He didn't want her jumping out a window.

Ilsa couldn't stand the noise.

"Try putting your fingers in your ears. That cuts the sound back."

Her husband was no help. All day she'd endured, and she was ready to snap. "That's not the point. I can't believe there's a world with this much noise in it."

"We'll be in Denver any minute. Remember, the whistle is going to blow."

"No. Not the whistle." She put her fingers in her ears. The blast of that whistle had happened every time they'd come into a town, and it'd blown over and over. "Can't you go tell them not to do that anymore?"

"They need to warn people the train is coming so they get off the tracks."

People had gotten off and back on in these towns. Ilsa thought she saw her chance to get away, but Mitch wouldn't even let her stand up.

And since she didn't want him to sit on her again, she battled her need to escape.

"Are we getting off in Denver?"

"Yep. We'll find a hotel for the night."

"Can you please get your own room this time? I don't want to share a bed with you anymore."

She saw Mitch's cheeks pink up a bit, and he looked up, away from her, then back down. She followed his gaze with her own and saw people staring at her. Some smiling.

She had no idea why.

Leaning close, he whispered, "Hush. That is a very personal topic, not to be discussed in front of strangers."

"Is this another of your rules?" she whispered back.

"It absolutely is. If you could read, I'd write the rules down so you could memorize them."

Ilsa had never wanted to learn to read less than she did at that minute.

"Look out the window. You can see the first buildings in Denver now. The train station is still a few miles ahead, but the train needs to warn people that—"

The whistle again. The train changed sounds, its rattling noise slowed but also seemed to be louder. Ilsa had no idea why this thing was so noisy. Why didn't they build it so it wouldn't break through her ears and pound on her brain?

And then she saw the buildings. She was sitting with a window on her right and houses rushed past. Or probably they were the ones rushing, but that wasn't how it seemed. The houses seemed to move, racing past the window. There were horses and wagons, and she saw pens full of as many cattle as the Wardens had driven into her high mountain home.

If she had that many cattle, she'd have to learn to count higher.

The cabins were crowded together. People stood out front of them or walked behind them. The cabins were of a size with the one Ilsa had grown up in, but then there were buildings that were taller, then taller yet. She looked beyond the buildings that lined the tracks and saw more, and behind them even more. She tried to count, but they whisked by too quickly.

"Here's the depot ahead." Mitch leaned close. The whistle blasted. He didn't talk until it quit. "You hold on to me, Ilsa. There are a lot of people out there, and I don't want us to get separated. I'll hold on to you as tight as I can, but you have to work with me. Hang on tight."

He reached out a hand, and she grabbed it. Swallowing hard, she watched the buildings get taller with rows of windows on top of rows of windows. There'd been several buildings like that in Bucksnort, including the hotel where they'd stayed. She'd gotten to climb stairs.

Did that mean there were even more stairs inside, and rooms stacked on top of other rooms?

The whistle blew again, and the train slowed and slowed. A terrible squealing sound came from underneath where Ilsa sat, and white clouds shot out from somewhere, as if the train were driving right into a fire.

Ilsa covered her ears and longed for her mountaintop. To think she'd wanted to come down and see a city.

Mitch woke up in the wee hours of the morning with a beautiful woman in his arms.

Just like yesterday morning, they had to hurry. There was no Pinkerton Agency in Denver, and he decided it was probably no use to look in Omaha. So it was on to Chicago. He was up and dressed before she started moving. He got things packed while she pulled on her dress. He had to tie the fancy bows on the boots he'd bought her. She didn't know how.

Mitch had ordered a carriage to take them to the train station, and it was waiting for them.

He had managed to find a private train car that wasn't in use. Now that he wasn't trying to hide his identity, he found plenty of people he could call on for favors. And he'd found that the Panic had made a lot of things very cheap. It was easy to find cars like this one for sale for pennies on the dollar as wealthy owners went bankrupt, and creditors sold everything to try to regain their losses.

It made it simple to travel in comfort.

Ilsa's eyes went wide as he guided her into the car. "This isn't like the train we rode to Denver."

It most surely was not. It struck Mitch then that he hoped very much to make his wife happy. And to do that, he'd spent a great deal of money. Fortunately, he'd brought a fine supply of his gold along. Now he stood eagerly, like a boy hoping to impress his sweetheart.

He thought of all the women who'd cast out lures to him back in New York. Even more, he thought of the times a woman had attempted to compromise herself in some way to trap him into marriage.

He'd ignored the lures and escaped the traps, and he hadn't cared much who was outraged or insulted. And now here he was, trapped into marriage by a woman who wouldn't know a feminine lure if it bit her. And he didn't mind being trapped at all.

Well, not much.

"We'll be traveling day and night for a while, so I didn't want us to be stuck sitting up. There is a bedroom in this car and more comfortable seating."

"This is so beautiful." Ilsa ran a hand over a settee with padded seats upholstered in blue velvet. It faced an arm-chair splashed with vivid blue flowers. A low table was set between the two. It was a far cry from the simple bench they'd ridden on before.

The doors and windows were trimmed with stained

oak so shiny it glowed. The walls were papered in brocade cloth with a regal blue design against a white background. An oval mirror with a gilded frame hung next to a door between the bedroom and a small room that was set aside for a chamber pot. Beneath the mirror was a large glass washbasin, elaborately painted. In the basin rested a pitcher. It sat atop a white-painted chest, all carefully anchored so it wouldn't slide or tip if the train ride got rough. A towel in matching blue and white hung neatly from a rack on the wall by the washbasin.

That mirror was at the back of the train, and they were the last car before the ones carrying freight. No one need come through that door ever. At the other end of the car was a door that led forward. They could walk out there to see who else was riding. But Mitch knew from experience there would be no need to leave the private car.

There was also a dining table with four chairs, but the train they were on didn't serve meals. Mitch had been on some back east that had full service of that sort, but this train didn't offer it.

"We'll stop for meals, but other than that, we can travel in privacy for the entire trip."

The windows were hung with heavy brocade curtains, tied back so they could enjoy the view. But Mitch would close them when they went to sleep, making the car a near cocoon where the two of them could be alone together. He remembered Ilsa saying she wasn't interested in sharing . . . married things with a near stranger. Him.

Remembered it? For heaven's sake, her words practically echoed in his head.

Well, here they were, alone and in for a long ride. Getting to know each other would be his top priority.

They had some real big states to ride across.

Knowing that, he relaxed. He had all the time in the world to get to know his wife, teach her about everything in the whole world, and woo her into becoming fully married to him.

In fact, because it was so early, and they'd had so many long days that he was just plain exhausted, he decided to put off their discussion for a while. He showed her the bedroom, and as soon as the whistle quit blasting to warn the folks of Denver a train was leaving, they were both back asleep.

Mitch's plan to spend a leisurely trip getting to know Ilsa was foiled by a blizzard that followed them across the country. He spent time every day of what should have been a four-day journey from Denver to Chicago outside with a shovel while the train huffed and steamed, waiting for the way to be clear. He and the rest of the men were called upon to clear the tracks in weather that almost froze them to icicles.

When he was inside his oh-so-luxurious train car, he was either shivering or sleeping.

He learned that the attraction of train travel sank with every mile, but his wife went undiscovered.

16

T hat's Chicago?" Ilsa had her face pressed to the window, looking at the tall buildings ahead, and so many of them. Her breath shortened. Her heart pounded.

Bucksnort had amazed her. Denver stunned her. Chicago left her reeling. And now she realized the difference between a town, a city, and a big city.

Chicago was a big city.

They whipped past yards full of cattle, then they left that behind, and the train slowed, passing small houses, then bigger ones, then what had to be businesses, but so many of them. Bucksnort had a general store. One general store.

Now, business after business, first two stories then three, then five.

What little time they had together on the train ride, they'd spent talking, and Mitch was teaching her to read from the book Ma sent along. Mitch called it a McGuffey Reader, and he'd insisted they spend time working from it every day.

But now words painted on buildings whipped past the window. It was all too fast for her to even begin to read.

She saw clothes in some windows and saddles in others. Food and furniture and more clothes and more food. And people. She had to learn to count higher than one hundred. That number wasn't close to high enough.

Even with the train slowing, she couldn't begin to see it all. She had to force herself to blink her gazing eyes before they dried out, because she was unable to look away from all that came rushing toward her.

The train whistle blew again and again. The huge beast seemed to want to announce to all and sundry that they had arrived. Then a terrible thing happened, another train came rushing right toward them.

Ilsa dove for the floor. The train whizzed past. She rolled on her back, propped up on her elbows, and watched the black monster whip by the windows so close she could have reached out and touched it.

What a terrible close brush with death. Was all train travel so dangerous?

"It's not going to hit us. It's on another set of tracks that run right alongside the ones we're on." Mitch jerked the curtains closed and helped her to her feet. He seemed to be used to her panicking by now. And who could blame him? She'd done it a lot.

"Yes, this is Chicago. It's our destination. And we may stay for the winter. The train ride was harsh with the snow and cold. I don't look forward to making the return trip."

She wanted to look at her husband and demand he tell her how there could be buildings so big and tall. Instead, she rushed to the window and peeked out. The other train was gone. Much as it stunned her, she couldn't tear her eyes away from the city they were rushing through.

The buildings bigger and taller. Built of some kind of stone.

"Let's gather our things. We'll check into the Grand Pacific Hotel. We'll wash up, have a meal, then go see the Pinkertons. I just hope coming to Chicago is enough. I hope we don't end up in New York City. I have no desire to go back there."

"H-how many people did you say lived there?"

"In New York City?" He brushed the front of her dress as if she'd gotten it dirty, but it seemed fine. He did knock her skirts down into order so maybe he liked them dangling near the floor.

She nodded, wishing she hadn't asked. They'd talked about numbers some but mostly adding and subtracting small figures.

"It's not a million yet, but it's growing fast and will reach that soon. And Chicago burned down two years ago. That's why there's so much brick."

"Burned down?" She stared at the city whizzing by. The train had slowed down, but it still seemed mighty fast to her. "But there are buildings everywhere."

"They built new ones."

"And brick?"

Mitch came up beside her to look out. "The red stone the buildings are made of. That's brick."

They were passing red buildings every moment. She marveled at what must be brick.

"It's the fastest I've ever seen anything come back." Mitch stood there, watching along with her. "It's inspiring. But it's stopped now. I sold everything and got out of my holdings just months before the Panic."

"The what?"

Mitch shook his head. "It's complicated and not something we need to worry about. But I started selling off property and cashing out stocks about a year ago. I walked away with almost everything I owned converted to gold, then came the Panic. Banks all across the country were failing. I'd planned to find a secure bank and leave my money locked up somewhere, but I didn't trust any of them to survive. When I left for home, I stopped in Chicago for a while. Went south to St. Louis and stayed there, then came back north to Omaha."

He tried to explain a financial panic to her. He'd spent a lot of time talking, telling her things. She tried to remember it all, but a lot of it was jumbled.

And reading was a slow but interesting skill. The sounds the letters made, how they went together to make up words was interesting. And there'd been a Bible in the train car, but only one. It was a lot like the big black Bible they had at home, but there was no sign of the second Bible. She could now read the word *Bible* printed in big letters on the front of the book.

He'd taught her to write her name. Ilsa Warden. Not Nordegren, like it had always been. She wanted to learn to write her old name, too, but there were enough things to keep her busy.

And he slept beside her every night and kept her warm.

She was getting used to sharing the bed with him, but she wasn't ready yet to share anything else.

17

Mitch had a firm grip on her. And he was noticing that she had a firm grip right back.

"If we get separated, I will never see you again." Ilsa squeezed his hand until it hurt. "If I'm lost forever, will you please tell Ursula and Jo that I love them?"

"You're not going to get lost." He hoped.

They'd disembarked from the train into snowfall driven nearly sideways by the blustery wind that came off Lake Michigan, a stiff breeze that was as much a part of Chicago as the lake. Juggling their meager baggage while hanging on tight to Ilsa, Mitch arranged for his private car to be stored. He then found a messenger boy and sent him with a note to the Pinkerton Agency saying he was in town and wanted a meeting this afternoon. He gave the boy a coin and told him to wait for an answer and bring it to the Grand Pacific. Then he led her to a horse-drawn streetcar other people were climbing onto.

"This will take us to the hotel." He had to reel her back when she tried to pet the horses. "The hotel we're staying in was a month or two from opening when I came through Chicago on my way out west."

The horses set off while Ilsa clung to his hand, looking at all the people and horses and wagons loaded with crates of goods. "Is this hotel as big as the one in Bucksnort?"

With a smile, he thought of the Grand Pacific Hotel. "I told you there was a great fire in Chicago about two years ago."

"Yes, and you said they started rebuilding right away."

Nodding as he settled her into a bench seat on the streetcar, he said, "The town was barely done smoldering when they began to rebuild everything bigger and better. I had a chance to invest in the rebuilding, but I was already yearning for home, so I decided not to sink money into anything new. Most of the time it was easy to say no, but this hotel tempted me."

"You mean like Satan, the great tempter?"

"No, not like Satan." Though Mitch had to wonder about that, the lure of money that had kept him away from home for so long. Maybe a little like Satan. "Now I get to see it. I could have arranged a tour when I was here last but I was—" he glanced around and leaned close—"traveling under a false name. I had business acquaintances in town who could have gotten me in, but to approach them, I would've had to reveal myself."

"A false name?" Ilsa sounded mystified, and she kept flinching when a carriage or wagon passed right by her window.

"Yes." He was sure he'd talked of this before. But he didn't worry about reminding her. She had a lot to keep track of. He talked until they reached the Grand Pacific Hotel.

As the streetcar drew to a stop, he pondered how someone had found him.

He'd emptied out his New York City home, but before he had, there'd been letters from Ma. Had someone gotten in his house? He'd kept his New York mansion locked up tight, had servants who lived with him, and he'd seen no sign of a break-in. But if they didn't steal anything and just snooped around to find out more about him, he might not have noticed.

Mitch shook his head to clear his thoughts and keep his eyes open. A man in this bustling town needed to pay attention.

He descended to the street and turned to help Ilsa down. She leapt and landed lightly on her feet.

He watched his little wild woman's eyes light up.

"This building is as big as the mountain we live on."

He needed to talk to her about streets—could she read well enough yet for signs to do her any good? But few buildings were this tall. She could use the height as a landmark to get back here. He'd write *Grand Pacific Hotel* on a slip of paper, and she could keep it in her pocket. She could pull it out and point and maybe she'd get directed here—unless she asked some street criminal, in which case they might rob her, or try, then she'd pull her knife. Then maybe the robber would pull a knife, then there'd be a fight and cutting and doctors and police.

Mitch couldn't stand to think about how bad it could get. He needed to put more notes in her pockets. For now, he just kept a tight grip.

"It's ten stories high, and I've heard it has shops." They both needed clothes. "And a fine restaurant, beautiful

171

broad staircases, grand promenades, massive columns and rich carpeting, and beautiful windows that light up the whole place during the day and thousands of gaslights to keep it bright at night."

"But does it have a place for us to sleep?"

Mitch laughed out loud and only a firm sense of propriety and the surging crowd all around kept him from hugging her. He decided then and there that he was going to show Ilsa more of the world just to hear what she had to say about it. Maybe not on this trip and maybe not until they—or he—built a train spur closer to Bucksnort.

Somehow, someday, he'd show her the world. He loved seeing it through her eyes. To her it was all a wonder, except the terrifying parts. Although this hotel was a wonder to him, too.

"Yes, Mrs. Warden, it most certainly does have a place for us to sleep." He wove his fingers through hers. "Let's go in."

They walked up a flight of stairs and entered a huge hall with high ceilings.

Ilsa gasped, then she said, "What is the point of trying to shut all the outside in?"

"What is the point, indeed?" Mitch was at a loss to explain it beyond beauty . . . which was reason enough.

"Chicago's weather seems every bit as cold as our mountaintop. Who cuts the wood to heat this place?"

Mitch didn't want to think about that, and he wasn't sure how to talk about coal or radiators or steam heat . . . come to that, he wasn't sure how they heated this place.

"It is pretty, though." He swept a hand toward the grand stairway and around the whole majestic entrance.

He pulled her toward the registration desk, but she pulled back because she'd stopped to run her hand over the smooth stone wall. "How do they make stone this smooth?"

"Marble." He pulled harder, and she came along quietly. Mitch signed the registry using the name he'd gone by in New York City. Mitch Pierce. All his sneaking on his way to Colorado had done no good, so if someone wanted to come for him, let them come.

He had qualms about danger catching him while Ilsa was at his side, but she was good with that knife. She might end up protecting him.

The clerk gave him a note that had been waiting for him confirming an appointment with the Pinkertons. They had no baggage beyond the satchels and bedrolls, so Mitch asked that the baggage be taken up, then led Ilsa back outside into the bitter December chill.

"I'm hoping we can conduct our business quickly, then I can show you Chicago for a bit before we head home." Unless they stayed all winter. The train ride across Colorado, Nebraska, Iowa, and Illinois wasn't pleasant. He didn't relish the idea of shoveling his way back again.

They climbed on another horse-drawn streetcar, and the horses drew the heavy cart along on the tracks embedded in the street. They were surrounded by freight wagons, carriages, people walking or mounted. The crowds, the noise, the motion, it was all overwhelming and painfully slow going.

Something would pass too close, and Ilsa would cringe and duck her head, then she'd stare outside again, transfixed by it all.

"Ilsa, stop looking out the window."

"No. I need to be ready to run or fight." Her hand slid to the knife she'd tucked into her boot.

Mitch didn't really blame her. The roar of the city nearly shook the streetcar. "After being back home in Colorado, on that quiet mountaintop, Chicago seems like a madhouse to me. I can only imagine how impossible it seems to you."

"Well, I have read about the tower of Babel. So, I knew there were places where large groups of people lived together. I just never could quite picture it—in fact, I realize now I never even tried to picture it."

Mitch led her off the streetcar. He descended and reached his hand up to help Ilsa down . . . just as she leapt and landed beside him. He needed to either have a talk with her or get used to that.

He turned to face a building with a large eye painted on the door. Curved over the eye were the words *Pinkerton National*, and below the eye the words *Detective Agency*. And in smaller print on the bottom were the words *We Never Sleep*.

"There's an eyeball on that door, Mitch. I feel like I'm being watched."

"That's the message they're trying to send. They want you to be confident they are watching—only they are watching the people we hire them to watch."

"It's making me nervous."

He waved through the window and saw a man inside nod.

Mitch walked on by.

"Aren't we going in?"

"No, we don't meet in there." He hustled her across the street, dodging carriages and riders. They went into a café. "I sent them a telegram from Omaha telling them we hoped to arrive today, and a message from the train station here in Chicago. They had a message waiting when we signed the register at the hotel telling me to come here to this café across from their office."

"If they're hired to watch people, do you suppose that man who is after you hired them to find you?"

It gave him pause. Could it be? The Pinkertons wouldn't be any part of hiring killers, but they found information. Did they always know what it was used for?

A man wearing a dark suit approached their table. He was about Mitch's height but thin where Mitch was solidly built. This man had dark hair cut short and barely visible under a hat with a thin brim and a rounded top. He had sharp, dark eyes, nearly black, that seemed to stare into Mitch and Ilsa. She was no hand at reading expressions, but this man's eyes made her shiver. He had a solid silver badge on his shirt, which he flashed by lifting open his suit coat when he got close enough no one else could see it. His coat dropped over the badge as he sat down at their table, but not before she caught a glimpse of a gun tucked under his arm.

"Pierce, I'm Gerald Locke, an agent for the Pinkerton Agency. After your telegram, I looked into the case you hired us for back east." He took the seat straight across from Ilsa on the small square table, and right next to Mitch.

"Locke, glad you could come. I'm Mitch Pierce, and this is my wife, Ilsa." Mitch had warned her he was using that

175

name at the hotel and everywhere else, and she was to try to remember to act like it was her real name.

Mitch rose from the table and extended his hand. "Good to meet you, Locke."

They shook. Locke nodded at Ilsa. "Mrs. Pierce."

Ilsa, not sure what rules applied to this, started to stand up like the two of them. Mitch rested a hand on her shoulder. It seemed like a friendly sort of touch, but his hand tightened on her enough that he held her in her chair.

From where she sat, she nodded back at Agent Locke, distracted by the concern that Mitch was going to make her learn to spell yet another name.

"Tell me what made you contact the Pinkertons. Is it connected to the trouble you had before?"

"It is. I've got plenty of suspicions and have for a long time. But now I hope I have proof." From his pocket, Mitch drew the note he'd taken off the dead man who'd come to Hope Mountain and told his story.

The Pinkerton agent's eyes narrowed and focused right on Mitch as he listened. Just like a man who'd never sleep.

18

Ilsa had a hard time listening. People buzzing like a hive of bees. Plates made of fragile-looking glass. A fork that shone like silver sunlight.

The noise wasn't a roar like the train or the dangerous dashing like they did on the streets, but there was a continual clatter of low voices and utensils clinking against plates. Chairs scooting in and out. Quiet but constant movement. All very distracting when she wanted to listen.

More than that, she found that she wanted to focus on the delicious food people just came and set in front of her without her having to get out her skinning knife or stoke the fire or anything.

Someone brought her coffee. She'd never had such a thing in her life until she'd come to the lowlands, and now they served it every time she stopped moving. Her first swallow was awful, burning hot, but that wasn't the coffee's fault, though the burnt taste held no appeal until Mitch poured in some cream and sugar. She'd gotten to enjoying the dark, steaming brew, even looked forward to it.

She'd eaten beef. Another thing she'd rarely had before the Wardens invaded Hope Mountain. Now she'd come to love the tender meat and the creamy gravy that went with it and the fluffy mashed potatoes. They were just always bringing something that left her in awe.

Then they brought Ilsa her very own dessert. It was a saucer full of some small, round red fruit, sweet and tart at the same time. They reminded Ilsa of the Indian berries they found near home. They were baked into a fluffy crust of some kind that reminded her of Ma's biscuits, except it sparkled with a snowdrift of sugar on the biscuit. Each serving was topped with a cold white ball Mitch called ice cream.

This dessert was almost as good as Ma's apple pie, and Ilsa ate it and drank her coffee and tried to listen.

She learned more details of Mitch's story. She'd heard a lot of it before. Between him talking to his pa, the sheriff, the marshal, and the time on the train . . . when Mitch wasn't shoveling snow. But she learned a few new things every time he talked. About him and about the outside world. He added to his story about the two attempts on his life. How he'd killed one man and let another get away, badly shot up.

She was so disgusted with those men for trying to hurt Mitch. She wished she'd been there to buy into the fight.

Then Ilsa heard stories of Mitch's investigation. The man who died had a thousand dollars in gold in his pocket. The shot-up man had the same amount. And that man had admitted who hired him—Pete Howell, Mitch's business partner.

Mitch had gone to work proving it. But he never could,

not enough to get a sheriff in New York City to arrest the man. He mentioned a woman's name, too. Ilsa wasn't surprised. Women could be as tough as any man. She proved that every day of her life. So why not be as bad as any man? It stood to reason.

Then Mitch talked about the men who'd come to Hope Mountain. Mitch knew their names, knew what they'd been paid, was sure he knew who paid them. Hired guns. Paid to commit murder.

"Let me read that note." Locke reached for it, and Mitch handed it over. He studied it a long time. Certainly longer than it took to read it. Even with her meager reading skills, she could have read it faster.

Locke handed it back. "Any law in the land would hold the man who hired murder as guilty as the man who pulled the trigger."

"Is this enough that I could take it to the police and get Howell arrested?" Mitch folded the paper again and shoved it deep in his pocket.

"You pulled it out of the gunman's pocket in front of witnesses?"

"I did. Ilsa was there, and several hired hands and my ma."

"You showed it to the sheriff?"

"Yes, and my ma, Ilsa, and one other witness came with me to the sheriff when we took the dead man and his wounded partner in, told our story, and showed him this note. And we repeated it all to a US Marshal with the same witnesses, except the sheriff had let my ma head for home by then."

"Can I reach the lawmen through the telegraph?"

"Yes, I know where the sheriff lives and where the marshal is headquartered." Mitch gave the names to the agent, and Ilsa watched the man write them down.

Detective Locke picked up his fork and tapped it against his pretty plate of dessert as he stared at something, or maybe nothing. Ilsa felt like he was looking through Mitch rather than at him.

Mitch didn't seem to mind. He had a drink of coffee and ate a few bites of dessert.

Ilsa leaned close and whispered, "Can I have his if he's not going to eat it?"

Mitch turned and smiled at her. Then looked around and waved a finger in the air. A man, who must be another one of those waiters, hurried over. Mitch whispered something, then the man hurried off. No waiting about it.

He brought back another whole dessert, whisked Ilsa's empty plate away, and set the new dessert in front of her. Then he poured her another cup of coffee. Food was so much easier here than on Hope Mountain.

Bowing, the waiter said, "I'm delighted you're enjoying the cherry cobbler, ma'am. It's one of our specialties." Then the waiter hurried off.

She wished he'd've waited so she could have said thank you.

"I'm going to pull all the details together and get them to our agency in New York City," Locke said. "We work together with a great degree of speed and skill. You may be required to talk with the Chicago police, but I see no reason you have to go to New York yourself, especially considering the threats against you are centered back there. Do you want to hire a Pinkerton detective as a bodyguard? We can provide 'round-the-clock service."

Mitch mentally debated it. "I've underestimated Howell and his reach too often."

"We can rent the room next to yours, on both sides if you want. We can provide armed guards, and our own secure carriage service."

The thought of it bothered Mitch, and he knew exactly why. "Howell found me out west somehow. What if I have your crew guarding me and another Pinkerton agent uses your information to track me down?"

Locke stiffened like a fireplace poker. "I assure you we would never be a party to hired murder."

Shaking his head, Mitch said, "You have it wrong. I'm not accusing you of being hired assassins, but what if your company was simply hired to find a missing person? You do that all the time, don't you? If you did and you passed the word on to your client, say Pete Howell, you wouldn't know what he did with that information."

Locke's expression changed from anger to interest. "If that's true, it would strengthen the case we turn over to the police. I'll look into it immediately. What about the guards?"

"As soon as you've cleared this up, let me know. Then I'll decide about hiring you. For now, we'll take care of ourselves. Four men have tried to kill me—skilled gunmen all. I've done all right at taking care of myself." He looked sideways at his gluttonous little wife scraping the last bites off her plate. "And my wife is more dangerous than I am, so we're fine on our own until I'm sure whose side the Pinkerton Detective Agency is on."

Locke nodded and rose from his chair.

"One more thing." Mitch reached into his pocket and produced a slip of paper. "This man, Morris Canton. He was involved in a crime in New York City. He turned everything he had to cash, then he vanished just ahead of the law. I found him out west, ranching in southwestern Colorado near the town of Bucksnort, under the name of Bludgeon Pike. I want you to find out whether he is a wanted man and what the police will do about tracking him down. I've already given this information to the US Marshal I talked to, but I'd like to know more."

"This is the kind of thing the marshals handle. I'll track down information on Canton, then use the name you gave me for the marshal in that area to see what can be done. I'll be in touch." He took the paper, read it swiftly before tucking it in his pocket, and left the room like a man with a firm purpose.

Mitch turned to smile at Ilsa.

"Do you think your ma knows how to make this?"

"Don't talk with your mouth full." He was watching her mouth overly.

"Why not?" She licked her lips to make sure there was no cherry juice on them. He was fascinated by that, and she glanced at his own lips, even though his dessert was long gone, and there wasn't a speck of a crumb anywhere on his face.

Mitch shrugged. "I don't know why. It's one of those rules."

"You mean like how a woman isn't supposed to be out alone at night or she'll end up married?"

Mitch chuckled. "Maybe not quite as serious as that one, but it's still a rule." Then Mitch shook his head. "You know what, wife? You just go ahead and do what you want. I find myself uncommonly fond of you just the way you are."

He looked down at her empty plate, then said, "Let's go see Chicago. And I think I need to buy you a couple of new dresses."

"We can't get much. It won't fit in my bedroll when we're riding back home."

"That is very true." Mitch swiped his index finger gently along her lower lip. "But maybe we can solve that with a packhorse." His eyes flicked to her lips again. "Or maybe a string of them. Let's go."

19

Ilsa wasn't a good fit for shopping.

And that's what Mitch spent the next week doing. Over her protests.

But the woman only owned two sets of clothes: one, the shirtwaist and riding skirt bought for her in Bucksnort's general store, the other made by his ma, who made it more interested in speed than style. Considering the woman was happiest clad in leather trousers, the two dresses she had were a fine improvement and possibly all she needed out west. But now she was in the most beautiful hotel in Chicago, and the woman needed clothes.

He'd've had an easier time of it taking measurements of one of Pa's longhorns.

She asked too many questions. Considered reticules and bonnets and even dresses foolish. When the seamstress tried to get her to try on a corset Mitch heard the shouting from where he waited in the front of the dress shop.

One of the reasons this was taking so long was because several times now, despite the money Mitch waved in front of the merchants, they'd been kicked out.

Usually when Ilsa brandished her handy knife.

She came storming out of the fitting room, her eyes flashing like blue lightning. "She wants me to suffocate myself with a piece of cloth wrapped around bones!"

As a description of a corset, it honestly wasn't bad.

Ilsa came right up to his face and whispered, "And she's trying to make me take my clothes off. It's indecent."

The harried dressmaker came out of the back room dangling a corset in one hand, a look of dismay on her face. "Mrs. Pierce. I'm sorry, but to wear the newest fashions, a corset is absolutely necessary for a proper, modest fit."

Mitch saw Ilsa go for her knife, and he caught her hand fast as a striking rattler. No bite or poison, of course. But he moved quick.

Hissing, his own snakelike attribute, he said to Ilsa, "No knife, please. We've been thrown out of every other store in the area."

She growled.

"I'll take you out for more cherry cobbler."

No growling. She perked up and asked, "Right now?"

"Give me one more minute with this woman." He turned to the poor dressmaker. "No corset."

Mitch honestly didn't blame Ilsa for that. He hadn't given much thought to ladies' underpinnings but bone? It sounded uncomfortable and more than a little creepy.

The woman's jaw firmed with stubbornness. As if she would save Ilsa from being unfashionable even at the cost of her own life. Too bad the woman didn't know Ilsa might take that literally.

Mitch dragged Ilsa back toward the fitting room. "Have you finished with her measurements?"

The woman, her eyes flashing with defiance, said in a snippy tone, "Yes."

Mitch stopped by a stack of fabric, and still firmly gripping Ilsa, he tugged five different colors out of a stack of floral and plaid wool. "Make her a dress in a fashionable style in each of these colors."

"The cobbler isn't back here." Ilsa yanked hard against his grip.

He went on to a stack of solid colors and tugged out a brown and a gray. "She needs riding skirts in these colors. Riding skirts, not habits. Don't make them fancy. Very plain. I don't want a bunch of ruffles and, for heaven's sake, no trains. Floral calico shirtwaists. Six of them. Any color that's stylish."

"Calico cannot be stylish, sir."

If there'd been even one more dressmaker, he'd've walked out. Instead, he doggedly went on, "Her safety is more important than style."

"That is most unfortunate." The woman sniffed, but she didn't say she wouldn't do it.

Then he went to a draped row of beautiful silks. He pointed at a bright blue nearly as lovely as Ilsa's eyes. "And a dinner gown. Suitable for evenings out or parties. Not too wide of a skirt. I doubt she'll agree to a petticoat, but you can include one."

He didn't see them getting invited to any parties, but he wanted the seamstress to know his intent. He had a vision of Ilsa dancing with him, and she would be spectacular in this color.

"How am I supposed to climb a tree wearing that?"

The shopkeeper looked scandalized. Mitch quickly pulled

out his purse of gold coins. The shopkeeper kept her opinions to herself as he handed over much more than she could've hoped to charge.

"All right, we're done here. Time to get that cherry cobbler."

As they left, he glanced back at the seamstress, still watching them with a horrified expression on her face, then her eyes dropped to the stack of gold coins in her hand.

Mitch wondered if the seamstress was in financial straits and if that was the reason he was able to bribe her to persist. There was a financial panic, after all. Gold was hard to come by.

Ilsa left the shop without a backward glance. As they walked to the café they'd eaten at the first day, he tried to explain corsets to her. She looked at him like he'd run mad.

All the shopping was just too much work, and he couldn't imagine her wearing most of this once they left the city. But they might be spending the winter here, so she needed a few things.

The dressmaker had orders to deliver the clothes to the Grand Pacific. They wouldn't be back for a fitting. Mitch decided Ilsa could sew in her own hidden knife pockets.

After they'd eaten more of the promised cherry cobbler, they strolled down the busy Chicago sidewalk until Mitch saw a window displaying ready-made coats. She already had a new coat from Bucksnort, but he decided on a whim to get another for her made out of dark gray wool with a black collar.

"This is nice and so warm." Ilsa touched the soft shearling

wool of the collar and smiled. The gray made the blue of her eyes even brighter, and the dark of her brunette curls shone as a few of the escaped coils dangled on her neck and in front of her ears.

He'd finally found something she liked. He'd give his whole fortune to keep her eyes this bright.

But Ilsa didn't want his fortune, so he could think that, and it cost him nothing.

It wasn't just Ilsa who'd had no things. He now wore a new suit. It felt like he was bound by ropes. The clothes he'd worn to Chicago were loose fitting. Before this fancy suit, he could move easily and with comfort. He'd had boots that kept his feet warm. Now he was back in a suit he'd never noticed was strangling him. He wore a vest and shirt, a necktie, and overly tight boots of thin leather that weren't warm and pinched his toes.

He wore clothes that no longer fit him. And he was in a city that no longer fit him.

When they walked out, her in her warm coat, him in a suit and overcoat, they were, at least in appearance, in step with town life. He didn't think any clothing would make him happy to be here.

Another day, he led her to a shop she really liked. It sold knives.

She helped choose a new one for herself, then sharpened it right there in the store. He bought her a leather sheath. She strapped it around her waist, lamenting that she couldn't hide it better so she'd have the element of surprise should she need to stab someone. He was glad his bloodthirsty wife at least wore it under her coat.

He armed himself better, too. And found he was a bit

more comfortable walking down the Chicago street with a loaded gun tucked in a shoulder holster under his suit coat.

He'd talked with her about finding her way back to the Grand Pacific should they become separated and was able to let go of the viselike grip he'd had on her hand. And they'd spent time every night working on her reading, and she now carried the note with the hotel address on it should she need to ask directions.

Nearly a week after they'd arrived in Chicago, they strolled along in the cold, her hand through his arm.

"Do you ever get tired of all the noise and crowds?" Ilsa asked.

"It didn't bother me at all before I went home to the Circle Dash, or maybe that's not right. After the first murder attempt, I started to flinch all the time." Mitch adjusted the shoulder holster and slid his hand into his own pocket to bring out his knife.

"What is that?"

"I got this from a dead soldier in the Civil War." Mitch frowned at the ugly memory of battle, though the knife handle itself just looked like a piece of beautifully carved bone, innocent enough.

He looked around and saw a small, heavily wooded park ahead, deserted in the cold weather. He led Ilsa away from the crowds. When they were beyond prying eyes, he said, "Watch what it does." He pressed a button, and a blade shot out of the end of the handle.

Ilsa gasped. "What is that?"

"I've heard it called a spring-operated knife, but a more common name is a switchblade. I've never gone out without it, not since the war." He pressed the tip of the blade against a tree trunk to get it to slide back into the handle. Then he returned it to his pocket.

Waving, leafless branches overhead sheltered them from softly falling snow. Tired of the shopping Ilsa didn't want, and despite the cold, Mitch said, "Let's take a walk in the woods."

Snow sifted down out of the leaden gray sky as they walked.

Ilsa's eyes flashed with pleasure. "How did trees survive in the middle of the city when people started putting up these huge buildings?"

"It's called a park. Cities always put aside a stretch of grass and trees so people can escape from the brick and stone for a few minutes. The noise is less, the crowds thin out, and, on a cold day like this, it'll be empty. I'm not familiar with this park, but some of them are big enough to feel like you've left the city behind. There's one in New York called Central Park that is hundreds of acres."

Ilsa's smooth brow furrowed. "What's an acre?"

Mitch shook his head. "I just mean it's really big. A big beautiful stretch of grass and trees."

"That's the first smart thing I've heard about cities."

He took her hand and led her across the grass, white with a layer of snow. His feet sank into the crisp, winter-dried grass with a gentle crunch. It was nice to walk on something soft. "We can't stay long. It's too cold. But just for a few minutes, we can walk in here."

He pointed to a clump of evergreens in the midst of a bunch of the bare-limbed trees. "Maybe those firs will get us out of the wind."

20

Stepping into the line of trees, away from the busy streets of Chicago, was like breathing for the first time in a week—no—longer than that. She hadn't been in the woods since they rode away from the mountain. Ilsa paused and dragged the crisp air deep into her chest.

They hadn't gone into the evergreens yet. Where they stood now, there were no leaves, and the leafless branches clattered together as the snow coated them. Huge snow-flakes fluttered onto her new coat. There were evergreens scattered among what looked like oak and maple trees. Grandpa had taught her the names of trees and plants, flowers and moss, the many things that could hold medicine. Now she looked at the bare-limbed trees among the evergreens. The green needles broke up the dreary gray of the trees in their winter sleep.

Even gray and bare, the trees welcomed her like old friends.

"Why are they in such tidy rows?"

"They were planted." Mitch lifted a branch out of her

way. "The trees you're used to in your forests grew from seeds that fell off of older trees. Ancient trees beside young, tall trees beside newly sprouted baby trees. Here they plant the trees in a tidy row."

"It seems like this way is a lot more work." Ilsa smiled and stayed close to him. His warmth was the perfect addition to this pretty place.

He said, "This part of the park must have survived the fire."

"That's right, you said there was a fire that swept through the city, and that's why the hotel is so new."

"Yep, everything is new in Chicago. At least around here." Mitch reached out a hand to push aside more thick branches that dipped low under the weight of snow. They reached a deeply forested stretch, and he touched a broad tree trunk. "But not these trees. Here they're not all in neat rows. Some of them must have been spared when the city was being built because these are older and not in straight lines or all the same age."

She itched to climb, to get overhead where she could look around, to leave the ground. Sometimes she felt as foreign to the ground as if she were a bird not yet old enough to fly. But baby birds sprouted feathers and took off on their wings, while she could only climb and swing.

Until her feathers appeared, the treetops beckoned.

Figuring there would be more city when she reached the other end of the park, she slowed, not wanting to leave this haven.

It was impossible to believe there could be this many trees in the middle of this strangling crowd of people. She grabbed the woolen lapels of her cozy coat and turned in a circle, looking up through tree branches blurred by ever heavier snowfall.

As she turned, a rifle barrel poked from behind a tree. Diving, she hit Mitch with all her weight. Surprise took him down more than her strength. As he tumbled over backward, a gun fired and fired again.

They landed with a thud on the rough, cold ground. Snow puffed up in a cloud around them.

Mitch swept her before him. He dragged her, though she was crawling fast enough he needn't have. They got behind one of the old trees with a wide trunk just as a row of bullets cut into the bark.

Her knife filled her hand with no conscious decision to draw it.

Mitch's pistol was out and in action. He fired.

Ilsa was too close to him. She knew from her years of hunting that if two targets were a distance apart, it was harder to hit both. Keeping the tree between her and the peppering gunfire, she reached overhead, snagged a low-hanging limb, and launched herself upward.

A hard hand grabbed her leg and yanked her to a halt. She looked down.

Mitch's eyes met hers. He whispered, "Don't kill him if you can help it."

She nodded with one jerk of her chin, her heart almost hot with the respect he'd just shown her. Then her bossy husband let her go, turned back to the gunman, and fired.

A bullet clipped the tree near where her hand held the trunk. He must've seen her go up.

If he did, and he took aim at her, that would draw his

fire away from Mitch and give Mitch a chance to eliminate this deadly threat.

She didn't dare move if he was trying to get her. Then the bullets were lower, aimed for Mitch, as if a single shot went wild.

Ilsa climbed on up, careful not to show herself. She struggled with her cumbersome skirts and wished for sturdy trousers, disgusted that she'd left hers behind on the mountain.

Finally, she was well above whizzing lead.

With the gun battle below her, she carefully peeked around the edge of the tree she'd scaled. She looked down on a single gunman far below. The man, slim and dressed all in black with a dark woolen cap covering his head, focused solely on Mitch. Her eyes skimmed along the branches. A path through the treetops as clear as a game trail opened before her. She walked along, careful not to let the branches sway, silent as a stalking beast of prey.

Inching along, she made her way over.

Once she was above the rifleman, she was in the most danger. There were branches from the top of the tree to the bottom, but they weren't as sturdy as a tree trunk, and they were all that lay between her and a would-be murderer.

She eased out and saw Mitch now across from her. From his angle, he could look right at her without being seen by the man shooting at him.

She pulled her knife from her hidden pocket and clamped it in her teeth.

Mitch stopped firing and lowered his gun so it pointed

at the ground. Clearly telling her there'd be no bullets to come flying in from him.

She braced herself to swing down. She had to hit hard enough to knock the man into a sound sleep.

A movement off to the side stopped her.

A second man crouched down, gun aimed. Scowling, Ilsa noticed a clump of acorns clinging to the oak tree she was on. She tore them free and hurled them straight at Mitch.

He glanced up at her. She pointed at the second gunman.

With a wild leap, Mitch vanished behind the tree just as the second man opened fire. Now men shot at him from two directions.

Ilsa held her breath, trying to decide how to stop both men. If she plunged down from overhead, the second man would see her. And he would notice when his partner stopped firing anyway.

Mitch opened fire again, now aiming at the man off to Ilsa's right and leaving the way clear on the man below her. With a hard, silent breath, she lowered herself, fighting to get close in utter silence. Branch after branch, soundless, quick, she was as deadly as any clawed animal. She passed the last branch, the last barrier to the man, still firing. He paused, reached for a belt full of bullets.

Like lightning it went through her thoughts that she was going out as a sheep in the midst of wolves. Jesus told His followers to be harmless as doves and wise as serpents. What did that mean? A dove could hurt no one, no matter what. But were serpents wise? Hadn't a serpent brought sin to the world through his temptation of Eve?

One thing she was sure of, these men below her were neither doves nor serpents. They were wolves, and she was right in the midst of them. Knowing that, she believed God would understand about defending her husband in a dangerous world. She'd have to ask Mitch what he thought about that later.

For now, she took the knife from between her teeth and plunged.

21

The first man who'd opened fire fell silent. Mitch couldn't look out, but he knew what had happened. Ilsa had happened.

Dropping flat on his belly, Mitch used the overgrown grass and underbrush as concealment as he crept on his belly toward the second man, still firing. But the bullets were man-high while Mitch slithered along. And Mitch was no longer worried about being seen from the direction of the first of these dry-gulchers.

A wave of something powerful swept through him as he realized how much he trusted Ilsa to have taken care of an armed man.

Then he thought of how the first gunman had aimed and fired, and his blood ran with cold rage. Ilsa had seen him in time to tackle Mitch. She'd saved him.

But that man had kept up the deadly assault, shooting at both of them with no care for the woman who was in his line of attack.

These men had been hired to kill Mitch—he knew it.

But they'd been willing to kill Ilsa simply because she was walking with him.

Furious, Mitch slipped forward. He'd learned to sneak in the war. He'd learned to use every inch of concealment. But true care took time, and Mitch had none.

He had to get to this killer and do it fast, before he noticed his partner's gun had fallen silent longer than could be explained by reloading.

Once the second man turned toward the first assailant, Mitch had to charge the man, even right into the teeth of flying lead, because otherwise the would-be murderer would open fire on Ilsa.

Mitch's stomach twisted as he pictured his feisty little wife, knife in her teeth, facing an armed man.

He wouldn't bet against Ilsa. But that didn't mean he wanted her being a target any more than she already was.

Pushing recklessly forward, knowing there was no longer a solid tree trunk between him and a hired killer, Mitch angled sideways along bushes heavy with snow, fought for silence, and hoped to take the man by surprise. But by coming from this direction, he would be shooting more toward Ilsa. No, in an effort to save his own life, Mitch had made a mistake and endangered his wife, because he couldn't be sure where she was. He holstered his gun without losing a second. He had to go in without firing.

Then the second man stopped shooting. He'd noticed his partner was out of the fight. Whether Mitch had a good angle of attack or not, there was no time left.

Mitch erupted from the ground and charged low around a dense evergreen shrub. He came at the man from the left side. The shooter held his gun in his right hand. That made the shot awkward because he had to turn to bring the gun around.

Mitch got three long strides before the man noticed. The gunman looked. His right arm came around his body.

With a low, diving tackle, Mitch plowed his shoulder into the man's gut just as the gun blasted. A sharp slash of pain tore at Mitch's back. Mitch tumbled, clawing at the assailant. He had to finish this fast. If his wound was serious, this man had to be down to stay before Mitch was out of the fight.

They quit rolling. Mitch slammed a fist into the man's face. Then another to the jaw, one to the belly.

It took him that long to notice the man wasn't hitting back.

He lay limp, unconscious, sprawled flat on his back.

A gray rock, smeared with blood, lay beside the gunman's head. It told its own story of why the man was knocked cold.

Before Mitch could struggle to his feet, Ilsa was at his side. She had her knife in hand and would no doubt have saved Mitch if he hadn't managed to subdue this killer on his own.

It hit him harder than that gunshot wound.

Pride. Respect. Love.

I'm in love with her.

"It wasn't necessary for me to kill mine." Ilsa blinked as she looked from Mitch to the unconscious outlaw. "How is yours?"

Mitch didn't answer, but the unconscious man was breathing.

"Let's get them together so we can keep watch over them until we decide how to transport two heavy-looking men," she continued. "Jo showed me how to build a travois. Perhaps we can haul them to Chicago's jail like a couple of felled elk."

Mitch stood, then his knees gave out, and he fell forward.

Ilsa gasped and rushed to his side.

"I've been shot." His voice was faint.

Ilsa saw a hole in his new coat, near the top of his shoulder. She shoved at his overcoat and got it off well enough that she could see a hole in his new suit. Still no blood. The suit coat went next. Mitch groaned, but Ilsa didn't need even the smallest bit of her medical skill to know she had to see how bad this was. A blood-drenched circle coated the whole of the upper part of his back. She used the hole to rip the new white shirt open. A nasty slit carved by a bullet ran in a furrow the length of his left shoulder blade.

"It's just a cut. The bullet scraped a line from the top of your shoulder, down a few inches, but it never went into you, thank heavens."

His cheek was pressed on the snowy ground. She knelt beside him and lowered her face until their eyes met. "Can you get up? I'm not sure if I can build a travois big enough for all three of you."

"Having all my clothes torn off in the icy cold is clearing my head."

"I suppose it does wake a man up."

"Plowing my face into the snow helps, too."

Ilsa smiled. "You're welcome."

"I wasn't exactly saying thank you, but if you want to take it that way, it's fine." He shoved himself to his hands and knees. Then looked at the man he'd captured. With stiff movements, he went to the man's side and dug around. He handed Ilsa a gun found in a boot, a knife up a sleeve, and a small, heavy pouch. It clinked just like the gold Mitch had found on the men who'd invaded their mountain. He took everything from the man's pockets, then despite wearing only a shirt, he took the strange cloth he'd wrapped around his neck—he'd called it a necktie—and bound the unconscious man's wrists.

With shaky hands, he ripped his shirt down the front into two strips, tied them into one long strip, and knotted them around the outlaw's feet.

At last he said, "Let's go check on the other one."

Ilsa brought the remains of his shirt and his two discarded coats along as they walked the few yards to Ilsa's man.

They found him unconscious, sprawled facedown. "I knocked him into a sound sleep with the hilt of my knife."

When she saw him again, this man who'd intended to sneak up on Mitch and attack like the worst kind of cowardly coyote, a wave swept over her, igniting her blood and sending it roaring through her veins. Her hand tightened on the knife.

Before she was overcome by an urge to do something wicked, Mitch patted her on the shoulder and distracted her.

The man didn't so much as groan when Mitch rolled

him onto his back. His eyes didn't flicker open even for a second.

With a disgruntled motion, Ilsa thrust her sturdy new knife into the sheath she had belted around her waist.

He looked up at her and grinned. "I'm glad you didn't kill him."

"Because you think it's not proper? Like it's not proper to be alone with a man? These rules are never-ending."

"No, well . . ." Mitch shook his head as he ripped loose more strips from his dwindling shirt. Ilsa saw him wobble, even kneeling as he was. He was bleeding badly. He had to be hurting and terribly cold. She was tempted to whack both of those men another solid blow.

Mitch braced one hand on the snowy ground for a moment. "No, I'm just afraid killing a man might bother you, give you bad dreams maybe. I'm glad you don't have that on your conscience."

"I most certainly don't want to kill anyone. Why, the way they're acting, what are the chances they'll make it to heaven? It would take something very severely dangerous for me to fight with enough force to send a man to hades. Now, that would give me bad dreams."

Considering the tatters of Mitch's shirt, Ilsa said, "We should start carrying a handy lasso like all your father's cowhands do back home. It will be easier on your clothing. Your shirt is beyond saving, I'm afraid."

"There are bullet holes all through my clothes so none of them can be saved."

Ilsa snorted. "There's still plenty of good wear in your coats. If anyone comments on the hole, we'll just explain that you were shot."

204

Mitch tied the man's hands so fast, so well, that Ilsa had to ask. "Where did you learn to bind a man like that?"

Mitch glanced at her and smiled. "It's how we hog-tie a calf."

"Hog-tie? We have wild hogs on the mountaintop, but we've never tried to tie one up. Jo just shoots them with her bow and arrow."

"We call it hog-tie, but we use it on calves."

She blinked at him in silence.

"A baby cow is called a calf," he said.

"I know, but why would you wish to tie up a baby cow?"

"Mostly we do it during spring roundup, but can we talk about branding and cutting cattle some other time?"

She didn't think she wanted to talk about it ever. Cutting sounded bad for the baby. She breathed in and out slowly, wishing like anything the man would make sense but a bit afraid to ask more questions. She still didn't know where a hog came into this.

"Anyway," Mitch went on—and Ilsa thought that was for the best—"now that they're tied up, how do we move two unconscious men? I want to take them to the Pinkerton Agency. It's much closer than any police station, in fact, I don't know where a jail is to be found."

"Police?" Ilsa hadn't heard that word before—she didn't think . . . heaven knew she'd heard so many new words she couldn't be sure.

Mitch shivered, and Ilsa tore most of the rest of his shirt into pieces and fastened a bandage over his freely bleeding gunshot wound. Then she helped him into his suit coat, followed by his overcoat.

When she slid the heavy coat around so he could fit his

205

arm in, a low groan of pain escaped. But once the coat was in place, he wouldn't be so cold. She regretted causing him pain, but it had to be done. She needed to get him back to the hotel and care for him properly.

"And you don't know where there's a jail?"

"Nope."

"A large city is much less convenient than a small one. And what are police again?"

"A *policeman* is another word for *sheriff*."

"And why do they change the name?"

Shaking his head as if his hair was wet, Mitch didn't answer. Instead, he ran his hands through the second man's clothing. He dropped a very nice knife into his pocket, then removed the belt full of bullets. He found a second gun up the man's sleeve and a third one strapped to a cunning little holster around his ankle. Mitch handed the weapons to Ilsa, and she took the ankle holster to keep. He wouldn't need it in jail, and it seemed handy.

Her pockets were quite full by now. Mitch kept searching until he produced a small, lumpy, leather pouch that clinked.

"More gold. I'll bet it's mighty near five hundred dollars, just like his partner had." Then he found a note.

"It says much the same as the note we found back home." Mitch went back to the first man they'd tied up and dragged him over.

"You shouldn't do that. It will make your shoulder bleed faster."

"I want to be able to watch them both at the same time in case they regain consciousness." Frowning, Mitch asked,

"How could Howell have found me this fast in Chicago? And how could he have gotten money to a gunman?"

"Locke said he would find out if any Pinkertons had been hired to search for you. He may have asked a man who informed Howell."

"Maybe we shouldn't go to the Pinkertons." Mitch stood, looking down at the men.

Ilsa wasn't sure she'd ever seen him hesitate over anything before. He was a man who made fast decisions and acted on them. Now he stood, rubbing his mouth.

Ilsa was sure he was trying to make one of his fast decisions, but his bleeding shoulder was distracting him. She was reading that from the way he stood and the expression on his face. Her spirits rose as she realized she might understand what the look on his face meant. She was slowly learning to understand people better.

"It wouldn't be hard to wire money from New York to Chicago."

"Wire? Isn't that what you called the telegram? A wire?"

"Yes, and the money doesn't actually get wired, but rather *permission* in the form of a telegram comes to a bank and allows them to pay out money. Howell could do it using the right instructions, knowing the right account numbers."

"I was trying to picture some way actual gold pieces could roll along the telegraph wires. Very confusing. They would be forever falling to the ground."

"I thought I knew all the money Howell had, but he is smarter than I thought, or maybe I'm not quite so smart. My partner had hideout cash."

"Could he have gotten gold from you without you knowing it?"

Mitch went very still. "Of course. He embezzled from me. That would explain a lot." He was silent for a long moment. Ilsa liked silence so she didn't urge him to tell her what *embezzled* meant. It sounded confusing—but then, what wasn't?

"I'm so used to trusting my gut instincts, I didn't look deep enough. Pete Howell and Katrina Lewis are two excellent examples of my gut not being infallible."

"So, does your gut, whatever that is, tell you to trust that Pinkerton agent, Gerald Locke?"

Shrugging one shoulder, Mitch winced, then said, "It does, but now I'm not sure of anything. I do trust the Pinkerton *Agency*, though. One man could be turned, bribed, and blackmailed into helping Howell. And I think this man's presence here is proof of that—if Locke informed those at the New York branch of the agency that Howell was up to no good. Someone checked incoming wires and let Howell know where I was. One agent or employee saw that wire and was well-paid to pass along the news that I'm in Chicago."

"Do we take these men to the Pinkertons or go find the sheriff? We need to decide so I can get your shoulder properly tended."

A shrill whistle sounded from the street beyond the barrier of trees. "This is the police! Come out of those trees with your hands up!"

With a quick smile, Mitch said, "I think that relieves me of making a decision. The police are here. We'll tell our story to the police, hand these men over, *then* go to the Pinkertons. But I'm not dealing with one agent alone this time. Every agent in that building is going to listen to my story, so no single dishonest agent can betray me."

"Someone reported gunfire," a booming voice shouted. "Come out of there."

He looked at her, and she thought he seemed sad. Again, she was reading the look on his face. She rested a hand gently on his left forearm, thinking of the bullet furrow on his back.

"What's wrong?"

"I'm sorry my troubles put you in danger. It happened in Colorado on Hope Mountain, and now it's happening here."

She patted his arm, careful not to jostle him, and said, "Don't be sorry. I found a tree and got to climb it. Can we come here every day?"

"It's going to keep getting colder."

She shrugged. "I'm used to the cold. I live on a mountaintop, for heaven's sake. I'm finally starting to like Chicago."

"Officer, a man shot me." Mitch raised his voice. "Two men attacked me and my wife. They're unconscious and tied up. Come on in."

It took some careful talking. Ilsa considered it an insult that Mitch had to keep his hands up but she didn't. As if she wasn't every bit as dangerous as him.

Finally, though, things were arranged so the men were hauled away. Mitch and Ilsa answered a lot of questions before going back to their hotel room so Mitch could be properly bandaged. Then they were on their way to the Pinkerton Agency.

22

We are taking this very seriously, Mitch." Agent Locke sure sounded sincere.

"I don't know if I can trust you, that's why I asked for several people to sit in on this."

"It wasn't necessary." Locke looked and sounded offended. "My integrity and the integrity of the whole agency are beyond question."

"I'm the one with a bullet crease in my back. So I don't much care if I trounce with hobnail boots on your tender feelings."

Locke didn't defend himself further.

"I don't know if I can trust you. I've turned everything over to the police. I told them I suspect those killers found us using information that came from the Pinkerton Agency."

Locke's eyes narrowed. His lips went thin. His eyes shifted to the man who sat behind an imposing desk. Allan Pinkerton, the man who'd created the agency. They were in his office along with five other agents. Every single one who was in the building. Mitch probably should've called in the secretaries and the men who swept the floors.

"I'm a wee bit peeved you've turned police suspicion on

us." Pinkerton's heavy Scottish burr resounded through the office. He stroked his full beard as he studied Mitch with cold eyes.

Mitch was inclined to trust the man just because if Pinkerton himself wasn't trustworthy, then the whole agency was corrupt. And the agency's reputation was too formidable for the corruption to go all the way to the top.

Or at least Mitch hoped so.

"I didn't expect you to like it. I know the Pinkertons like acting with independence from the police. But whether you're upset because I've insulted you, or upset because I messed up plans you've made with hired gunmen, I just can't tell. That's why I talked to the police, but I'm here telling you, making it clear and looking for help. I still have every hope you're trustworthy."

"We've found that when we work on cases with the men in blue, we often end up tripping over each other, Mr. Pierce."

Mitch thought that might be for the best. "Look into this, Pinkerton. Get to the bottom of it. The leak came from your office, almost certainly. You're the only people who've been in contact with New York. If Pete Howell is getting information from the Pinkertons, it would be easy for him to know where I am."

"You told me you came to Chicago using your real name," Pinkerton stated. "You're staying in a prominent hotel. If those gunmen found you in the wilderness in Colorado, then they could surely find you at a grand hotel here. But, aye, it looks bad. To put their plans in place, get the money paid, would take a bit of time. And we're the ones who wired back east the first day you were in town. We will find the man working for the Pinkertons who betrayed you or prove it was no one of ours. Either way, we will find out how Howell got word. If he's wiring money, transferring funds out of a bank account, we can track that."

"While you're at it, find Pete Howell and keep an eye on him."

"That's a fine notion. Locke, make arrangements for that. And you'll nae be payin' us, Pierce. The reputation of my agency is in question, and I'll not take a penny to fix this. If I can't get to the bottom of it, I'll shut the doors on my business and fire every man in this room, including myself." Pinkerton rose from his desk.

"And now, I'm going to talk to the police. They may be in good spirits because you've turned over two would-be killers. You said they have already identified them and they are wanted men, have I got the right of it?"

"You do."

"Both men alive and with charges enough they could hang. We might get a confession, and they might swear to who hired them to keep them from getting the noose." With a firm nod, Pinkerton said, "Let's hope the police feel like they have enough to arrest Howell and put an end to your troubles."

He rounded the desk and took his coat, hung with many capes down the back, and a bowler hat from a hall tree. He held the door open for them to leave. "Be cautious, Mr. Pierce."

Mitch found it irritating to be called Pierce now that he'd left New York City. But that's how everyone knew him, and he'd used it deliberately to flush out a killer.

It had worked all too well.

Mitch and Ilsa left the office. He was no longer hauling Ilsa along, hanging on tight to keep her from getting lost. Now it just felt right to hold her hand. They headed back to the hotel. His gunshot wound ached more every minute.

As they entered their room, he looked sideways at her. He wasn't overly tall, but she was petite and made him feel like he was. He thought of that moment in the park when his heart had opened to her, and he almost told her he loved her. Instead, he thought of something more practical. "We've never talked much about how I got up on Hope Mountain when I first came home."

The startled look told him she'd never given it much thought. "You're right. You came from that high valley where Ursula lives. There's no trail down to the lowlands. When we were sent away while you were sick, my sisters and I scouted around and found the place you entered the high valley, but the way down was sheer. How in the world did you get up there?"

"The mountainside is steep, and you have to cling to it with your fingertips and toes. You can't walk up a trail, you have to climb."

"Climb? Like I climb a tree?"

Nodding, Mitch said, "Yep, and you're great at that, aren't you? I told you we couldn't get home until spring, but maybe that's not true. There is every chance we could claw our way up that mountain and go home—even in the winter."

"I have a new knife. I'm ready. Let's go home."

He looked at those eyes. Looked at the black corkscrew curls that tended to escape her bonnet. Looked at the woman who filled a place deep inside that he'd only realized was empty when it wasn't anymore.

As they hung their coats and gloves, he knew he wanted to be closer to her. To be truly married to her. And he didn't know how.

They would have to learn together, and they could only do that with honesty.

"We can't go until I can be sure I'm not taking death home with me. I have to put a stop to these attempts on my life. But—" His voice broke.

She turned to face him, reached for his hands. "What is it, Mitch? Is your shoulder hurting?"

He fought for control. Torn nearly in half by the choices he'd made. The mistakes. He looked at their hands as he said, "I should never have brought you with me."

"But . . . I thought you wanted me to come?"

He heard the hurt in her voice and was able then to look at her, to control himself. "I wanted you with me so bad I swept you along with my plans. You'd have been safe on Hope Mountain. Instead, I brought you here. You could have been killed."

Squeezing his hands until they hurt, she snapped, "No, *you* could have been killed. I saved you. Thank heavens you brought me."

She really had saved him. Three times. Once when she knocked him out of the path of the first bullets. Once when she'd climbed that tree and spotted the second assailant. And once when she'd knocked the first man cold, which set Mitch free to hunt down the second.

"I'm here with you so we can settle your problems and get you back to your mother alive and well."

"Is that why you're here?" He was pretty sure he'd next thing to kidnapped her. "I remember sitting on you on the train to force you to come with me."

She squeezed harder, and he flinched. She was really a tough little thing.

"Ilsa, I wanted you with me something fierce. But you'd be safer back home."

"Where two hired killers attacked us only a short time ago? It didn't feel that safe."

"Good point."

"And we can't go home until whoever is behind this has been stopped, so don't talk foolishness. We're here, we're staying to fight. We'll get your enemies behind a jailhouse door, then we'll go home."

Mitch felt something warm in the center of his chest where his ruthlessly cold heart usually beat. Warmer every minute. Hot if he cared to admit it. And he had no idea what to do to find Pete Howell and bring him to justice. He felt like he'd done all he could.

So what to do while he waited for the police and the Pinkertons and the next attack on his life?

"Before we go home, I want to—to—" How did he ask? What did a husband say to a wife who wasn't yet truly his wife? "Ilsa, do you trust me?"

She looked down at their hands clasped together and didn't look back up.

"I don't like it that you're not answering." He lifted her hands and pressed them against his chest.

That got a smile out of her as she looked up. "I'm not all

that worried if you like it or not. I'm trying to be honest. And the honest truth is . . . yes. Yes, Mitch Pierce or Warden or whatever name you're calling yourself. Yes, I do trust you."

He lifted her hands even higher and kissed the backs of her fingers. He thought his cheeks were warm and feared he was blushing. But he forged ahead. "Then let's have ourselves a honeymoon."

A frown crossed her face. "Are there going to be bees? Because you have to be very careful collecting honey."

Mitch laughed and leaned down to kiss her, one loud smack on the lips that cleared away her frown. "No bees. But it's called a honeymoon because it's very sweet."

Together in a city far from their true home, with a day of terror and a new realization from Mitch that he was in love with his wife, Mitch and Ilsa became truly, beautifully, completely married.

Ilsa woke up with her head resting on her husband's chest. Just like she did every morning. But this morning was different. This morning she was truly his wife.

She brushed her hand gently over his chest, and her fingertips touched the edge of his bandage that had wrapped around his shoulder to protect his back. Swallowing hard, she thought of how close she'd come to losing him.

She'd been all too willing to go into his arms.

It still rang like the purest song, the way he'd spoken of her saving his life. She had, but he'd spoken only of her part. And he'd spoken of it with respect, kindness, and pride. The truth was, they'd worked as a team to save each other. And they'd come through.

Then came the moment when "the two shall become one" had been shared between them. An experience with mutual sweet innocence.

The stresses and fears that pursued them had been swept away by her joy that they were alive and their enemies had been defeated, again. For now.

Running her hands over that bandage, thinking of their danger, and the loveliness of being married, she felt his heart speed up right under her hand. She raised her eyes, and they locked on his, the brown rich and bright. And happy.

That's when she noticed there was no smile on his face—and yet she saw happiness in his eyes. She was reading his expression.

Of course, she was so happy herself she might be imagining his mood.

"Good morning, wife."

"Good morning, husband."

He lowered his head to kiss her, and she decided she had it all about right.

Wax Mosby looked out the window half-covered by snow. Winter was fully upon him. He didn't pay much mind to what day it was, but he thought they'd finished with November, and it popped into his head that it was nearing Christmas.

As he watched fat flakes of snow drift down, he had a rush of childhood memories from that happy season. A lot of hurt came with those memories, and a lot of pleasure.

Pa had died when Wax was nine—his memories of Pa

were mainly tramping around in the woods, hunting for game to feed the family. Ma hadn't liked speaking of Pa, so Wax's memories were faint.

Wax had two brothers just a year each younger than the other and below them, two little sisters. Every one of them needed to eat. He'd gone out hunting when his ma fretted that he shouldn't even be allowed to hold a gun. Right from the first, he'd shown a rare skill with a firearm.

Wax and Ma had scraped by with their rough little homestead. It was in a rugged stretch of western Colorado, and they'd barely scratched a living out of that stony soil. But thanks to Wax's hunting, they never lacked meat on the table. They had a milk cow and a few chickens, and Ma kept a good garden. They got by.

His two brothers wandered off way too young and were swept on to the westward lands. It'd hurt Wax because he'd given his whole life to raising them, and when they were old enough to help, they ran off.

Wax had taken up the idea of marrying and bringing a wife home to be a family with him and Ma and his half-grown sisters.

Then while Wax was out hunting one day, Ma and his sisters had been killed by passing outlaws.

Wax had hunted them down and found his hunting skills could put terror in the hearts of evil men. There'd been a reward on those men's heads, and Wax had collected enough money to live well for a long stretch. But instead of leaving the killing behind and using the money to start a farm somewhere else, he studied wanted posters. He went hunting with a fire in his heart to bring killers to justice. He'd earned good money as a bounty hunter and earned a reputation. Men wanted to hire his gun. That gun earned him a living.

He'd hunted bad men ever since. And now, today, he looked out a window and remembered Christmas.

And wanted his family. Four of them dead, Ma and Pa and his sisters. And two gone forever.

That left him stranded in a cabin, and stranded in life. For the first time ever, he saw that his life had been created by the acts of evil men. In his hunger for revenge, he'd let those men make him into a killer. Now he had to ask, Was he an evil man himself? His choices had, step-by-step, led him away from his ma's teachings. His faith. His chance at a decent life. His chance at a decent afterlife.

It was never too late to be forgiven, but to do that he had to change.

And to do that, he had to get out of here, and to get out of here, he needed the money coming to him from Bludge Pike.

For one bright, tempting moment, he wanted to run to his horse, throw on a saddle, and ride away. Now. Make the changes he had to make right this second.

He'd always justified his gunslinging because he fought on the side of right, but not this time. This time he'd chosen the wrong side. And he'd made a good, strong man angry.

God might forgive him, but Quill Warden never would.

An avenging angel watched over the ranch. And with the end of winter came the beginning of the Wardens' revenge. They'd ride in, guns blazing, to send Wax to the afterlife he deserved.

23

Mitch had the best morning of his life. And he wasn't even counting waking up with Ilsa. That was an entirely separate bit of wonderful that didn't belong with any other event.

But after they lingered in bed, Mitch had helped Ilsa into the new city clothes that had been delivered.

Because they were both in a good mood and because Ilsa's gaze kept straying to his bandaged shoulder, which made her very gentle and—even better—cooperative, they'd enjoyed getting ready for the day.

She'd even let him comb her dark curls.

They'd eaten so often at the hotel restaurant the staff greeted them like family. Ilsa was usually impatient with civilization, but today she let him teach her about all the extra forks, knives, and spoons the restaurant in the Grand Pacific Hotel put on the table. She made no secret of think- ing one spoon was sufficient to meet her needs. But she smiled over his instructions, and he was so happy he didn't care if she ate with her hands. Or her feet for that matter.

This morning, he was inclined to think every move she made was brilliant.

Then he'd taken her to a bank and spent time discussing loans and interest rates and vaults. If she wasn't fascinated by it, she made a good show of pretending. And he was learning that even though she had little interest in money and banks, she was smart as a whip and stored information away and stewed over it and asked questions that helped him know what didn't make sense.

Next, he took her to the Lincoln Park Zoo. She was appalled by the elk shut up behind fences. The placid wolves and the mountain lion made her sad.

"These are wild animals that run miles every day. They're not meant to be locked up like this."

"Are you sure they run miles? The elk I've seen mostly just walk along slowly grazing. Sure, they can run. But they don't really, not that much. And mountain lions tend to rest on tree branches, lunge on the occasional slow-walking elk, then rest some more. Not that different from here." Mitch stared at the sleeping mountain lion and the wolves that were, well, not all asleep. One licked himself while another gnawed on a joint of meat. "They don't look all that upset. In fact, they look fat and happy."

They walked on past a bison. Ilsa had never seen one before. They couldn't get to her mountaintop, it seemed.

There were a bear and foxes, which she recognized. Then she stopped so suddenly she stumbled. He caught her to hold her upright.

"Eagles," her voice squeaked as she pointed. "In a cage?"

"Now, honey, this way a lot of people can see animals they might have never even believed existed. They learn about wilderness animals and besides—" He swallowed hard, thinking fast because frankly those eagles bothered him. He'd seen them soaring on the updrafts and screeching as they dove for a fish in a rushing stream. They looked miserable caged up. "The bald eagle is our national bird. People should be able to see it."

She turned away from the eagles to glare at him with her arms crossed. "I suppose you think I should be in a cage. People might not believe a woman lived up in those mountains. You could cage me up and educate people."

That earned her a grin. He shrugged and gave up. "All right. I agree it's hard to look at them. I'll sneak back here with you tonight and let them go free." He had no intention of setting the eagles free. Partly because it was no doubt against the law. Partly because they really were fat and tame looking, so he figured they'd flutter out of their cage, then just perch on it. He also worried that they'd had their wings clipped—but he didn't mention that to Ilsa. He suspected she'd be outraged. And if that was the case, and they did get out—or some scoundrel (like him) released them—they wouldn't be able to fly. Which would make him feel even worse. And finally, because they'd have to sneak in under cover of darkness, and he had plans for himself and his pretty little wife tonight. Plans that didn't include going out in the cold.

He had a wily notion. "I only hope they aren't so used to having food given to them that they've forgotten how to hunt. If that's true, setting them free could mean they'd die."

Ilsa's brow furrowed as she looked back at the beautiful birds. And then she saw the peacocks. One called out to her in a voice that sounded like a woman screaming.

Her mouth gaped open as the bird lifted its tail feathers and fanned them in a high, wide arch. "That's beautiful. Why would a bird have feathers like that?"

"I'm not sure. I suppose we could ask one of the men who works here at the zoo." Then he tapped into a lesser side of himself, a manipulative side, a side he'd used a lot in business. "Aren't you glad you can see strange animals you'd never see anywhere else? Isn't it interesting to learn about them?"

Her eyes narrowed, and she gave him a baleful look before turning back to the peacock with his brilliantly displayed tail feathers. She said somberly, "It is nice. I'm just sorry animals born to run free through deep woods and vast prairies have to spend their lives in small cages so I can learn."

Ursula felt like she lived in a small cage, and she wanted to be free.

Snowed in. Alone. Only the winter wind and an occasional soaring eagle for company. The elk were there if she wanted to hunt. Before the heavy snow came, she'd seen a bear lumbering through the deep woods at the far side of her valley. It was probably sleeping the winter away in a cave.

With nothing to do but chop into kindling the wood Dave had left for her, she let her mind bounce around ideas as she worked. She spent time daily hurling her ax at a broken-off stump that stood ten paces from her chopping block, about head-high.

She got a strange satisfaction from the little act of violence. She worked off her loneliness and anger and self-pity by honing her skill with the ax.

She also remembered Mitch had come to the mountaintop through this valley. She and her sisters had scouted out the place. Now she was drawn to it.

She had no intention of climbing down, but she was curious to see how he'd done it. She began tramping in the snow for hours any time the weather wasn't dangerously bitter. She learned where the ground was protected from the deepest snows and where it filled in until it was higher than her head.

She worked her way around the edges, peering over cliffs, pondering parts of the mountainside swept clear of snow. She looked over the spot where they'd found his tracks entering the high valley and tried to pick out handholds. As she hiked around, she began to know her home.

And she missed her sisters until the loneliness of it ached like a broken bone. But there was much to learn about her valley, about reading. It pushed back the isolation if she took on the challenge of learning and exploring.

She wasn't sure how long she'd been up here. But what did time mean?

It was dark and light, long days and short, cold and not cold. Grandma had always kept track and known when Christmas was, but Grandpa didn't pay the calendar much mind.

The Nordegren girls had celebrated a simple Christmas about the time they realized the days were getting longer.

The days were still getting shorter, so it wasn't Christmas yet. As she tramped around, she sang Christmas songs, and she sang verses from the Bible about the baby Jesus.

She was careful to always be back in her cabin before nightfall, not because she was afraid of being lost, but just because that seemed orderly. To work in the light and be home to eat and read and get warm in the night.

She was sure that she'd found the cave the bear hibernated in. But then she found a second one and wasn't interested in poking around in both, to possibly awaken a hungry, cranky bear.

She found where the elk slept, and she found oak trees with acorns thick on the ground and cold, frozen berries she ate right off the branch.

Often she went to the place Mitch had climbed. On her knees, bent far forward, she looked over the edge of the mountain and wondered. She thought she saw a way down. Not to walk, it was far too steep for that, but ledges.

The ledges curved around an outcropping of rocks so she couldn't be sure the way would continue to be so climbable, but Mitch's presence here proved it could be done. Much as she disliked that disease-bearing vermin Mitch Warden, she had to give the man credit. Only someone very determined would have climbed so hard and so far on the chance he might find his family up here.

She looked down at those ledges again and, because she wondered how to keep from going out of her mind while she waited for spring, was tempted.

Just to climb down a ways. She wouldn't go all the way down. She didn't want to be all the way down. But just to see if she could do it. Just to have something to occupy her mind.

Turning away, she lowered herself to sit on the ground

and rested her head on a rock behind her. Despite all Grandma's endless warnings, she was tempted.

Tempted.

Her sisters had gone down, and they'd survived.

Ilsa had even gotten sick, and she'd survived.

A person could go down there, live down there, and still make it to heaven. It wasn't as if the lowlanders were all doomed.

They just weren't safe.

She turned around, got on her knees, and looked over the ledge again.

Just a few yards. She'd climb just past that outcropping to see if she could continue to go down.

Temptation. Just give your Savior a kiss, and we'll give you all this silver.

Shaking her head, feeling more alone than ever, Ursula left temptation behind and headed home. There was plenty of time to decide about climbing. She didn't have to do it today.

24

A hard rap on the door jerked Mitch out of a sound sleep.

"Yes, just a minute."

Ilsa was up and heading for the door, wearing . . . very little. Mitch jumped out of bed and dashed after her to stop her.

He reached the door just as she took hold of the knob. It inched open. He slapped it closed with the flat of his hand.

He'd seen through the thin opening before he'd slammed it shut.

Mitch was a man who thought fast in a crisis.

He snapped at Ilsa. "Get dressed—fast." He leaned to whisper. "Make sure you have your knife."

Ilsa dressed with lightning speed. He saw from her expression that his first order annoyed her, but the knife . . . that spurred her on. If Mitch didn't hurry, she'd get back to the door before he did.

"Let me in, Mitch." The pounding on the door got louder. He'd have everyone in the hotel awake in a minute. Well, good. One of them could send for a policeman.

"I'll be right out." It was mighty calm for what Mitch really wanted to say. Ma would wash his mouth out with soap for even thinking it.

He might even hand her the bar of soap.

Mitch jerked on his trousers, dragged his shirt over his head without tucking it in, and yanked on his shoulder holster with motions so fast and sure it hit him how faithfully he'd been carrying a weapon of late. He seated his gun, then dragged his suit coat on over it with the tails of his shirt hanging out. He shoved his feet into his boots without socks.

One quick glance told him Ilsa was lacing up her shoes and was fully decent. She finished the second shoe, looked up, and nodded. "Ready."

"So am I," Mitch snarled. He ripped the door open and stared at his former partner.

"What did you do to me, Mitch?" Pete Howell swung a fist.

Mitch ducked. Pete stumbled forward, carried by the force of his swing. He blundered right into Mitch, who shoved him back, grabbed the front of his shirt, dragged him into the room, and slammed the door. Then he swung hard at Pete's chin. Pete crashed against the door so hard his knees gave out and he sank. Mitch held him up with one hand, then swung with the other. Pete took a fist to his belly, then dropped so hard he slipped through Mitch's hands. He collapsed like a limp dishcloth, flat on the floor.

Out cold.

Mitch had a lot more punches to throw, but his no-account partner was out of the fight. As big a weakling as Mitch always figured him for.

Mitch looked around. Ilsa stood behind him, knife in hand. Mitch frisked Pete and found no weapons. Nothing. Pete had never been one to arm himself. Add that to him not being able to take a punch, and it stood to reason the man would hire his killing done.

Why after all this time, after all the attempts on Mitch's life, had Pete come here personally? Why had he thrown a punch instead of drawing a gun?

Moaning, Pete tossed his head from side to side. His eyes fluttered open. Mitch tied Pete's hands with a necktie—he'd gotten it back from his prisoner the last time someone had come gunning for him. Sinking both hands into the front of Pete's white shirt, Mitch jerked him to his feet and banged him down hard in a chair by the small table in their room.

Pete whined, and Mitch remembered that Pete had been sharp-witted and hardworking, ambitious and diligent, but he'd never seemed dangerous. That soft, peaceable look was how he'd gotten away with all his treachery.

"I'm calling the police," Mitch snapped with soaring satisfaction. "They'll be here in a few minutes to arrest you for murder."

That jerked Pete's lolling head up straight and got his eyes wide open. "What? Murder? I haven't murdered anyone."

"Not for lack of trying."

Pete blinked. He stared at Mitch, his mouth opening and closing like a landed trout.

Ilsa came up beside Mitch. "This is the man who hired someone to kill you?"

With a violent shake of his head, as if to clear his thoughts, Pete said, "That's a dirty lie. I didn't hire a killer."

He sounded so sincerely shocked that Mitch stopped. Listening was better than beating an answer out of Howell anyway. Besides, he could always keep the beating in reserve in case he had a good enough excuse to do it later.

Mitch grabbed Pete's shoulders and lifted him out of the chair. "I caught a man who had nothing to lose. He had at least two of my bullets in him already, and if the wounds didn't kill him, men hunting him to gain a reputation would. He told me you'd hired him. And I found your name in the pocket of two other would-be killers."

Pete's eyes darted around the room as if looking for a way to escape . . . he had a fair resemblance to a cornered weasel.

He finally seemed to give up on escape because he looked back at Mitch. "How could I hire someone to kill you? I'm bankrupt and you know it. Hire him with what money? You sold everything out from under me and you knew I was overextended—on your advice. Borrowed up to the hilt. Then my businesses were gone, my partner had vanished, and the creditors were at my door. If I hadn't already married Katrina, she'd've left me."

That almost earned him a closed fist.

"So you admit you and Katrina were sneaking around behind my back?"

Pete's eyes flashed with defiance. "I waited until she told you. She'd chosen me, why would I kill you over a woman I'd won?"

"No, she did not tell me. I caught you together one night when I followed you."

"Sh-she didn't tell you?" Pete swallowed hard. His eyes shifted, looking again for an escape. Then he lifted his chin as if begging Mitch to punch it. "I refused to get involved with her when she was seeing you. She came to me and said things were over between you. Then when you left so abruptly for Europe, I thought it was because you were upset over losing her. Any man would be distraught over losing someone as beautiful, ladylike, and pure of heart as Katrina Lewis."

Mitch's brain felt foggy. Nothing Pete said made any sense. He studied his old partner, sitting at Mitch's table, telling a version of a story that rang true but settled none of Mitch's problems.

Mitch asked, "Why would a hired killer have a note on him bearing your name and a thousand dollars?"

"A thousand dollars?" Pete snorted in angry laughter. "And where was I supposed to get that much money? I'm bankrupt. And Katrina and I would've been all right even after you ruined me, because I could've gone to work for her father, except for the Panic. Her father went bankrupt. I heard, just today, you were here in Chicago. I didn't come here hunting you. I just met a mutual acquaintance who said you were staying here in the Grand Pacific."

Mitch had seen several men he knew from old business dealings. Because he wanted it known that Mitch Pierce was back in town, Mitch hadn't hesitated to greet them and visit awhile.

"I thought you did all your financial shenanigans, then took off for Europe knowing I'd be too broke to come after you. Now you surface in Chicago. What are you up to, Pierce? I want some answers, and I want the money you stole from me."

"I stole nothing from you." Mitch slashed a hand so

close to Pete's face he ducked. "And if you're bankrupt, how could you afford to come to Chicago?"

"It took my last penny to get here, and that's even including the fact that two train tickets aren't expensive. And I'm in Chicago because—well, I had my reasons for coming here." He got that shifty look again. "I had no choice but to leave New York City. I left town the morning after someone tried to kill me."

"Someone tried to kill you?" Mitch asked.

"*Two* train tickets?" Ilsa added.

25

A rapid, frantic knock on the door turned their attention. "Pete, are you in there? Pete, are you all right?"

Mitch recognized the voice, turned to Pete, and growled, "You brought Katrina with you?"

"Open this door, Mitch Pierce. I hear you in there. What have you done to my husband? I'm going for the police right now, you've—"

Mitch yanked the door open and glared at the cool little viper he'd nurtured. "Katrina, well, now the party is complete. The ice is here."

Her brow furrowed, no doubt wondering what he meant. He wasn't dealing with the finest mind.

Although, honestly, right now he was feeling mighty stupid. Who was he to judge another's mind?

Katrina strode into the room, her blue eyes flashing, her mouth a tight, angry line. He gave way before her even though she was a willowy, frail-looking woman. She was dressed in . . . rags.

Shocked, Mitch really looked at the beautiful woman.

She, who had new gowns for every season, who always wore the newest styles made by the most celebrated dress-makers and rarely wore the same dress twice, had on a worn gown, badly faded, the wrists frayed, the collar stained. Her bonnet was drab and limp. The dress was wool, more suited to warmth than style. Style had always been her first consideration, far above comfort.

He noticed her boots as she headed straight for Pete. Down-at-the-heel. The leather worn and unpolished.

And beneath her bonnet a braid hung. Tidy, but when had Katrina ever dressed her hair so simply? She always had elaborate curls artistically arranged on her head. A hairstyle only a skilled lady's maid could manage with an hour to do her work.

Katrina and Pete really had fallen on hard times. But Katrina's spine was straight. Her chin lifted as she looked down her nose at first Mitch, then Ilsa.

She approached Pete's side. He reached for her with his bound hands, hesitated, and dropped them. She turned to Mitch, looking as fierce as a mama wildcat. Well, no, more accurate to say as fierce as a mama kitty cat. Because she looked to have claws, but he couldn't ever see Katrina being dangerous. Of course, he'd thought the same about Pete, so again, he was no judge of anyone.

"All right, both of you, I'll tell you straight, I have given Pete's name to the police and to the Pinkerton Agency. I've accused you, Pete, of attempted murder. I've been set upon by killers four times now. Twice it was two men, so I'm counting it as six times."

"I'm not the killer—you're the killer."

Mitch scowled. "Who am I supposed to have killed?"

Pete jabbed himself in the chest with his thumb. "Me."

Mitch found himself at a loss for words. Finally, he managed to say, "Uh, you're not dead."

"Your hired killer missed. But that doesn't make you any less guilty."

"You're wasting my time. I didn't hire a killer—you did. I suppose you've decided to muddy the waters by accusing me of the crimes you're committing?"

"You leave Pete alone. Haven't you already done enough damage?"

This from a woman who had always expected Mitch to protect her from so much as a gust of wind. Her cool, regal fragility, her need for a big strong man, had made Mitch feel like a hero.

He noticed Ilsa sharpening her knife. "I'd say you two are the ones who've done damage. Why did you—"

Ilsa moved to stand between the bed and the table. "I'd say I'm the only one here no one can suspect of anything. I didn't know any of you when the first murder attempts were made. You say you've had a killer attack you? Well, Mitch has had multiple attacks aimed at killing him, and your name was found in the possession of killers twice now, and a third one said you hired him."

"I did not—" Pete shoved himself to his feet.

"Hush!" Ilsa jabbed the tip of her knife right at Pete's nose. "Sit!"

There were four chairs by the small table in the room. Katrina had her eyes on Ilsa's knife and quietly sat beside Pete. She shook her head defiantly and began untying Pete's hands.

Mitch didn't try to stop her.

"You are like the Bible story of 'The Wolf in Sheep's Clothing.'"

Katrina frowned.

Pete said, "'The Wolf in Sheep's Clothing' isn't a Bible story."

Ilsa stabbed the tip of her knife straight into the tabletop. "You are a sinner before the Lord."

Flinching, Pete arched a brow at Mitch, then scooted his chair up beside Katrina.

Mitch pulled up a chair. "Ilsa, you sit here, honey."

With a cold look that made both Pete and Katrina edge back in their chairs, Mitch said, "Ilsa is my wife."

He wanted to add, "If she says 'The Wolf in Sheep's Clothing' is in the Bible, then I'll punch any man who says different." But he just couldn't quite speak the words. Best to get back to the problem at hand.

"If you didn't try and kill me, then someone went to great lengths to make me think you had. I didn't hire anyone to kill you. I suspect the same person made both hires and deliberately pointed the finger of guilt at the two of us. We need to figure out who that is."

Then he looked at the two of them together. Clinging to each other. "But one thing I know. I saw the two of you together, in a way that was undeniably, well, romantic, and Katrina never broke off our relationship. If she told you that, she lied."

Katrina's hand tightened on Pete's until her knuckles turned white. She gave Pete a frightened glance, then looked back at Mitch. "You were traveling to Europe— and I only knew that because someone else had heard you were going and asked me about it. You didn't even tell me. We'd hardly spoken for a month."

"That's because I was hunting for evidence to prove my business partner had tried to have me killed."

"I did not—"

"Let Katrina finish explaining her lies first." Ilsa pulled her knife free of the table and inspected the tip for damage as she spoke.

Katrina swallowed. "I knew you were no longer interested in me. I did tell Pete I'd talked to you. But the truth—"

"Your truth is a lie," Ilsa hissed, not unlike the noise the train made when it blew off steam.

"You lied to Pete. You admit that." Mitch talked fast before Ilsa took up the story of that stupid fleece-wearing wolf again.

Katrina nodded her head. "Yes, I admit that. But you were through with me. You can force me to admit I didn't say the words to end things between us, but *you're* the one who was no longer interested. Well, I wasn't interested either, but, well, anyway, we were done. We both knew it."

And honestly, she had a point. Mitch decided not to admit it.

"Two men tried to kill me in New York. Two separate incidents. I killed the first one. The second, I wounded, and he told me you'd hired him. He was bleeding bad. I said I'd get him to a doctor, but I wanted a name. I'm a good judge of a man, and he told me your name. I took it for the truth."

Ilsa whispered in a very kind voice, "Look at the two of them. You're a terrible judge of people."

She had a point, too. He decided not to admit that, either.

"I did not hire a killer, Mitch. I am an honest man." Something shifted in Pete's eyes that Mitch couldn't quite understand.

"What are you not telling me? You say you didn't hire a killer, and I'll admit, until that man said your name, I'd've never believed it of you. But you aren't telling me everything. I've decided you could afford thousands of dollars to hire killers because you stole money from me."

The rasp of that whetstone stopped. Ilsa raised the knife, and even with the table between them, she reached it toward Pete. "Tell us the truth."

Her voice was chilling, frightening. His wife the barbarian had joined them. "You're going to hang for hiring a killer. If you want to live, tell us what you're lying about."

Mitch would have confessed to everything he'd ever done—maybe confessed to things he hadn't done. And he was a lot tougher than Pete Howell.

"I did it."

"You hired killers?" Mitch slammed his fists on the table and launched himself to his feet.

"No!" Pete shoved his chair until it toppled, and he nearly fell over backward. Stumbling to his feet, he said, "No, not that. I stole money from you. I am not—" His voice broke, and for a horrifying moment Mitch was afraid he was going to cry. Truthfully, Mitch considered him more the crying type than the killing type.

"I'm not a killer." He looked wild-eyed at Ilsa, who slowly stood, knife drawn, that feral look in her eyes.

Mitch was so in love with her.

240

He had no time to tell her right now.

Pete was brilliant and mild-mannered but with a sharp way about him. A way that had reminded Mitch of himself. It was why he'd taken Pete on as a partner, given him more responsibility, increased his wages, then advised him on his own investments and planned to let Pete buy into Mitch's mills.

"How did you do it?" Mitch admitted that he'd trusted Pete with a lot. Ilsa was right, Mitch was a terrible judge of people. In fact, now that Mitch thought about it, he'd gotten rich as fast as he had because he didn't trust anyone. Pete and Katrina were the exceptions.

"I kept two sets of books. The ones you saw listed iron ore at higher-than-market price, only by a few pennies. But I skimmed off those few pennies—"

"You stole a few pennies hundreds of times a day, every day, for years."

"Spread over five steel mills. And that second set of books had the sale price of the finished steel at a few pennies lower than market price."

"Again, a few pennies for every pound of steel, it adds up to thousands of dollars."

"And I kept it all in a bank you didn't do business with."

"Jay Cooke's banks. I refused to put my money there because he was my competition." Mitch paused, thinking of all that had happened with the Panic. "All his banks went broke."

Nodding, Pete said, "I lost everything."

"My father lost everything, too," Katrina said, "so there was no help from him. My mother had family who'd gone to Georgia after the war and taken over a stretch of land.

My parents moved there. They were furious with me for marrying Pete. They already knew he'd lost everything, even before the Panic. They'd hoped for better for me. In their anger, they didn't invite us to join them."

Mitch well remembered Katrina's wealthy, arrogant father and wasn't surprised he'd gone south with the other carpetbaggers. "Your father will prosper on the misery of the South. No doubt he's wealthy again already."

"That left me with no recourse but bankruptcy," Pete said. "Which I declared before we came here."

Ilsa broke in. "What in heaven's name does all this mean?"

"It means," Mitch said in his coldest voice, "Pete borrowed money. He was sure he could pay it back because he had a nice comfortable source of income—the money he was stealing from me. Then all of a sudden, he finds out his fool of a partner is gone. The steel mills sold. There was no money left to skim. And the money he'd already stolen vanished when the banks closed. He went from a wealthy man to a pauper overnight."

Pete said, "I was still struggling to bring things to rights when someone tried to kill me. I had money in a bank here in Chicago."

"More stolen money?" Mitch snapped. "And you declared bankruptcy, cheating all those you owed, while you had funds here?"

"I scraped together the last of what I had, and we ran." Pete didn't deny that he'd left people holding debt while he claimed bankruptcy. "When I went to the bank, it had just locked its doors for good. My money is gone."

"Not your money. You stole it from me, then you stole it again from those you owed."

Pete ignored Mitch's statement. "There was an angry mob outside the bank. A man there recognized me as your business partner. He said he'd seen you at the Grand Pacific. He sneered at me. Said it was a strange sort of partnership where I could be losing everything while my partner was living high in the most expensive hotel in Chicago. I was furious at you for selling off the mills."

"So, you could no longer support yourself by stealing." Ilsa resumed sharpening her knife.

Pete's fury faded, and he picked up his chair and sat back down . . . out of Ilsa's reach. "Here we are. Both of us with a killer on our trails. We're a fine pair."

"But you got out with your money, didn't you, Mitch?" Katrina watched him with cold, greedy eyes. "You sold before the Panic."

Pete's eyes lit up. "That's right. You sold out, got all your holdings turned into cash, right before the banks closed. You're sitting on a fortune while the whole country is in financial ruin. You could buy up most of New York City with the cash you have on hand. You can get land and buildings for pennies on the dollar."

Mitch didn't mention the majority of his cash was hidden in a cave in Colorado.

"The country will straighten out in a couple of years, you'd own property that would boom, and you'll be one of the richest men in America. Maybe the world. You need someone to help you. I've learned my lesson. Katrina and I have been going to church. Since we lost everything, we've learned what's important in life. I could—"

"I will never go into business with you again." Mitch clenched his fists and rose from his chair. "In fact, if I don't like what I hear from you in the next few minutes, I'm going straight to the police and have you arrested for stealing. I'll include Katrina for aiding and abetting your crimes. You'll both go to prison."

Katrina gasped so loud it was almost a scream. "Prison? Mitch, no!"

Mitch leaned forward, fists on the table. "You'll have a roof over your head."

The avarice faded from Pete's eyes. He leaned back.

"I still suspect these two of hiring those killers. They need to hang." Ilsa sounded like the most bloodthirsty woman who'd ever lived.

He turned and saw a gleam in her blue eyes that many would've taken for true desire for a hanging. Mitch was getting to know her better all the time, though, and he could see amusement.

Ilsa was just playing her own part in scaring first a confession and now cooperation out of these two half-wits.

She was a true partner. And since he was now a rancher, he wondered if she'd be good at breaking wild mustangs.

"What is it you want to know?"

Mitch went to a long cord hanging against one wall and tugged it. Ilsa had noticed it before and asked him what it was, but then she wondered what most everything was.

Mitch went to a desk and scribbled a note. Except for the scratching of a pen, they sat in a grim silence. Before long, a knock sounded at the door.

Mitch went and yanked it open and thrust a note into a man's hand along with a coin.

The man nodded eagerlly and ran down the hall before Mitch got the door shut.

Mitch turned, grabbed his chair, pulled it up to the table, and sat. "Start at the beginning, and tell me every single thing you stole."

245

26

Mitch pounded Pete with questions, and his old partner answered every one of them. That's when Mitch hit a stone wall in his reasoning. "The first attempt on my life was made before I sold out. In fact, it *caused* me to sell out. So it couldn't have been one of the businessmen who bought companies from me that you'd already bled dry—though I'm sure they're plenty mad. But if you really didn't hire the killers, then who did?"

Mitch narrowed his eyes as he sorted through all the pieces of information he'd collected since the first shooting.

"The murder attempts were to scare me into selling."

"Those killers were only to scare you? Not kill you?" Ilsa asked. "They were supposed to miss? Does that include the two who came to Hope Mountain? Because they seemed very serious."

Shaking his head, trying to put the pieces together, Mitch said, "Did this start out as an attempt to kill me or scare me?"

"Maybe whoever hired them didn't care which happened," Ilsa said. "Maybe he thought if you died, they'd move in. If you lived, you'd leave the city."

"If you died," Pete said, "whoever was after your property would turn his attention to me."

"How many people knew you longed for home?" Ilsa asked.

Mitch held up a hand. "Let me think. I need a few minutes of quiet. I've had this all wrong from the beginning."

Who wanted him out? Who wanted what he owned badly enough—

A hard fist on the door cut off the quiet. Frustrated, Mitch went to the door. He opened it to find Allan Pinkerton himself standing outside.

Mitch needed quiet and time to reason. But he had things to say to Pinkerton, too. "Come in. I've found a piece of this puzzle that throws everything into disarray. We can talk it through."

"Nae, Pierce, I'll not come in. It's nearly noon. I'm a civilized man. We'll hold this meeting in the hotel dining room." Pinkerton slammed the door.

Mitch glared at it for a long minute, annoyed by Pinkerton's brusque behavior.

Mitch looked Pete in the eye. "If you run away from me—"

Pete waved the coming threat aside. "I'm not running. You keep threatening me with hanging, but I haven't done a thing to deserve that. But whoever is trying to kill us isn't going to let me tell my side of any story."

Mitch thought again of those two attempts on his life before he sold everything off. There was more going on here than a buyer who'd gotten robbed. Or maybe it'd started as an attempt to scare him off and changed when the plan worked and the buyer found he now owned, at great expense, something worthless.

"Let's go."

Pinkerton stood when they reached his table. He went to the chair Ilsa had approached and pulled it back.

She said, "Get your hands off that chair. That's the one I'm going to sit in."

Pinkerton blinked, then he gingerly released the chair, his hands raised like someone pointed a gun at him. He slowly went back to his own. Mitch watched Ilsa sit and scoot into the table with no need of assistance at all.

Mitch was pretty sure Pinkerton would have moved farther away from Ilsa, except Pete and Katrina took the chairs beside him before he could rearrange the seating. Mitch sat beside his wife.

Mitch clenched a fist as he told Pinkerton all he'd found out since Pete and Katrina had appeared at his door.

When he'd finished, Pinkerton turned to stare at Pete Howell, then his eyes shifted to Katrina.

Mitch couldn't tell what was going on with the man, but much like Mitch needed time and quiet to figure out what was going on, Pinkerton seemed to want that, too.

Turning his thoughts to all Pete had confessed, Mitch sorted through it.

The rest of the table was busy eating, and Mitch joined them, eager for a stretch of quiet.

When the meal was nearly finished, Pinkerton said, "We sent a wire from the office here to New York concerning your case. We have reason to believe that wire went to someone outside the office. It reached my agent, but there is a time discrepancy, enough that someone could have copied it down, maybe even left the building with it and returned to send it on its way. The wire was touched by three people—two who work for me, the third the telegram deliveryman—before it reached the agent who took on the investigation.

"All three had good reason to have the wire, the man who brought the original message from the telegraph office to the agency building. The man he handed it to, who would take it to an agent, and the secretary who took the wire and held it until my agent returned from a case.

"It shouldn't have waited. Locke requested our best agent, but instead he should have insisted it go directly into the hands of who was most readily available. We are very quietly looking into the three people who had access. They'll be followed, we'll look into their finances and correspondence. We'll see if one of them has suddenly come into money that can't be explained. I run a company that operates on trust, Pierce. If I've got people who will sell our information, then my agency can't be trusted, and I won't stand for that. The people at the telegraph office feel the same. Their service is supposed to be above suspicion. We'll find out who passed on this message, if someone in fact did."

"It's good to know something's being done." In fact, Mitch was fiercely glad Allan Pinkerton seemed as determined as Mitch to get to the bottom of this. To Pete, Mitch asked, "Are we going to find out you got your hands on that wire, and that's why you came to Chicago? The timing is too perfect to be a coincidence."

"I've already confessed to my crimes. And if someone

is trying to kill me, then doesn't it make sense the same man is after you?" Pete kept eating.

Mitch got the impression he was really hungry. Katrina, too. Hungrier than could be explained by missing breakfast. Just how broke were they?

"I'm a cynical man, Pinkerton, but I couldn't believe Pete would hire my death. Of course, I'm astonished he stole from me, too. But anyone who knew me and wanted to cause trouble might mention Howell. But the gunman I'd shot was facing death, not from his bullet wounds, those wouldn't have necessarily been fatal, but I'd shot his right arm up, broken it. His days of making a living with his gun hand were over. He and I both knew men hunting a reputation would come for him, to put a notch in their gun. He was as good as dead, but rather than let me get him to a doctor, he ran."

"So this man might still be alive." Pinkerton rubbed his beard thoughtfully for a long time.

Mitch let the man think. He'd heard Pinkerton had a sly mind and a clever twist to his thoughts.

"You say you didn't find enough evidence in New York to confirm what the man you shot said. Enough to convince you, but not enough to convince the police to arrest Howell."

"Yes, I had Pete here followed by Pinkertons, you should know that." And Mitch saw by the way Pinkerton narrowed his eyes that he indeed did know. "I searched Pete's desk. I checked his finances." Mitch slid his eyes to Pete. "Obviously not closely enough."

Pete flinched but kept chewing. Almost like a man eating his last meal.

251

"There just wasn't solid proof. Not enough for the police to act. And I found people who told me they didn't trust him and were no longer doing business with me because of him. I knew I'd lost some business, but I'd never laid that loss at Howell's feet until the gunman I shot spoke his name."

Mitch glanced at Ilsa before he went on. "And I found him with Katrina, who I was . . . seeing at the time."

Katrina scooted her chair just an inch closer to Pete.

Pinkerton nodded.

"They were going around on the sly, both of them lying to me." Mitch watched Ilsa draw her knife and test the edge for sharpness without giving him a single look. She'd brought it to dinner.

"We were not." Katrina jabbed her fork at Mitch. "Pete and I talked and spent time together, but nothing happened between us until you and I were as good as finished."

Ilsa finished her meal, and while they waited for dessert, she began running her thumb over the blade of the knife that'd come from the restaurant kitchen. He hoped she wouldn't sharpen it enough someone in the kitchen would cut himself.

She didn't seem like the jealous type. But she did seem like the stab-someone type.

"Katrina and Howell married within two weeks of you leaving New York," Pinkerton stated.

Mitch looked at them, sitting so close. What a pair of polecats.

Pinkerton reached into the watch pocket of his vest and extracted a timepiece. He snapped it open, then studied the dial.

"I need a list, Pierce. Everyone you sold to. Everyone who might've known of your interest in going home."

"I'm going to assume," Mitch said, "those men came to Hope Mountain because they searched my home in New York. I don't think they could have followed me. I was too careful."

"They were probably there waiting for you." Pinkerton snapped the watch closed and repocketed it. "Do you want me to take these two into custody? I can escort them to the police station."

Mitch gave Pete and Katrina a considering look. "I wonder if there's a way to stake you out as a Judas goat and trap whoever's trying to kill us."

"Judas goat?" Ilsa piped up. "Is that like the Bible story about 'The Fox and the Goat'?"

"No, it's more like the Bible story of Jacob preparing goat stew to feed to his father."

"There's no Bible story about a fox and a goat." Katrina scowled at Ilsa.

"Don't you talk to Ilsa that way. You shouldn't even utter the word *Bible*," Mitch snapped. "Not when you're missing some really big things like 'thou shalt not steal.' Not to mention about a thousand verses that tell you to repent of your sins. Until you get your own soul sorted out, don't correct my wife."

Mitch supposed that was his job. He really needed to talk about this with Ilsa. Probably when they were alone, which was usually at night in their room. But now that they'd found out what really went on between a man and woman in the marriage bed, he wasn't one bit interested in talking when he was alone with her.

Ilsa leaned close and whispered, "Are you going to fin-ish your apple dumpling?"

Mitch slid his plate over to her. "Once we're done here, there's something I'd like to show you."

Pinkerton took Katrina and Pete to another hotel. Ilsa was glad to see them go and wondered why Mitch said he'd pay for the room. Money was confusing.

Ilsa walked down the crowded sidewalk, sticking close to Mitch.

He held her hand. It was different now. He didn't hang on tight to her wrist and drag her along. Though she hadn't minded that at first. She had no idea where to go, and Mitch was always headed somewhere, and he seemed to like to hurry.

He tried to explain things to her, too. But sometimes it was all just too much, and she just let him take charge. And there was just a little part of her that suspected that, especially at the very beginning, he was afraid she'd run off if he didn't hang on tight. When they'd been in Buck-snort and she knew Jo was headed back to Hope Mountain without her, Mitch might've been right to worry. The tight grip had helped keep her from running for home.

But it seemed different now. He only held her hand. He still didn't want them to get separated, but she wanted to be with him. An escape was no longer a threat. He held her hand, and she held his.

He'd been moving along, fast as the cold wind, but he slowed and edged her close to the buildings, out of the line of streaming people.

"You're getting better at reading, aren't you?"

"I am. I can read the Bible now, the one we have, and it's interesting to read the words I've always known. And I like the McGuffey Reader. I've been through it several times, and it makes good sense."

He pulled her on along the street to a wide window full of books. So many she couldn't count them all.

"Let's go in." He opened the door. A tinkling sound rang overhead. He let her go first.

"So many books." Ilsa looked back as he closed the door with another ring of the bell. "And once I can read, will I be able to read all of them?"

Nodding, Mitch drew her along to a wide shelf on the right side near the front. "You can read the title of this, can't you?"

"Yes, of course, it's a Bible. I've never imagined seeing so many Bibles in one place." Ilsa reached out and ran one finger over a smooth cover. Leather, she thought. The words *Holy Bible* were in big golden letters on the front, and that was all.

A stoop-shouldered old man came up beside them. "Are you thinking of buying a Bible? We have several beautiful ones."

"Do you have a copy of *Aesop's Fables*?" Mitch asked.

"Yes, certainly, over here." The man headed toward the back corner. Ilsa looked up at Mitch, felt her brow furrow.

"*Fables*, you've said that word before."

"Let's look at it." Mitch headed after the man, and for the first time in a long time, Ilsa didn't want to follow. But she went along.

The man picked up a book with a drawing on the front of

a fox looking up at a cluster of grapes. Ilsa reached for it. It was slim, and the cover was hard, not leather like the black Bible.

"Can we look at it?" Mitch asked the bookstore owner.

"Of course, take your time. We encourage folks to browse. We have several different copies of this book, too, larger and smaller." He swept a hand along in front of books that were of different sizes. "There are many different fables. Different books contain different stories, though the best-known ones are in each volume."

He let Ilsa take the book, and he headed back toward the front of the store.

Mitch flipped the cover open and ran his finger down a list in the front. He turned to a page that read "The Boy Who Cried Wolf" and turned the book toward her.

"Can you read this?"

Ilsa did. It was the same story as the one she had at home. Slowly she read the familiar tale.

"When we get home, you'll find that the book we left there isn't written in this language."

Ilsa narrowed her eyes in confusion. "What do you mean?"

"Do you remember the story of the tower of Babel? We speak the English language, but not everybody does. In fact, Alberto, who rode to town with us and has worked with my pa for years, can speak Spanish, read it, too. The book of fables you have back home is written in a language I can't read. You can't read it. Neither can Ma or anyone I know. But I think it's written in the Danish language. Your grandma was Danish, wasn't she?"

"Yes, she was very proud of that."

"I suspect that book came over with her family from a country that speaks Danish. And she might have been able to read the language, then translated it to English. Or she might've just known and enjoyed those stories so she told them to you, probably because she recognized the pictures, just as you do."

"So once I can fully read, I still won't be able to read my second Bible."

"I'll buy this one for you, and you can read it and compare it to the Bible that's up in front of the shop." Mitch ran his finger over a beautifully drawn picture of a wolf draped in the hide of a sheep. "You gave Ursula your copy to take up to her solitary house on the mountaintop. Now you can have your own. My family has a Bible, but we don't have our own copy of *Aesop's Fables*."

Ilsa looked at it, then she turned and looked at the big, plain Bibles at the front of the store. "You've told me many times there is only one Bible. But I've always been taught there are two."

She looked away from the books and into Mitch's kind eyes. "Why isn't this book up with the other Bible? Why put them so far apart?"

"This one says *Aesop's Fables* on the front cover." Mitch closed it so she could read the words above the picture. "The other says *Bible* on the front cover. They are apart because that is the Bible and this is not."

Ilsa stared back at the book in her hand, then hugged it close, her thoughts rabbiting inside her head. "I-I don't understand. Why would Grandma and Grandpa tell us they were both Bibles?"

There was a stretch of silence, until finally she looked at Mitch again.

"I don't know why they'd do such a thing." Mitch hesitated. "Are you sure they did? Can you remember them actually saying that this was a second Bible, or is it possible they just had both books—the only books in your home—and read them both a lot? Maybe they read from both of them every night, and you were so young when they died, maybe you just got confused and thought they were both Bibles."

Ilsa opened her mouth, then closed it. "I-I can't remember." She clutched the smaller Bible closer. "I feel like I don't believe in God anymore if I abandon this."

Mitch slid his arm across her shoulders. "Of course you still believe. You remember what Ma said, believing in Jesus is how we get to heaven. 'For God so loved the world, that he gave his only begotten Son, that whosoever believeth in him shall not perish, but have everlasting life.' All the meanings of every word in the Bible are there to teach us. To help us understand more about God and guide us in our faith. But the one most important thing is belief."

Ilsa listened. She tried to tame her thoughts. She was nearly overcome by the fear. "I'd like this book. Can we get one for Jo, too, and maybe one for your ma?"

"I think that's a good idea. And one for Ursula. And we'll buy our own Bible." They'd read from one in the hotel, but they couldn't take it with them. "You and I, Ilsa, are a family now, and we need a family Bible."

As they left the store, Mitch carried the books, wrapped carefully in brown paper.

"Thank you," Ilsa said, "and I will think seriously, and pray seriously, over what you've told me."

He tucked the books under one arm and took her hand. And even more than earlier, it felt as if he really just liked being connected to her.

She walked beside him and tried to think and pray and remember what Grandpa really said, as opposed to what Ursula said. Ursula had the most solid memories. Had Grandpa ever called the smaller book *Bible*? Or had they, the Nordegren sisters, just believed it, accepted it, and never questioned it or discussed whether it was true?

She prayed, dug for true memories, and fought the fear that she was losing her faith.

27

A scratching sound from the window snapped Ilsa awake.

She grabbed Mitch's arm and shook it.

"What—"

She slapped a hand over his mouth and breathed the words into his ear. "Shh, get up, get dressed. Someone's coming."

Ilsa dove for the dress she'd tossed on the floor when Mitch started kissing her last night. She yanked it on, hearing Mitch doing the same on the other side of the bed.

As she scrambled into her clothes, she heard it again. A scratch at the window.

By the palest of moonlight, she saw movement outside. They were high up, many floors off the street. Ilsa didn't question that someone was out there, though. She was a woman who knew climbing.

Her shoes on, but with a care for silence, she rushed for the hotel room window, knife ready.

Mitch grabbed her before she got close.

"Out—now."

He dragged her to the door. It stirred her anger. She didn't like running.

She jerked free, rushed to the window, and flattened her back against the wall beside it.

Mitch was right behind her, but the first gust of cold air came through as the window slid up.

Mitch threw himself to the far side of the window, across from where Ilsa stood. It was pitch-dark in the room, but she had excellent night vision, and she saw Mitch's gun, pointed straight at the ceiling. Her hand clenched on her razor-sharp knife.

The muzzle of a gun led the way as the man slipped in so silently a chill of fear rushed up Ilsa's spine. The man moved like a ghost, like the most silent of hunting animals.

But he was quick. He had to know the cold air would wake them before long.

He rushed the bed and unloaded his gun. Blankets were jarred, a pillow exploded. Before he could realize the bed was empty, Ilsa leapt on him, the way a wildcat leapt on a running deer.

The man roared as her arms took a choking grip on his neck. Mitch grabbed his gun arm and shoved it toward the outside wall. The man fired and fired until the gun clicked, empty of bullets.

In the darkness, it was hard to know where everyone was. To prevent harming the wrong man, Ilsa clung like the most determined predator to the right one. She had her knife in hand, but she didn't use it. Even to slam it into the man's head, she'd have to let go, and she could barely hang on using two arms.

Something heavy, probably the killer's gun, hit the floor.

A sickening thud shook the man. A second time and a third. After a muddled moment, Ilsa knew it was Mitch landing blows. The would-be killer stumbled backward and fell. Ilsa slammed to the floor, her breath knocked out. She still clung to him, refusing to be shaken off. All she could do was make things harder for the man who'd come to kill.

Another thud. The weight of the man shook as Mitch punched and grappled with him.

Finally, the man went limp. A second later, his weight was gone. Ilsa gasped for breath that wouldn't come.

"Ilsa, are you all right?" Mitch lifted her into his arms.

"Yes, fine." Her voice sounded high and weak. "Don't let him get away."

Ilsa was laid gently on the bed, Mitch's treatment of her so at odds with the violent pummeling he'd just given their attacker.

The gaslight came on, and Ilsa blinked against it.

Mitch loomed over her, frowning. Finally, she drew a clear breath and said, "I'm unhurt. Falling to the floor knocked the breath from me, but it's back now."

Mitch watched with keen eyes, then finally he turned to their attacker and knelt. Ilsa turned on her side to see Mitch binding the wrists of the unconscious man with a necktie. It was a good thing Katrina had untied Pete, and they'd left the necktie behind. Mitch needed to lay in a supply.

Once he was secure, Mitch sat back on his heels and looked at Ilsa. "We have to get out of here."

"Not until that man tells us who sent him."

Mitch held up a pouch that even Ilsa, with her little

exposure to money, recognized as of a size with those owned by the other men who'd attacked.

"And is there a note with Howell's name on it?" Ilsa asked.

"No," Mitch said. "Not this time."

"The killer who hired this man knows there's no use in pretending your partner is the one behind these murder attempts. And Pete said someone tried to kill him. That means—"

Mitch leapt to his feet. "It means he might even now be sending men after Pete and Katrina. We've got to go."

Pete and Katrina had left with Pinkerton. Mitch had later explained to her that he gave them enough money for a hotel room because he wanted to be able to find them, and they had no money for a place to stay. But he didn't want them next door, so he sent them to a different hotel.

The only reason Pete was free was because Mitch was devising a trap for the killer. A trap that had not yet been set.

Ilsa said, "Where did they stay?"

She felt her husband grab her wrist and drag her, stopping only for their coats. She didn't mind at all. Honestly, she had sort of missed being towed along.

In the hotel lobby, Mitch sent one alarmed night watchman to stay with their prisoner and another running for the police. Then they were outside. Mitch spotted a horse-drawn carriage parked out front of the hotel.

He shouted directions to the man. "And hurry. A man's life is at stake."

Ilsa was neatly tossed inside, and Mitch jumped in behind. The carriage took off before the door closed.

—o○o—

Ilsa was thrown against Mitch as they careened around corners. The speed didn't keep Mitch from raging inside.

Why hadn't he hired bodyguards for himself and Ilsa, and for Pete and Katrina? Why hadn't he sent Pete to jail?

Why hadn't he just gone right back up that slope to Hope Mountain with Ilsa and his family? The snow would've closed in, and come spring, he could've kept an eye on the trail for trouble.

Weary from the short night, the brutal fight, and the endless attempts on his life, Mitch wanted home so bad he could hardly bear it.

Ilsa took his hand firmly in hers. Could she tell he was near his limit? Or maybe she needed someone to hang on to as much as he did.

He held her small, sturdy hand tight and shuddered. "What if I'd married that coldhearted Katrina?"

The carriage veered, and Ilsa toppled onto him, then sat back up. She found a smile. "It would never have happened. She was right, wasn't she, that you weren't spending time with her anymore?"

Mitch nodded. "I was finding excuses to not spend time with her. I'd had business discussions with her father and wanted no part of him. And I got the feeling he wanted me married to his daughter for all the wrong reasons. Katrina and I went to the theater and out for dinner, dancing, and on carriage rides." He didn't tell Ilsa that, at first, it had appealed to him to have the beautiful, fragile woman on his arm. He'd felt protective, even heroic. Her cool nature seemed like the correct demeanor for a proper and decent woman. But about the third . . . or maybe fifth time she'd shrieked at the sight of a bug or wept over a rip in her long, dragging gown—for heaven's sake, how was it supposed to *not* rip—Mitch started comparing her to Ma.

Katrina had not compared favorably.

The carriage veered hard to the left as they rounded another corner. Mitch fell nearly on top of Ilsa. He caught himself, both arms braced on the seat beside her. Their eyes met. Their faces were close enough that Mitch leaned forward to kiss her.

"I know I should stay and solve this, but everything in me wants to go home." He kissed her again.

The carriage straightened, and Mitch was on his side of the seat again.

Ilsa grabbed his hand. "I'm not sure we can leave until we put a stop to these attacks. If those men hadn't come to Hope Mountain, I might think we could find a peaceful life. But we both know—"

Mitch kissed her. No reckless ride necessary to bring him close to her.

"You're right. We have to solve this. And then I want to go home, all the way home, and stay there with you forever."

The carriage driver shouted, "Whoa!"

The brakes came on, and the horses slowed so suddenly Mitch and Ilsa both pitched forward until they were nearly on the facing seat.

"We'll get it settled by questioning the man we caught entering our hotel," Ilsa said hopefully.

"The men we caught hunting us in the park didn't talk. Or rather, they did talk. They told us all they know. Pete

Howell hired them. It's not enough to talk to our prisoners if they've been fooled." Mitch nearly ground his teeth in frustration.

With a wrench of the carriage door handle, Mitch was out. Ilsa landed lightly on the ground before he could turn to help her—he was used to that now. She darted for the front door of the hotel, even though she didn't know where they were going.

Mitch caught up to her and passed her, catching hold of her while he ran.

Inside, Mitch rushed for a stairway. They were one flight up when a single gunshot echoed through the building.

A woman screamed—loud, long, shrill—until it hurt Mitch's ears. Worse yet, he knew that scream. He'd killed bugs because of it enough times.

Plunging upward, Mitch heard voices added to the scream. Glass shattered. They reached the second floor. Mitch knew which room Pete and Katrina were in, but he didn't need to because the screaming never stopped.

Doors popped open as he ran.

"What's that?" A growing blizzard of voices filled the hallway.

"Was that a gunshot?" A shrill, panicky woman.

"I'm sending for the police." A man, taking charge, except no one came out rushing for the stairway to get help.

"Who is that screaming?" Another woman, her voice rising until it, too, was nearly a scream.

The babble of voices rose. Every door in the hotel was open, noses poked out, men and women wearing robes and nightgowns.

Feet on the stairway coming from behind Mitch told

him the shot had been heard from the lobby. Or maybe they'd seen him come rushing in and followed.

Mitch reached the door and twisted the knob. Locked.

He backed up a step to kick it in, when it swung open hard enough to slam against the wall. Still screaming, her hands soaked in blood, Katrina rushed out and flung herself against him.

"Pete's dead." Her screaming turned to sobs that wracked her body. Mitch saw two bloody handprints now plain on his white shirt.

"Someone came in—in—" her words broke, she struggled to go on—"came in the window and sh-shot him."

Mitch saw the night clerk come up; he thrust Katrina at him. She clung like poison ivy, but Mitch tore her grip loose, then rushed into the room, gun drawn.

"He's gone," Katrina screamed. "Pete's dead, and his killer went back out the way he came in."

The window stood open. Cold Chicago wind made the curtains twist and dance. And Pete Howell, Mitch's partner and his enemy, lay flat on his back, one clean shot through the heart. His thieving days were over, and a murderer, and whoever had hired the murderer, still roamed free.

And Mitch's name was still on their list.

28

Ilsa rushed to Pete and knelt beside him. He sure looked dead, but Ilsa thought it was only right to check.

She couldn't put her hand on his heart. Too much blood. She felt for the place in his neck where a heartbeat could be found. She pressed hard, waited, pressed harder. Nothing.

Mitch was beside her then, pulling her to her feet. They stood, side by side, looking down. "He was my chance to find out what's going on."

Ilsa's eyes went to the window, and as her gaze slid there, she saw something. "Look, the killer must've dropped his gun."

Then more people were in the room. Security guards for the hotel, then a policeman arrived, and people milled in the hallway, peering into the room.

In the madness, time crept along. A man came with a stretcher, and Pete was hauled away. Katrina followed, weeping at his side.

Ilsa had a slash of guilt as she watched Katrina, a woman she didn't like and hadn't been nice to, weep until her grief seemed beyond bearing. It was enough to make Ilsa want to just plain bolt. Run for Hope Mountain.

She wanted to see her sisters, listen to Ursula sing, eat food hunted by Jo's skilled hand, and sit with Mitch at a fireplace with logs burning and crackling.

She wanted home, and she told Mitch just that. He'd told her the same thing earlier, and she'd answered just as he did now.

"How can we until this is settled? We'd just take the danger with us and leave behind any chance of finding the one who wants me dead."

In the confusion, neither Mitch nor Ilsa had thought to mention the gun to the police. Now she noticed it again where it had fallen, nearly under a small table. Ilsa studied it. "We should take that to the police."

Mitch went and crouched beside it.

"Don't touch it." Allan Pinkerton was at the door, scowling. "I had a man in this hotel watching over them."

"A bodyguard?" Mitch asked.

"No, a jailer. I was afraid they'd run."

Mitch rose, stepped away from the gun, and came back to Ilsa's side. "Where was your man?"

"Right next door. I just found him knocked out cold. Whoever came in here got my man first. And he's been out awhile. A knot on his head has had time to bruise. His window is wide open, too."

"So, two men?" Mitch looked at the bloodstain on the floor where Pete had lain.

"One man could've done it." Pinkerton went to the window, opened it, and looked out. "There's a wide ledge. And look, this building has a fire escape. They're going up all over town since the fire." Pinkerton turned in disgust. "One man could've climbed up here and gotten to my man, then come in here, killed Howell, and gone out the same way he came in."

He turned to Mitch. "Why did he leave a witness alive?"

"A witness?" Ilsa asked.

"Yes, Katrina. She was screaming. I was running. Maybe he heard the footsteps and panicked, but that's a two-shot pistol, and we only heard one shot. I never even asked Katrina what the man looked like."

"If she's seen a killer and survived, she's not safe." Pinkerton rushed for the door, Mitch right behind him.

Mitch, out in the hotel hallway, shouted, "Where'd they take the body?"

A faint voice, behind a door, said, "Quiet down."

Ilsa ran after Mitch. He was nearly to the stairway when he skidded and whirled as she came up.

Smiling, she said, "You forgot me."

He grabbed her hand and said, "Not for long, I didn't."

He turned, now a half a flight of stairs behind Pinkerton. She asked, "Why are we running? Why did you ask about the body?"

Mitch didn't look back, he only moved faster, but he did manage to answer her question. "We're running because the only witness to murder is wandering around without any protection."

"Katrina."

"I can't believe I just let her walk out alone."

"I thought the police took the body, so she's with them."

"Yes, but we didn't even warn them to keep a protective

eye on her. Not to mention, we need to talk to her. Her description might help us catch the killer."

They rushed through a lobby far more modest than the Grand Pacific's and out the door. Pinkerton was clambering into a carriage.

He shouted over his shoulder, "Get up here! They took Howell to a mortician. My driver overheard where they were going."

Mitch and Ilsa got in, and the carriage sprang forward.

The group rushed along the empty, snowy streets of Chicago. Suddenly they heard their driver shout, "Whoa!"

The carriage stopped abruptly, and Mitch and Ilsa, facing forward, were thrown across the seat and landed on either side of Pinkerton.

As they scrambled off the poor man, Pinkerton shouted to the driver, "What's going on?"

"It's the carriage I saw earlier, sir. The one following the hearse with the widow in it. Something's happening."

A shrill scream pierced the night. A gunshot.

Pinkerton opened the door and climbed out. Mitch was next, in time to see a man drag Katrina from the carriage. He saw them, fired a gun.

Mitch threw himself back into the carriage. He dragged Ilsa beneath him as multiple shots drilled holes in the carriage.

Then came the sound of running feet. Katrina's scream.

Mitch scrambled out to witness Pinkerton coming around from the side of his carriage away from the gunfire.

A small buggy darted away.

Katrina's screams accompanied the sound of turning wheels.

Their driver clambered down. "Their coachman's been shot. I know him, let me see to him, Mr. Pinkerton."

"Go, yes, quickly. There'll be a doctor in the morgue. It's nearby."

The driver sprinted toward the other coachman.

Pinkerton shouted at Mitch and Ilsa, "I saw which way they went. Get in the carriage." He climbed to the top of the high driver's seat. Mitch leapt back in with Ilsa, and the carriage rolled, throwing both of them into the back seat.

Mitch opened the carriage window, gun in hand, and looked forward. The carriage wheeled around a corner. "There!" he shouted. "Turning left two blocks down."

"Got it. Keep watch, I can barely handle this thing."

The streets were empty in the dark hours of the night. Their tearing wheels were all that could be heard, except the faint crunch of speeding wheels ahead.

Pinkerton slowed, then made a tight turn. There was no way to do this faster.

The buggy ahead had stayed too long on one street, and they were visible, but it was fast and took the corners better. It was leaving them behind.

Was Katrina dead? Mitch kept expecting to see her body flying out of the vehicle. What did the man want with her other than to silence her?

Mitch watched the streets, watched ahead.

Pinkerton narrowed the distance. Mitch found himself willing the carriage to a faster speed. The buggy, still well ahead, zipped around a corner. They'd left the businesses behind and were driving into an area of big homes.

When they reached the turn, Pinkerton took it fast enough that Mitch clung to the window frame with one hand and to Ilsa with the other, afraid their shifting weight might be all it took to tip the carriage.

They straightened and . . . nothing.

The street was empty.

Mitch listened for all he was worth, but he couldn't hear wheels turning ahead. Couldn't hear the clop of horses' hooves.

"Stop!" Ilsa's voice carried like a general in combat.

Pinkerton heard it and obeyed. She went flying out the side opposite Mitch and landed on the street. Mitch rushed after her, then turned to Pinkerton and hissed, "Keep going so they won't realize we've found them. They might be listening for the wheels. Then get some of your agents and get back here."

Pinkerton nodded, then slapped the reins and sped off.

Mitch went after Ilsa, running toward a wide lawn surrounding a mansion. One of a row of them. Ilsa rushed between the huge houses and Mitch wanted to shout to stop her but held back. If she'd heard something, then Mitch might be warning the kidnapper that they were on to him.

Could her tracking skills in the wild be of any use here? He couldn't catch her to ask.

They reached an alley behind the mansions, fenced-in gardens surrounding them. Mitch ran into Ilsa. She'd stopped so silently, he hadn't heard her. He caught her before she was plowed into the ground. They stood. He matched her frozen stillness and heard hooves in the distance. To the north. Was it Pinkerton or the buggy they pursued? He started up, and she grabbed his arm.

274

Leaning close, she whispered, "The riders got out back here, and the buggy went on, just like we did. But I don't know which house they went into."

She thought for a moment. "This way." She started north, the direction the buggy had gone.

Ilsa slipped forward, the dark almost complete. Fences, hedges, and big houses surrounded her. Clouds moved overhead, blocking out the meager moonlight. She smelled dust. Overlaid with the scent of the horse and something else. She wasn't sure what stopped her. She could see no tracks, but something . . .

She reached out and touched a tall hedge, thick and smelling of pine. What was it that told her this was the place? She didn't know, but she trusted herself. Then, focused on every smell, sound, touch, and sight, she heard something more than whatever it was that drew her here.

Footsteps behind a hedge, quiet as a whisper. The very quiet of them was attention getting. Not people walking normally.

Next a door opened and closed almost, but not quite, silently.

"They went in here. There must be a way in."

Mitch's hand settled on her shoulder. Then he went ahead, his hand brushing the pines. His trust in her struck Ilsa to her heart. For a moment, her head felt strange, light, like she might need to sit down for a bit. She knew so little about men, but she had memories of her grandpa. Gruff and short-tempered when anyone questioned him or if a small girl felt like she knew better.

Yes, she'd been a child, and probably he did know better, but she realized she'd expected Mitch to act like that. With all the dragging he'd done. With all his knowledge of this strange world he'd taken her to, he'd been very much in charge, and she'd had no choice but to let him be. But not always.

He'd trusted her when those two men attacked them. He'd told her she'd saved his life three times. He'd known when she sharpened her knife and spoke harshly to Pete and Katrina that she was on his side and trying to scare them into admitting all they'd done. He'd known and encouraged her methods.

And he'd trusted her when she woke up earlier tonight and said there was someone at the window. On her word alone, he'd acted.

Now he did it again. She said those they sought were here, and he never doubted, he just searched for a way in.

The bits and pieces of respect and trust he'd given her, and the respect and trust she had for him, all swept through her like the coldest, cleanest mountain breeze. She was in love with him.

"Ilsa, here." Mitch's voice was the barest whisper. "I found a gate."

They had to save Katrina and arrest the kidnapper, who must be the enemy who'd been after Mitch, then they'd get back to their room, where it was warm.

And then she'd tell him of her love, and then she'd do her share of dragging. She'd drag him back home to Hope Mountain. Although she suspected he'd come along without protest. He might even lead the way.

—o◯o—

Katrina was dragged along at a near run, her wrist caught in a viselike grip.

Pete was dead. It still shocked her to think of how he looked lying there on the floor of that hotel room.

And now here she was, in the clutches of the one man she feared.

She had no great love for her husband. He'd failed her. He'd promised her a life of ease and then lost everything. While there was a chance to get that money in Chicago, she'd had hope.

Now all hope was gone.

The man held fast as they whisked past armed guards.

"Be vigilant," the man said sharply. "I think we lost them, but I can't be sure. I want one of you in the front."

Three men stood by the back door. One left the door and followed them while the other two kept watch.

Katrina saw two more when they were near enough to the front door.

The man dragged her into the plush library with the sentry closing the door with him still on the outside. The hollow sound of a lock clicking twisted her stomach as she thought of all that had happened tonight, and all that might happen yet.

Her wrist was finally released, and the man walked away—straight to a crystal decanter with brown liquid in it. She smelled the sharp fumes of whiskey when he opened the bottle and poured himself a drink.

Here she was in a fine home. So new she could smell sawdust and paint. She was in one of the mansions that had sprung up in the city when it had grown with almost desperate speed after the fire.

And then the Panic had ground everything to a dead stop.

Many of these houses had belonged to men who'd overextended in their rush to rebuild, then lost everything in the financial collapse. The man who'd brought her here had purchased it for pennies on the dollar.

The man who'd taken her was white-haired and gaunt, when he used to be a man in robust health. He might have lost weight, but his new suit fit him perfectly.

"Is your husband dead?"

"Yes."

"But Mitch Pierce managed to survive . . . again."

Katrina was a fool for giving up on Mitch when they'd been involved back in New York City. She should have been nicer to him, tended to his needs, and catered to him. Maybe he would have remained interested. Maybe she'd now be married to a strong man who survived murder attempts and had deep pockets full of gold.

It was easy to look back and see where she'd chosen poorly. But Pete had seemed like a more appealing choice, friendlier, kinder, more easily manipulated—although she hadn't recognized the thief and liar in him until it was too late.

It gave her some satisfaction to goad the man. "Mitch came to our hotel room just after Pete was shot. So he definitely survived tonight's attack."

The old man scowled and shoved his hands deep in his pockets. "That man has nine lives."

"Just like a cat."

The man snorted. "More like a two-hundred-pound mountain lion. His survival is more than just luck."

"Can it be enough? Can this end now?"

"Pete's dead, and you're here with me, unable to testify about what happened to him." With a curt shake of his head, the man said, "No, I can't allow Pierce to live. He came all this way to investigate. There'll be no peace while he's alive."

"There could be. You wanted Pete dead. Now he is. Haven't you figured out that Mitch is a hard man to kill?"

He sank into a comfortable settee. Katrina marveled at how well he moved. Despite the gray hair at his temples, he still moved with the athletic energy that had always defined him. Katrina couldn't bear to think of him aging. She didn't know what she was going to do when he was gone.

"All these men I've hired have done me no good. The way I've gone about this has been an expensive failure. Creating that account in Howell's name. Hiring a man to handle this and giving him the money to keep hiring gunmen. Your way worked better. I'm proud of you, Katrina."

"So, you're saying—"

"You're the one to kill Pierce."

A cold thrill swept through her like an icy Chicago wind. She poured her own glass of whiskey, then settled into an overstuffed chair by the fire. "I dropped my gun in the hotel. I'll need another one, Father."

29

Ilsa watched her husband fiddle with the iron gate.

"Give me your knife." His whisper was only a breath higher than the buffeting wind.

She handed it over, mindful that he was aware of where the cutting edge was. She wasn't sure why he needed it. He had his own, but hers was very narrow, maybe that was it. For the sake of staying quiet, she didn't ask questions. He bent over the gate, then after a few moments, hunkered down in front of it. The high, windswept clouds scudded overhead, and the moon peeked out. For a moment she could see him poking her knife in a little iron plate that was barely visible.

The metallic scratching kept her on edge as she listened for any movement behind the gate. The people they pursued wouldn't hear it because they'd gone inside. She hoped.

Then the gate swung open, and she knew it was the right place. The sound when it swung was near-silent, but she recognized it. That was what had stopped her before.

Mitch touched her arm, then settled her knife carefully in her hand.

She sheathed it and followed him, keeping ahold of his coat so they wouldn't get separated. With guns involved, it was best to know right where the one man was who was on her side.

Keeping close to the hedge, Mitch went along the edge of it, staying to the shadows rather than striking out across an open garden. The house seemed to sit in perfect, unbroken darkness, but Ilsa knew Katrina was in that house with the man who'd taken her. There were no lights burning, at least not back here where they could be seen.

Still holding tight to Mitch's coat, Ilsa reached out to touch the rough stone and slid her fingers along it as they walked along the back of the house.

"Knife."

She handed it to him again carefully. No sense cutting themselves to add to all the other trouble.

A sharp rap on the door turned Katrina's head.

The door shoved open, and she was shocked. No one interrupted her father. Unless—

"Intruders, Mr. Lewis. Back door."

"Someone followed us?"

The guard nodded. "There's the special exit, sir."

"Make sure the way is cleared."

The guard withdrew, leaving the door open.

Father surged to his feet and strode to his desk. He pulled a gun from the belly drawer and another from a second drawer. He thrust the second gun at Katrina.

She recognized it as the mate to the Derringer she'd used on Pete tonight.

"If it's Pierce who followed us, you may get your chance to kill him tonight." Father grabbed a lantern off his desk and rushed to the door of his library. He looked both ways.

Mitch attempted to open the lock for just a few seconds, then eased back. His gut told him no one lived alone in a house this big. They'd certainly be facing more than the one man who'd taken Katrina.

If not guards, there would at least be servants, maybe sleeping, but if they heard someone come in, they might call out a warning.

For the sake of speed, Mitch might have gone crashing in, taken his chances, but he wouldn't lead Ilsa straight into an ambush.

Instead, he opted for silence. He drew Ilsa along with him to a window. He still had her knife because hers was thinner, sharper, and more flexible than his switchblade. He fiddled with the window lock and heard a soft slide of wood.

Shoving the window up, he appreciated the new construction. The windows moved easily, no squeaking.

He could see into the room beyond enough to be sure it was empty. He grabbed the windowsill, which hit him about waist-high, and dragged himself up and in. He landed softly on thick carpet.

Turning back, he almost knocked heads with Ilsa as she leapt in. His woman-sized red-tailed hawk had next thing to flown in here.

Mitch could leave. It would be the safer choice. He could find out who owned this house. Alert the police and the Pinkertons and let them investigate.

Allan Pinkerton was even now coming back, probably bringing help. But he didn't know where they were. To wait might improve their chances of solving this. If Mitch and Ilsa were killed, it might ruin those chances altogether. Waiting would certainly be safer. They could even retreat and go for help themselves.

But what of Katrina? What would happen to her in the meantime? She was in the clutches of a killer. She was the only eyewitness to murder. And that murder was almost certainly committed by the man who had her.

There was no time to break off the search to involve the police. He moved ahead, risking his life and much worse, Ilsa's life, but he had no choice.

Moving slowly in the deep darkness, he found a long table and moved along, running a hand over each chair back. The room was cavernous, a formal dining room, no doubt.

Then he heard footsteps heading straight for this room.

Katrina kept pace as Father charged down the hallway and wrenched open a door.

Katrina had been in this house only once before. Her father had sent her a note saying he was in Chicago, after she'd wired him to tell him they were headed there.

He'd been working on silencing Mitch ever since he'd realized Mitch wouldn't do business with him because of his less-than-scrupulous business practices. When Mitch had shown no interest in her father's underhanded dealings, they'd turned their attention to Pete. And then the Panic hit with both Pete's and Father's bankruptcies.

Father had earned himself a new fortune in the South, and he'd put a price on Mitch's head and arranged for an agent to handle the payments. He'd decided to set Katrina free of Pete, too.

Two thousand dollars to kill Mitch Pierce. One thousand paid up front. Another when the job was done.

The agent was still out there, still hiring, and Father had given him a fat account and the freedom to hire without consulting him. If Katrina could end this tonight, Father could call the man off. Until Father did that, the attacks would continue.

Father thought he'd been handed the perfect chance to solve all his problems in one deadly night, but Mitch had dodged the attack again.

And now there was a good chance Mitch had followed them here.

Father plunged down a dark, narrow staircase, and Katrina kept pace. It flickered through her mind that they were both running. When had they started running? They'd always been the ones to make others run.

Now they ran as if the hounds of hell were after them.

Considering she'd become a murderer tonight, especially considering she'd enjoyed it and planned to do it again, they very well might be.

Mitch reached the door on the far wall and grabbed his gun, preparing for guards to come charging in. Instead, footsteps rushed past the door. One pair heavy, the next lighter—a woman's footsteps.

Katrina. There was a very good chance, this late at night, that if the kidnapper had brought her here, the kidnapper—probably Pete's killer—was leaving with her. Taking her where? To kill her?

Mitch eased open the door, holding his breath against a squeak. It led to a hall barely lit from a pair of turned-down lanterns. The door to his right swung shut with a firm click. Low voices echoed from the back of the house, near the door he'd almost come in.

He should go in there, deal with those men—because they might be coming behind him. But he couldn't. Even if he won a fight with them—and with Ilsa fighting on his side, he probably would—it would slow him down. He had to get Katrina out of the killer's clutches.

Grabbing the nearest lantern off the wall sconce, he went to the door that had just closed. He opened it and saw a long downward flight of stairs that looked dark and smelled of smoke. None of the sawdust and new paint smell here. These stairs smelled of ash and mold, and were older than the new house.

A house rebuilt after the fire, set on an old foundation, with an old basement, no doubt. Mitch stepped down, drew Ilsa beside him, and closed the door in complete silence, hoping the men upstairs didn't even know they were here.

Having them come from behind would make this much more difficult.

They might notice the lantern was gone. But maybe they'd think the kidnapper had it.

He started down, his hand steadying him on the rough stone walls. Footsteps below faded into the distance, still two sets. The darkness was barely pushed back by the dim lantern. He turned the flame high enough to see what was ahead and hurried down a straight, narrow staircase that led far too deep for a usual cellar.

Once he was down, even with the lantern set to a high flame, there was nothing to see, no one to follow, not even the distant tread of feet. Multiple doors opened off a barren, stone room.

Ilsa caught his hand. She turned the lantern down until there was barely a glow, and they moved forward. He wasn't sure what she was following, but he had no better ideas so he went along with her.

She quickened the pace and reached a heavy iron door set in a wall of quarried rock. The door stood open. The air ahead smelled dank. Mitch went through the door with the lantern held shoulder-high. The ceiling was only inches above his head, and there was no sign of light ahead. No sound. He moved forward, realizing he'd entered some kind of tunnel.

He and Ilsa moved quickly now. The tunnel wasn't wide enough to walk side by side, so Mitch led the way. He wore boots, but they had soft leather soles. He'd regretted that when he'd bought them, because they weren't warm, but now he realized they were quiet.

Ilsa was as silent as a ghost behind him.

Rushing along, they must have gotten closer because Mitch could suddenly make out the faint echo of distant footsteps moving fast.

Katrina and her kidnapper were just ahead.

—o◯o—

"We should stay and fight." Katrina tugged on her father's coattails.

He whirled around so fast she staggered back. He held the lantern. The dim flickering light cast his face in demonic red light.

"No. A man with money doesn't risk his own life. He pays others to do it."

A chill of anger went down Katrina's spine. "Like me, Father?" He'd raced down the hallway toward the cellar stairs. He hadn't even looked back to make sure she was with him. "You pay killers like me?"

The light continued to flicker. Pa looked beyond Katrina into the dark tunnel. His shoulders eased. "No pursuit. We got down here before anyone saw us."

Then he turned his attention back to her. "Don't call yourself a killer."

And yet that's what she was. She had to admit she'd enjoyed shooting Pete. Enjoyed it so much it was shocking. It had torn something loose inside her. Her heart, her mind, almost certainly her soul.

"And do you think I should take it up as a living? With Pete dead and bankrupt and no way to get hold of Mitch's money, and no invitation to come and live with you in the South, I have to find a way to support myself."

Anger burned in her chest and came out in acidic words.

There was a silence for too long. Then Father said, "You are speaking female nonsense. Of course you won't do it for a job. But helping me straighten things up between you and Howell, now you and Mitch, that's personal. It takes guts to do that. You found that kind of strength within yourself."

To be a killer. Katrina's stomach twisted. Her father cared nothing for her. A man she worshiped called killing strength. When the truth was, drawing a gun on an unarmed, unsuspecting man was the worst kind of cowardice.

Why hadn't she been better to Mitch? Of the three men in her life, she'd chosen two dishonorable weaklings and betrayed the strong, honest man.

But her father had decided he was proud of her. The broken part of her loved that and wanted more of it.

"Let's keep moving." Father turned and moved forward, slower now. Steady.

Ilsa loved the dark. She sometimes thought of herself as one of the night animals. The critters living on Hope Mountain did such interesting things at night. Many couldn't even be seen except at night. If she wanted to learn about them, she had to be comfortable in the dark.

The glare of the lantern was unpleasant, the sharp smell of the kerosene made the scent of their quarry harder to distinguish. They didn't need the lantern now that they were in this . . . whatever it was. They only needed to go straight ahead on a smooth stone floor.

But Mitch seemed to like the light, so she had to deal with it.

She wondered, as they rushed along, who'd built such a thing underground. And where it led. They had left the house far behind. The air was wet, like the depths of a cave that dripped water from the ceiling or had hidden ponds. There were caves like that on Hope Mountain.

Ilsa caught the flutter of fresh air. What would they find ahead?

Then she heard the scrape of a shoe too close ahead and grabbed Mitch's arm. She took the lantern from him and set it down in utter silence.

Then she moved on through the tunnel until she heard a voice.

"Are you still hoping I'll kill him, then?" Katrina should keep silent. But how could she? She'd killed once now and was making cold-blooded plans to do it again.

"I don't think we have much choice. Pierce knows too much. And he's too relentless. He won't stop now."

"Where are we going?" Katrina asked.

"To the hotel where Pierce is staying. We'll find our way up to his room. I know how the man I sent earlier was going in. You can do it as well as he did."

"Unless he's the one whom your guards said was at the back door."

Father shrugged. "If he was and he survives my guards, he'll find nothing. He'll return to his room eventually. When he does, we'll finish this."

"Using the fire escape?"

"Yes, it's perfect for this use."

There was silence. Finally, Katrina said, "No, I don't think so. That man failed. We're going to stop being sly. I'll walk up to his door as I did early yesterday and knock. He'll open the door, and I'll kill him the moment I see him. No more trying to sneak up on a man who's so suspicious. I'll face him, a foot away, and pull the trigger, the same as I did to Pete."

Katrina went on. "I'll probably have to kill his wife, too. She was an unpleasant, crude little creature. I'll enjoy that."

A chill rushed down Ilsa's backbone.

To hear such talk of murder, and the method was suggested by Katrina herself. She wasn't just obeying this man, she was taking charge.

Mitch leaned so close she felt his breath on her ear. He said, "I know that man."

Ilsa felt rage coming off Mitch in waves.

Mitch forced himself not to go charging in swinging.

It all made sense now. The man who had a part in driving Mitch out of New York City. Not because of any act on his part . . . although now Mitch knew that wasn't true.

Denham Lewis, Katrina's father, *had* acted. He'd hired murderers.

But that wasn't what had really made Mitch want to quit New York and go home. It was knowing he could grow into a man just like Lewis. In fact, he'd have to become more like him if they went into business together. There was no other way to do business in partnership with Lewis. Especially if Mitch had married Katrina.

Denham, more than Katrina, had made Mitch pull away from the relationship and the city.

And how long after Mitch had turned down Lewis's offer for partnership had the first murder attempt come?

A quick calculation told Mitch it had come within days.

Finally, he knew what had kicked off this whole hornets' nest. Or rather *who* had.

"Keep moving." Father tugged on the knob of a heavy door. It opened with a shriek that sounded like a tormented soul.

Father turned to her. "I'll get us a cab, then you go to the Grand Pacific and end this. I belong to a club that's open late. I need an alibi."

"And I don't?" Katrina heard the pounding of surf. The house had been near the shores of Lake Michigan, though not right on it. But that tunnel came out here. Probably an old smugglers' tunnel, or maybe a part of the Underground Railroad.

"No," Father scoffed. "No one will suspect you of doing such a thing. In fact, you should kill them and then start screaming just like you did with Pete. You'll blame it on the same mysterious intruder who killed Pete tonight. It's natural you'd go to your old friend in your hour of need. And it's natural that the man who killed Pete would also be after Pierce."

Katrina knew it could work. She also knew she was taking all the risks.

But from deep within her broken soul, she knew from killing the first time that there were others she might enjoy killing.

How far down on that list was Father?

She got a firm grip on her Derringer. "Let's go."

The damp was heavier with each step. Ahead, Ilsa heard a strange, high-pitched howl echo back toward them. The flutter of fresh air changed to a steady flow. Mitch, hanging on to her wrist as always, froze in place.

Her chill was gone. Ilsa's spine hardened. She was going to enjoy tackling this woman and knocking her out as cold as a mountain winter.

They heard every one of Katrina's horrid words. Heard the man's hateful plotting. To think—Katrina's own father!

Mitch rubbed her arm, trying to comfort her from such ugliness, no doubt. But Ilsa needed no comfort, she needed one good crack at Katrina.

Caution made sense when slipping up on a grizzly bear. But not right now. Since her husband trusted her to obey, and he wished her to stay close, he wasn't expecting her to shake off his comforting hand, rush past him, and charge for the door she knew was open. Katrina and her father weren't going to get away.

With speed matched only by complete silence, Ilsa rushed toward the voices, knife in hand.

Mitch was only a pace behind her and nearly as quiet. He could have grabbed her if he'd wanted. Instead, he came along to help.

It warmed her heart.

In a rectangle of moonlight ahead, and with the low flame of a lantern to guide her, Ilsa saw who she wanted. Who Mitch might be foolish enough to turn his back on. She slammed into Katrina.

Katrina went down screaming. Mitch could have predicted she'd be noisy.

Ilsa slammed the hilt of her knife into Katrina's head, and with a short, sharp wail, Katrina collapsed, out cold. Ilsa was getting good at taking prisoners.

Not something Mitch had hoped for in a wife, but useful.

Mitch passed her and hit Lewis. They went down in a tumbling heap.

A solid fist slammed into the side of Mitch's head. For being an older man, Lewis was strong. His muscles showed no sign of being reduced by age and soft living.

Mitch, his ears ringing, couldn't find a weak spot as he swung hard, again and again, taking as many blows as he landed.

Lewis roared harsh words Mitch didn't want Ilsa hearing. He hit harder, faster. Lewis did the same.

A roundhouse punch knocked Mitch sideways. Lewis rolled and staggered to his feet and took a step toward the door. Planning to run, the yellow-bellied coward. Hiring murder. Urging his daughter to kill. Leaving her behind while he saved himself.

Mitch dove and tackled him to the stone floor.

As they landed, they rolled near the open door, and in the moonlight, he saw Lewis draw a pistol. Mitch clawed at the gun. Lewis rolled so he was on top of Mitch, bringing the gun around. Before he could get it properly aimed, he fired. What if he'd hit Ilsa?

Then a little fury pounced.

Ilsa had tried to be patient and leave Mitch to it. Then a gun fired, and it finished off any patience she had. She dove into the fray, found the right man with no trouble at all, because he was on top. She jumped on his back and yanked on his hair.

The fight went out of him before Ilsa had a chance to use her knife hilt. He tumbled sideways with Ilsa still clinging.

Katrina's father was as limp as her. Ilsa definitely needed to do all the fighting for the family from now on.

Mitch was on his feet, jerking on the man's arm and tugging a gun away. "He's unconscious."

Mitch stepped out of the moonlight. A few hurried footsteps sounded, and within seconds a light popped on. Mitch carried the lantern they'd left behind—apparently not far back. Then he turned up the lantern Lewis had carried until they could see well in the dank tunnel.

Ilsa slid away from the man who'd come with Katrina just as the lights flamed high.

Blood trickled from the corner of Mitch's mouth. She dabbed it away while he stared at the man at her feet.

"Yep, Denham Lewis. Katrina's father." Crouching, Mitch pressed his hand to Lewis's neck for a few long seconds. "And he's dead."

Ilsa looked down. The man's white shirt showed red right in the center. "Did you shoot him?"

Mitch shook his head as he rose, then patted his pocket. "We were wrestling over his gun. It went off. I never even got mine out."

He turned and glared at her. The lantern light made his eyes blaze like fire. "The reason I never got it out was because you rushed ahead of me."

"I was afraid you might not distrust Katrina."

"After the things she said? I promise you I fully distrusted her."

"Yes, but you've got so many rules. I was afraid one of them might be not to whack a woman over the head. I have no such rule. I had to make sure she couldn't hurt you."

"I actually do have a rule not to whack a woman over the head." His gaze dropped to where Katrina lay unconscious. "But I'd have made an exception for her."

Katrina held a gun in her hand that matched the gun they'd found in Pete's hotel room.

"She was in on it. She and her father together." Mitch's jaw tightened, and Ilsa saw the anger in his expression without him having to yell. "They tried to have me killed back in New York City and again in Colorado, then here in Chicago.

"It makes sense. When I started my involvement with Katrina, I visited with her father many times. He was a wealthy man in New York City. Very powerful. I was impressed with his success, and we discussed very seriously doing business together. Until I got to know him better. I saw some of myself in him, and I didn't like it."

"You didn't like Denham Lewis?"

Silent for a moment, Mitch shook his head. "No, that's not it. I didn't like him, but what put me off investing with him and what made me back away from the relationship with Katrina was that I didn't like seeing what I was becoming. I considered myself a hard-charging businessman, but I also considered myself moral. I believed in God and always did business honestly. But Lewis, I wouldn't say he was dishonest so much as he enjoyed crushing the competition. He liked winning, and he liked hurting the people he defeated. I could see the day I might become him. Especially if I invested with him and married his daughter. I distanced myself from Katrina and told Lewis I wouldn't be investing my money with him."

"And once he realized you wouldn't go into business with him, he thought of Pete Howell and decided to push Katrina at him and kill you?"

"Or maybe Lewis and Katrina decided it together."

Mitch was silent awhile. "Lewis went bankrupt in the Panic. I suspect an investigation into his finances will show he was on very shaky ground before the banks closed. He acted like he'd be doing me a favor to let me invest, but he might have been desperate for someone to bring new money into his business. And he might have thought I knew more about his questionable business practices than I did."

"If he's bankrupt, that means he lost all his money. So where did he get all those gold coins to hire your death?"

"Pete was rushing to Chicago to get money out of a bank here before it closed. Maybe Lewis did the same thing, only faster."

"Do you think this was all him right from the beginning? He sent his daughter out to snare you?"

Mitch flashed a quick grin in the lantern light. "Maybe, but I'm more inclined to think he got the idea after I met Katrina. He saw a chance with his daughter's gentleman friend and took it."

"So all the killing was Lewis's doing, until for some reason, tonight, Katrina shot Pete."

"That may be hard to prove. She deserves to hang for shooting Pete, and we heard her confess to it. But when Katrina wakes up, I suspect she'll spin a fine tale. It's very hard to find a jury who will hang, or even jail, a wealthy young woman who can cry on command."

He looked at the pretty woman he'd thought he might love. And he saw that same ruthlessness-turned-to-evil in her that he'd recognized in her father. What he'd feared might come to life in himself.

"She'll say her father killed Pete. But she did it. She's a murderer. And she's good enough, beguiling enough, a jury may well believe every word she says, blaming everything on her father. Even to saying he kidnapped her off the street and was dragging her away with him."

"We heard her footsteps. She willingly followed right along. Is there no way to prove she shot her husband?"

Shaking his head, Mitch said, "I'll tell the truth, and the police and the Pinkertons will investigate. We'll see how it all ends."

"It may well have been him all along making the plans. Did she say she killed Pete, or did she just say she wanted to kill you? I can see how she might convince someone she was an innocent victim."

Nodding, Mitch said, "That's what the jury will think. But both of them were armed. Both were determined to find me tonight, and she had her own plans to kill both of us. We heard that."

"It's time to fetch the police again." She sheathed her knife and buttoned up her coat. "It seems like they should have to catch these criminals themselves and not make us do all the work."

Looking up from the night's madness, she saw her husband grin.

"What is there in this to make you smile?" she asked tartly.

"I just realized our problems are solved, and we can go home."

"As long as there aren't more men out there who've been paid to kill you and who will carry out their plans not knowing the ones who ordered your death are now dead."

The smile vanished off Mitch's face. "I wonder how many there might be."

"We'll have to keep a wary eye out, but let's go home to Hope Mountain." She found a smile for the first time in a while. "I don't want to be separated from you while you get the police. Let me tie this hog so she can't escape when she wakes up."

She frowned down at Katrina, who needed her arms and legs bound. Ilsa didn't want to tear up another petticoat. "I think you need to start wearing two neckties."

Mitch grinned. "Her father has one on."

30

Mitch sat at a table, talking over the case with Locke. He wanted this over so he could take his wife home. But the police wanted him to stay. They had endless questions. And Katrina was playing the helpless victim to perfection.

So far Ilsa and Mitch had sworn to what they'd heard, and the police were keeping her locked up.

"She always could cry mighty easy," Mitch said grimly.

"We've got something we're working on that may sway the police to your side," Locke said. "It's rarely used in trials, but the police are listening to us in this case."

"What's that?" Mitch watched Ilsa eating. She'd discovered chocolate cake.

"Fingerprints." Locke's eyes narrowed with cool satisfaction.

"Fingerprints, how can that prove anything?"

"No two people have the same lines and swirls on their fingers."

Mitch lifted his hand and stared at the fine lines on his fingertips. Ilsa stopped eating long enough to do the same.

"But what does that have to do with this case?"

"Mr. Pinkerton prides himself on using the finest scientific methods in his investigations. We've all known about each one of us having unique prints for many years. Recently we've learned we can use fingerprints to solve crimes. The police are reluctant to use it, but our detectives have convinced them in this case that fingerprints will prove Katrina's guilty. The gun in their hotel room had an unusual bullet, matching the one found in Howell's heart. On that gun is one set of fingerprints. Those of Katrina Lewis Howell," Locke said with satisfaction.

"If you'll remember, Mr. Pinkerton stopped you from picking up the gun in the Howells' room. There are no prints from some would-be intruder, as Mrs. Howell claims. And the police haven't touched it. No one has. Mrs. Howell claimed the killer dropped the gun. Also, she had on her person a second gun, an exact match to the one in the Howells' room. Both guns are engraved and numbered. The prints and those matching guns are enough to convict her. She's a very skilled liar and a sympathetic character, but those fingerprints outweigh her weeping protests."

"Investigating crime sounds so interesting," Ilsa said. "I'd love to learn about it."

Mitch signaled the waiter for more chocolate cake to distract her from signing up as a Pinkerton agent. He didn't want her to start liking the big city so much she wouldn't go home. He decided to order a supply of chocolate and a recipe book to take home.

They'd go back to Colorado in the spring and maybe just stay forever.

No more traveling. No more excitement . . . at least none worse than being charged by a bull elk.

Ma could keep her busy with chocolate cake until she settled back down to safe, sane, happy life on a mountaintop.

31

How is your mother going to figure out how to work something so complicated?" Ilsa shook her head as she watched boxes load onto a train car. Boxes and boxes and boxes.

"I owned a steel mill. I know so many things that would make life better out west."

"But a sewing machine? I know what sewing is, and while it's true the lady who demonstrated the sewing machine made two pieces of cloth connect together with thread, it's too complicated for any normal person to manage.

"I watched the woman. Pedaling her feet like some kind of duck. Moving her hands and feet, fingers shifting the fabric, doing all those things right at the same time. She has to know so many things and do them all exactly right at exactly the right time. And where does the thread go? And how can she help but be stabbed by that sharp, flying needle?"

"Why spend so much time worrying about the sewing machine? There's plenty more for you to fret about."

Mitch slung an arm around her waist, teasing her, she knew. He was just enjoying himself far too much.

"What about the pipes? The bathtub? The shower bath?" He leaned very close. "What about the windmill?"

That one baffled her. "It's ridiculous to talk of pumping water out of the ground when we have streams flowing fast right at arm's reach. And a bathtub inside a house? What for? Simply bathe in a stream instead of shipping so many crates across hundreds of miles."

"There's a water heater."

"We already heat water in the fireplace."

"You'll see when we get it all set up. It will be worth all the effort to take it on the train to the town nearest Bucksnort, then have mule skinners haul it to our place. I've already arranged to meet the freight wagons in Bucksnort when they get that far, but it will be a few weeks after we arrive. We'll be riding on horseback, and that will make the trip go faster for us."

"Five wagons of supplies, five mule skinners—and why would you want to skin a mule? Do they have a nice hide? Does it make fine clothing or warm blankets?" Shaking her head, Ilsa said no more. She had expressed her doubts, but it was easier to stop the sunrise than deter Mitch from buying all this.

He kept talking about plumbing, but none of it made sense. She did know he intended to build a home for them, and apparently cutting down trees and putting up walls was too simple. Even after watching his parents build a cabin in a few days, he still wished for something this complicated.

They watched the loading of their crates, then went to get in the private train car they'd ridden out in. Christmas had come and gone in Chicago, and Ilsa had to admit she loved the candles and decorations, the bright paper-wrapped presents, and all the delicious food.

She'd heard carolers. All the music would delight Ursula. It was the one thing Ilsa wished she could take home.

But she learned the songs and sang them often. And Mitch seemed to know them, and he remembered the words and tunes when she couldn't. He'd even bought a songbook and said they'd give it as a gift to Ursula.

He bought warm, soft fabric, as well as light colorful pieces of cloth. Thin tissue with markings he called dress patterns, which looked strange and confusing to Ilsa. How many ways could there be to make a dress or a shirt?

They'd been nearly frantic to go home once the trouble was settled with Pete Howell and Denham Lewis. Katrina was very firmly locked up in jail for killing her husband. All her pleadings had failed her in the face of those fingerprints and Mitch testifying to what he'd heard right from Katrina's lying lips.

But they'd delayed and delayed. The warnings of men Mitch had talked to made them wait out January and February. Men whose opinions he respected told him the train was unreliable and often stopped in wretched conditions for blizzards.

Ilsa knew that for the truth because they'd had to stop on the way out to Chicago. Mitch said he had no interest in shoveling his way across four states.

All that was finally done, the weather had grown more reasonable, and now they had to endure the long and loud train ride home.

During their time in Chicago, Ilsa learned to read quite

well, and she enjoyed one delicious dessert after another. And they had found out there was a baby on the way! Mitch had made her go to a doctor, which was strange considering that Ilsa was a doctor. The man had asked shocking questions. Mitch had answered many of them for her because she refused to discuss such personal things with him, for heaven's sake.

In the end, though, the doctor assured her there would be a baby come fall. This was something she was thrilled to take home from Chicago.

The train had already whistled multiple times on its way in. She hadn't done hardly any jumping and screaming. She took some pride in that, but in some ways it seemed wrong. Like she was allowing those around her to believe this mad noise was acceptable.

With everything loaded, they boarded the train, and she huddled in a chair, a very comfortable chair in their own car, dreading the days of travel ahead.

Finally, the wheels began to chug along, slowly at first, then picking up speed. Getting out of Chicago was dreadful. Fast-moving trains came hurtling toward them, barely avoiding one terrible collision after another. That awful whistle, the roaring engine. It was so much nicer to ride a horse.

But finally, they were out. And now they'd endure.

All in a quest to reach home and Hope Mountain.

Ursula threw the ax. Her bitter loneliness, her anger at herself and the whole world, her guilt at the way she'd betrayed her sisters, all gave her furious strength.

She strode to the stump of the broken-off tree that was taller than she was and yanked the small ax free. She'd hacked a good-sized hole into it by now. Thinking about Jo and her arrows and Ilsa and her knife, Ursula liked having a weapon of her own, relished honing her skill with it, enjoyed being fast and accurate. She suspected her ax throwing was a sign she was going furiously mad from the isolation.

But the only way to end the isolation was to get out of here. And the only way out was down.

Down to the dangerous forbidden lowlands. Even as terrified as she was, every day the temptation to go grew. She needed to go down.

She'd always loved being on the mountain. And thought being alone on the mountain sounded blissful.

But her life was a misery. Her songs were dirges. The loneliness gnawed at her like the teeth of a starving wolf. She was desperately alone. Miserably alone.

Spring was slowly making its way up the mountain, but the trail down to her sisters was still impassable. If she could have gotten through, she'd've gone. Even with the Wardens down there. That's how lonely she was.

To pass the days when the winter winds howled, she'd done endless hours of studying with the McGuffey Reader Jo had left. Jo had given her a notion of how to sound out the words. Enough that she was beginning to read with some bit of skill. The bigger, black Bible was full of very difficult words, and she stumbled badly with it, but it mostly made sense. She could sound out the words in the smaller Bible, but they made no sense. She couldn't match them to the stories she knew, nor make the sounds form into any words at all. It was something else that was causing endless frustration.

It had gotten her through the winter. But now the days were warmer, and she couldn't bear to stay inside.

Almost daily, she'd hike to the trail down to Jo and be turned away.

Then she'd hike to that rugged climb down the mountain where Mitch had come up, and long for a human voice. She wanted to talk to someone. And at the bottom of this mountain, she'd find someone who'd speak to her.

But each time she stood looking down, her courage failed. Grandma's voice echoed in her head about the dangers.

But Grandma had never been so utterly alone.

Grandma, I need someone. I need to go down.

Wax needed to go up.

He trod to the base of that mountain every day and stared up at the spot where he'd seen the avenging angel.

Spring was here. Snow melted and flowed. The trails were still deep so no one from Pike's had come over, but they'd be here soon enough.

Wax needed to go up and find out if the Wardens were up there. Find out if they knew what Pike was up to.

Good sense told Wax to fight his way to Pike's the first day he could get there and take his money and go.

But something about that mountain just plain called to him.

He didn't like thinking he'd fought on the wrong side.

He didn't like thinking he'd been lied to and used as a weapon against good people.

And he needed to go up before the trails opened and Pike sent orders for more harassment of the Wardens.

He needed to go up.

Mitch watched the land whip by, marveling at the miracle of train travel.

They flew along at a pace unimaginable with a horse or wagon. Home, all those miles west, was only a few days away. Well, more than that, because of the train they were taking. The new southern route of the Atchison, Topeka, and Santa Fe Railway ended at the Kansas-Colorado border. They'd have a lot of miles to ride on horseback.

He'd already arranged wagons and teams to haul everything he was bringing home.

He'd decided to ship things by train to Denver. From there, they'd haul everything in wagons to Bucksnort.

He'd been told not to expect anything to get there for at least a month. The weather was too unpredictable. But come late April, or maybe May, his purchases would arrive.

A little cringe of embarrassment swept through him thinking of what he was hauling home. He'd gone a little crazy. Even Ilsa's sensible skepticism hadn't been able to stop him.

Ma wouldn't care about all the finery. She'd be fascinated by the plumbing, though. But Ilsa couldn't fathom why he wanted these things.

Well, no mind. He'd have an indoor bathroom in his house. A windmill, if he could figure out where to dig a well in such a rocky land, that would bring running water inside, and a water heater to use for bathing and washing dishes. No matter what else happened, Ma could use that sewing machine. The Nordegren women would learn—Ma would see to it. But for now, Ma was sewing clothes for everyone, and her new daughters needed almost everything.

The rock of the fast-moving train lulled him into sleep, until he was jerked awake by the blast of the whistle. He saw Ilsa jump so high it was a wonder she didn't blast right out through the ceiling of the train car. She'd mostly stopped letting the whistle startle her, but if she was sleeping, it always came as a shock.

He knew her fear wasn't funny to her, but he had to fight to keep a concerned look on his face as her fear transformed to anger at his smile.

Then he looked around. "It's getting dark. The day must've gotten away from us." He sat up. "Did you sleep?"

Ilsa straightened her shoulders and wiped all her churning emotions off her face. He'd been impressed with her efforts to remain calm. The noise had been a constant torment to her.

"I must have since the train whistle woke me." She looked out the window. "We're pulling into a town. A much smaller town than Chicago, thank heavens."

"Look at that sunset." Mitch rose to stand at the train window. The bright orangey-red sky framed the last, small curve of the setting sun. The whole world was bathed in the beautiful color. "This train could take us across the country in only a couple of days if we didn't have to stop at every little town to pick up and drop off passengers, shipments of supplies, and mail. But it never stays long, and we'll be on our way shortly."

312

Ilsa came and sat beside him. He rested one arm around her shoulders and pulled her close. "Are you hungry? Do you want to eat? The train won't stop long enough for a meal in town, but I can send for our supper as soon as we're rolling again." Fortunately, this train had a kitchen.

"Yes, that's a good idea. Thank you."

They were traveling onward again soon, then a porter brought food and later returned to clear it away.

Mitch dimmed the lanterns. He took Ilsa's hand and drew her down beside him on a settee.

"We're headed home, Ilsa. Finally. Would you like to go back to Chicago sometime? For a visit?"

"You mean take this train again?" Ilsa asked in horror.

Smiling, Mitch pulled her closer and kissed her cheek. "I was thinking we'd wait until the train comes much closer to Bucksnort. But you don't sound like you hope for a longer ride."

Ilsa shook her head frantically.

"I've learned to appreciate home. Honestly, I agree with you."

A small gasp escaped her pretty lips, and they formed into a smile. "That's nice to hear. But I enjoyed seeing Chicago."

"Enjoyed?" Mitch arched a brow.

"Enjoyed might be an overstatement. But it was interesting." The train whistle picked that moment to blast, and her smile faded to a scowl. "I feel no great urgency to repeat it."

"We'll stay home, then. We'll build our house and—" He rested a hand on her still-flat stomach. "And we'll have a family. We'll spend time with my parents, with Dave and Jo, and try to talk Ursula into being less crazy."

Ilsa shook her head. "That will be a challenge. I don't suppose the trail to the top of Hope Mountain is clear yet. Things melt slowly up that high. We might be another month, even two, before I can see my sisters again. I really miss them. And I'd love to tell them about the baby."

And Mitch loved giving her everything her heart desired. "I lived there for years as a kid. Grew up there just like you. I'd say at least another month before we can climb the trail we came down. But you know how I came into the canyon, don't you?"

"I do. You didn't come up the way we did."

"Dave and I used to climb all over Hope Mountain as kids. We got to the top sometimes, but we couldn't get a horse up there. Dave and I used to talk about what a fortress the place would be, and Dave especially dreamed of finding a trail up there a horse could manage. When I got home, I didn't know what had happened at the ranch, but I knew things had gone wrong. And I knew that, if they could get up that mountain, my family was probably up there. When we came down, I could see that Dave and Pa had done a lot of work on that trail to make it passable for the horses and cattle. But when I wanted to go up at first, that trail was buried under snow, and I didn't recognize it as a useable trail. Instead, I climbed the steeper slope. And I got into the canyon with the stone building—which I didn't notice and had never seen, by the way."

"I know how you got up there, Mitch. When we went to that high canyon and found the stone building, it was because we were exploring the direction you came from."

"I just wanted to remind you of it, because—" He waited until he was sure she was paying attention. "I think, if we're very careful, and mindful of your . . . delicate condition . . . I don't see any reason you and I can't climb up there just like I did. We don't have to wait for spring to come to Hope Mountain and melt that steep trail. We'll climb right up there as soon as we get home and wait with our families to come down when the snow melts."

Ilsa smiled and threw her arms around his neck.

He laughed and kissed her. She showed more gratitude for suggesting they climb a mountain than she ever had for all the luxuries his money had bought her.

"I love being married to you, Mitch." She hesitated, then kissed him again, more gently, more deeply. When she pulled away, he watched her eyes flutter open. Their gazes held. Then she said, "I love you."

Had she told him that before? He'd been sure she loved him, but he'd never heard those exact words before. And he'd never said them.

"I love you, too, Ilsa."

The spark of pleasure in her eyes lifted his spirit until he could have floated to the ceiling.

"You're the best part of going home. Ma and Pa and Dave, seeing them again was what my heart longed for and what led me home. But the joy of seeing them isn't half the joy I found with the wild little bride who brought sunlight into my life. After my years of thinking I was such a fine businessman, I didn't realize how dark my life had become. I still believed in God, but I hadn't really worshiped Him for years, or gone to church."

"I enjoyed attending church in Chicago. Ursula would love the music. And to hear so many voices joined together. And hear the parson's Bible readings and prayers

. . . it was so inspiring. I regret there is no church near us back home."

"You don't need a parson or a building to have church. My family always spent Sunday morning in Bible reading and prayer. I'm sure they still do. Now we'll join them."

"But there'll be no piano or hundreds of people singing together. I can't wait to tell Jo and Ursula all about it."

"My parents would love it, too. They have lived out here for so long they haven't sat inside a real church for years, well, except for our wedding." Mitch thought of the churches back in Chicago struggling to rebuild after the fire. There had been few of any size. St. Patrick's had survived, but none of the others he'd heard of. But all were still worshiping as they built under their feet and over their heads.

Then he thought of how he'd lured Ilsa through that wedding ceremony with talk of babies. And now, here they were, with one on the way. He hugged her close as he thought of the wonder of having a child with this woman.

The racket of the train had settled in, until Mitch hardly noticed it. They rattled and chugged along again until he felt like he was being rocked to sleep.

They still had a long journey ahead, and they might as well rest up for the end of it, which would be spent sleeping under the stars and riding long days on horseback. The southern train they'd taken didn't get as close to home as the one to Denver. But the weather made the southern trip easier along the way.

"Let's go to bed, shall we?" Mitch said. "This was an exhausting day. We'll sleep well, and tomorrow we'll enjoy knowing we're closer to home with every passing minute."

She rested one of her strong, skilled, knife-wielding hands on his cheek—well, she wasn't wielding a knife right at this moment. "I can't think of a better way to go to sleep, or to wake up, than lying next to you."

He rose, took her hand, not dragging her along with him anymore. And he'd let her lead plenty of times. He planned for the back and forth of it, the taking turns, to last all their lives.

She rose, and they walked together, to rest and comfort and closeness. Side by side. And he wondered at this woodland creature who'd brought light back into his life. His feral wife. His only love.

His woman of sunlight.

About the Author

Mary Connealy writes romantic comedies about cowboys. She's the author of the KINCAID BRIDES, TROUBLE IN TEXAS, WILD AT HEART, and CIMARRON LEGACY series, as well as several other acclaimed series. Mary has been nominated for a Christy Award, was a finalist for a RITA Award, and is a two-time winner of the Carol Award. She lives on a ranch in eastern Nebraska with her very own romantic cowboy hero. They have four grown daughters—Joslyn, married to Matt; Wendy; Shelly, married to Aaron; and Katy, married to Max—and six precious grandchildren. Learn more about Mary and her books at:

maryconnealy.com
facebook.com/maryconnealy
seekerville.blogspot.com
petticoatsandpistols.com

Sign Up for Mary's Newsletter!

Keep up to date with Mary's latest news on book releases and events by signing up for her email list at maryconnealy.com.

More from Mary Connealy

Growing up in Colorado, Josephine Nordegren has been fascinated by, but has shied away from, the outside world—one she's been raised to believe killed her parents. When Dave Warden, a rancher, shows up at their secret home with his wounded father, will Josephine and her sisters risk stepping into the world to help, or remain separated but safe on Hope Mountain?

Aiming for Love
BRIDES OF HOPE MOUNTAIN #1

You May Also Like . . .

Arabella Lawrence fled on a bride ship wearing the scars of past mistakes. Now in British Columbia, two men vying for her hand disagree on how the natives should be treated during a smallpox outbreak. Intent on helping a girl abandoned by her tribe, will Arabella have the wisdom to make the right decision or will seeking what's right cost her everything?

The Runaway Bride by Jody Hedlund
THE BRIDE SHIPS #2
jodyhedlund.com

Determined to keep his family together, Quinten travels to Canada to find his siblings and track down his employer's niece, who ran off with a Canadian soldier. When Quinten rescues her from a bad situation, Julia is compelled to repay him by helping him find his sister—but soon after, she receives devastating news that changes everything.

The Brightest of Dreams by Susan Anne Mason
CANADIAN CROSSINGS #3
susanannemason.net

Caroline Adams returns to Indian Territory craving adventure after tiring of society life. When she comes across swaggering outlaw Frisco Smith, his plan to obtain property in the Unassigned Lands sparks her own dreams for the future. When the land rush begins, they find themselves battling over a claim—and both dig in their heels.

The Major's Daughter by Regina Jennings
THE FORT RENO SERIES #3
reginajennings.com